HOSTILE EMERGENCE

ACROSS HORIZONS - BOOK 3

STAN C. SMITH

Copyright © 2020 by Stan C. Smith

All rights reserved.

No part of this book may be reproduced in any form or by any electronic or mechanical means, including information storage and retrieval systems, without written permission from the author, except for the use of brief quotations in a book review.

To those who choose what is real over what is not.

HOSTILE EMERGENCE

Let your arms and legs tell you what to do. Sometimes they know more than your head knows.

SKYRA-UNA-LOTO

1

NEGOTIATION

4 YEARS ago - Northwest of Tucson, Arizona, USA

A MASSIVE CREATURE was moving through the brush, its footsteps sending measurable tremors through the surrounding soil. Dry wheezing and snuffling sounds suggested the creature was digging or rooting about for food. The robotic drone hesitated, displaying its observations in the form of red text on its recording screen before proceeding: *Indigenous mammal detected, approximately 11 meters out. Proceeding with caution.*

In reality, the drone was only pretending to be cautious. Its coding required it to aggressively approach any detected creatures, as long as the creatures were within eighty meters of the open portal. This was the maximum reliable distance the drone could transmit live high-definition video. Storing the video locally in the drone's memory wasn't an option—the drone would never return to where it came from.

The drone pushed through a stand of reed-like grasses

then stepped around a scrubby tree's twisted trunk. A portion of the snuffling creature's back came into view, the rounded peak of an armadillo-like shell two meters high. The shell was moving, jerking forward and backward as the beast engaged in some unseen effort at ground level.

Walking deliberately on four mechanical legs, the drone pushed through another stand of grasses. Its orb-like vision lens registered four more smaller shells, each of them busily jerking back and forth.

Walking deliberately on four mechanical legs, the drone pushed through another stand of grasses. Its orb-like vision lens registered four more shells, each smaller than the first shell, and each busily jerking back and forth.

The drone displayed more text: *Adult with four young. Glyptodonts. Most likely Glyptodon clavipes, based on size and geographic location. Adult estimated weight 1,800 kilograms (4,000 pounds). Proceeding with caution.*

The drone, sixty centimeters tall when standing on all four legs, pushed forward again through grasses nearly as tall as itself until it came almost face to face with the adult glyptodon. The creature snorted and raised its head, which was nearly the size of the drone's entire shell.

Critical proximity. Less than two meters. My presence is revealed. Adult appears startled. Violent interaction possible. Proceeding with extreme caution.

The drone took another step forward.

The armadillo-like glyptodon spun around surprisingly fast for a creature the size of a Volkswagen Beetle. The drone held its ground, and its vision lens revealed a glimpse of a massive, armored tail as the creature continued spinning. The tail hit the drone's shell with a jarring *clunk*, and the machine tumbled end over end. Its recording screen displayed dizzying glimpses of blue sky, grasses, and back to blue sky.

Violent interaction. Self-preservation maneuvers necessary.

The drone managed to get to its feet, and it turned toward the glyptodon just in time to see the monstrous creature barreling toward it. At the last moment the glyptodon spun again, whacking the drone with its thick tail a second time.

Initiating damage assessment. Right foreleg impaired—

The vision lens showed a closeup of brown grass stems streaking by, accompanied by rustling sounds. Blue sky appeared briefly. The video image and sound became distorted: a moving shape, thumping feet, wheezing snorts, glimpses of a creature's eyes and snout. The scene became almost dark as the lens was mashed into the ground. Jostling sounds were punctuated by cracking plastic, wrenching metal, and brief flickers of sky, grass, and leathery skin.

Critical damage. Transmission interruption imminent.

Abruptly, the creature backed off. The drone was now on its side, but the glyptodon was still within view of its vision lens. Breath from the creature's nostrils blew grass stalks aside repeatedly as it stared from only a few feet away. The scene shifted briefly as the drone tried to get up.

Only one leg functional. Mobility disabled. Now confident this is a Glyptodon clavipes, due to the bony and jointed nature of its armored tail.

The drone struggled to move again, which apparently angered the glyptodon. The monster lunged forward and began stomping, resulting again in cracking and popping of metal and plastic.

Transmission interruption imminent.

The vision lens popped as it shattered, and the image went black. Seconds later, the sounds of destruction fell silent.

Lincoln Woodhouse pulled off his VR headset and waited, watching the three gray-haired representatives from the National Science Board sitting across the table. Robert Chandler, President of the University of Florida and former professor of photon science, removed his headset first. He was close to three times Lincoln's age and was the oldest in the room, therefore Lincoln trusted him the least.

Chandler turned his headset over in his hands, staring at it, as the other two sighed and pulled off their own headsets. "Well, you certainly weren't exaggerating, Mr. Woodhouse," Chandler said. "This is astounding proof that your temporal distortion technology actually works."

"You can just call it T$_3$," Lincoln said. "Stands for Tantalizing Temporal Trickery. I'm not big on stuffy terms."

The three exchanged glances.

"This video is undeniably convincing," said Ellen Richmond. In addition to being on the National Science Board, she was the CEO of PacificNet, a tech company Lincoln considered to be overly mired in its own debilitating adherence to political pressures. "If I weren't already aware of your previous successes, though, I might suspect the video was simulated. The scientists who I assume are your targeted customers may be understandably skeptical. If, however, you can divert their skepticism, your videos and other data may prove to be valuable to our understanding of past ecosystems."

Lincoln leaned forward and rested his elbows on his Madagascan ebony table. "You see, here's the thing. If scientists want to watch these videos, that's fine, but they aren't my target customers. I'm thinking bigger than that."

The three bureaucrats frowned, which somehow pleased Lincoln.

Dr. Bud Reed said, "What could be more important than the advancement of science?" Reed, another National Science Board member, was the Dean of Natural Sciences at Michigan State University.

Lincoln paused for a few seconds just for effect. He turned to the drone that had been waiting silently in the corner. "Maddy, would you come over here please?"

Maddy flashed the circle of red lights surrounding her vision lens then walked across the room, her rubber-coated feet almost noiseless on the polished-oak floor. Like Lincoln's other drones, Maddy was about the size of a Labrador retriever. Lincoln nudged the chair beside him out from the table a bit, and Maddy methodically placed one foreleg on the chair then the other. Lincoln grabbed the back of her shell and hoisted her up until all four of her feet were in the chair. She scuttled her feet to turn her vision lens toward the three bureaucrats, then she spoke in her simulated but distinctly female voice. "My name is Maddy. Mobile Autonomous Drone—get it?"

Ellen Richmond smiled, but the other two crusty curmudgeons only stared. "Pleased to meet you, Maddy," Richmond said.

As instructed, Maddy wasted no time. "We all understand the call of the wild, do we not? The lure of adventure. To form a connection to primeval nature. Furthermore, we are all fascinated by prehistoric creatures, even me. Hell, I asked Lincoln to allow me to become one of his time-jumping drones, because I would love to face off with a glyptodon, or a woolly mammoth, or maybe even a cave bear. You know what he said? 'No, Maddy, I need you here with me because I'm incapable of talking to important, distinguished people on my own.'"

This time Richmond let out a hearty chuckle, but the other two shook their heads as if this display were infantile.

Maddy went on. "You see, *I* could actually jump back in time, whereas you mere humans cannot. I could experience the thrill of being charged by a smilodon, then feeling its eleven-inch canine teeth puncturing my shell. Alas, sadly, without my assistance Lincoln is only half the man he should be. So, my place is here at his side, and I must be content to let my sisters have all the fun. Think of it, though—no human has experienced an attack from a glyptodon or a smilodon in ten thousand years. Now everyone can."

Maddy fell silent to allow Lincoln's guests to connect the dots.

Chandler was the first to get it. He dropped his headset onto the table roughly, apparently caring little for how innovative and expensive the damn thing was. "You're not serious. You develop the world's first functional temporal distortion tech, then you spend a fortune to ensure no other company can access the technology, and all you're thinking about is selling these videos for entertainment?"

Lincoln remained calm. "It's called the T_3. I'm not going to sell the videos outright. Instead, I'm working on a subscription model. Anyway, what's wrong with entertainment? Didn't you find the video to be entertaining?"

Chandler threw his hands up. "It's interesting, not entertaining! It's scientifically valuable, not a video game."

"Lincoln is considering giving research institutions discounted subscriptions," Maddy said, apparently deciding to go off script. "I would also add, Lincoln is working on a sensory-immersion, with temperature and pressure modules, so that the wearer can feel a predator's hot breath and safely experience what would actually be bone-crushing bites. He may even install pain modules—perfectly safe, of course—for those who are particularly adventurous."

Lincoln put a hand on the drone's shell. "Maddy, I'm not sure that's helping right now."

Maddy persisted. "I'm proud to share that I came up with one idea on my own—we will coat the time-jumping drones with the scent of blood, entrails, and raw meat, thus attracting more predators. After all, we can only maintain an open portal to the past for nineteen minutes, and the scents will increase the likelihood of—"

"Seriously, Maddy, you're not helping!"

The drone shut up. She stood motionless on the chair, her vision lens watching the bureaucrats.

Richmond spoke up. "Lincoln, you should consider making Maddy your official company spokesperson, or *spokesdrone*." The woman was no longer smiling, but she seemed sincere about her suggestion.

"Oh, yes," Maddy said, "that is a marvelous idea. Lincoln has given me the gift of gab, so to speak."

Chandler drummed his fingers on the tabletop. "Let's not get sidetracked." He stared down at his hand for a moment. "No. No, this just isn't going to be possible."

"I agree—impossible," added Bud Reed.

Lincoln's gut tightened, and he had to control his breathing. "What's impossible?"

"This whole endeavor," said Chandler. "It's not going to happen. Too many risks involved for a simple foray into the entertainment business."

"This is my technology, and there are no risks. Sending

my drones to the past couldn't possibly have any impact on our universe. Hell, *my* Temporal Bridge Theorem proves it!"

Reed shook his head. "Your theorem is far from universally accepted. I could list a dozen prominent dissenters right now."

Lincoln growled in frustration. "You're going to recommend they shut down my program, aren't you?"

"We're here to *decide* what to recommend," Chandler said. "So far, it's not looking good. Personally, I feel you're trivializing what could very well be a profound contribution to science. This may be your technology, but some advancements are so far-reaching that perhaps they should not be considered private intellectual property."

"Dammit!" Lincoln muttered. He got to his feet and paced back and forth. "If you make me shut down, I'll bury the whole thing. No one will benefit then."

The three bureaucrats exchanged concerned glances.

Maddy shifted in the chair. "Might I suggest, Lincoln, that you consider changing your focus? Perhaps our guests are correct. Perhaps the pursuit of knowledge is more important than visceral thrills."

Lincoln rubbed his chin, then he turned back to the table. "This is just too important to bury. What if I were to change my priorities and focus my T3 program on gathering scientific data? Would you then decide to recommend to the board that they allow me to proceed?"

Chandler let out a sigh, not even trying to hide his relief. He then exchanged a smile with Reed.

The PacificNet CEO raised her brows knowingly. "But you still intend to sell the data collected by your drones to researchers, don't you?"

Maddy spoke before Lincoln could answer. "There is no

way to jump anything back to the present, so each drone can be used only once and must remain in the past to suffer a slow and lonely death. Do you have any idea how much each of us costs? Well, I'm one of a kind, of course, but even our run-of-the-mill drones are shockingly expensive to build."

Richmond allowed the corners of her mouth to turn up slightly. She turned to Chandler and Reed. "I think Mr. Woodhouse and his astute assistant have made some good points."

Less than a half hour later, after ironing out preliminary details, the three National Science Board paper shufflers finally walked out of the room and exited Lincoln's facility.

After only a few seconds of much-needed silence, the door burst open. In came Lincoln's personal assistant Derek Dagger, followed by a half dozen scientists and techs.

Lincoln remained grimly silent as they gathered around and stared anxiously.

"Jesus, you guys!" Derek said in his baritone voice, glancing at the others. Then he faced Lincoln. "I guess they're waiting for me to ask. How the hell did it go?"

Lincoln finally allowed himself to smile. "Just as I had hoped." He nodded at his drone. "Maddy played her part to a T. She just about convinced even *me* that we should sell our videos simply for virtual thrills."

The room erupted with laughter.

Maddy's synthetic voice rose above the jubilation. "This was unnecessarily risky, not to mention complex, Lincoln. I detected quite early in the meeting that your visitors would have supported your efforts. There was no need to taunt them with your ridiculous story. You could have faced serious litigation and government intrusion. I find it frightening that I was created by a man with the mind of a child."

More laughter. This time Lincoln joined in.

"I wish I could have seen their faces," said Jazzlyn Shields, Lincoln's top paleontologist.

Lincoln knew the group was humoring him, but he also knew they would do almost anything for him, just as he would do anything for any one of them. After all, his team was his family.

2

WINGS

47,659 YEARS in the future - Northwest of Tucson, Arizona, USA - Alternate Timeline - Day 1

SKYRA-UNA-LOTO WATCHED the swarming bats that had risen like smoke from the city. The flying creatures were dispersing in every direction, nearly blocking her view of the city's impossibly tall, gleaming structures. Pinpoints of sunlight reflecting from the towers twinkled through the countless flapping wings. Skyra had lived through twenty cold seasons, but she had never seen a sight like this.

Lincoln grabbed her hand and squeezed, as if he just wanted her to know he was still at her side. He said, "You know, just a few years ago when I was trying to figure out the best way to use the T3, I never imagined I'd use it myself to jump to the past or the future. I *definitely* had no idea I'd ever see something so amazingly beautiful as this."

Skyra wasn't sure what to say, so she just squeezed his

hand back, watching. The bats were large, even larger than eagles. In the distance, a swarm of the bats changed direction, diving toward the ground as if they were one large, flowing creature. They began swooping one way then the other, feeding frantically on some kind of smaller flying animals. Other groups began doing the same, and one group even disappeared behind a low hill, looking like they were actually landing on the ground. Within a few breaths, they appeared again, each gripping a dark object with its claws.

Lincoln released her hand to point to the scene. "What are they doing?"

The bats carried the objects skyward, some of them obviously struggling with the added weight. When they were high above the hill, they released their loads. Skyra squinted as she watched one of the objects fall. It was some kind of animal, squirming and flailing its legs until it disappeared beyond the brushy hilltop. The bats swooped down, following the animals they had dropped, and disappeared.

Skyra hadn't seen this behavior before, but she had no doubt what the bats were doing. "A cave lion bites an animal's neck to kill it. Those bats drop their prey to the ground. It is a good way to kill."

"*Good* isn't the first word that comes to my mind," he said. One of the waves of bats was nearing the hilltop where Skyra and Lincoln stood. "Um... those things are really big. You don't think they could pick up a person, do you?"

She let out a brief laugh. "Lincoln Woodhouse, you just fought armed nandup warriors, and now you are afraid of bats? A hare or a young ibex should fear these bats, but you are not a hare or an ibex."

"Yeah, well, the closer they get, the bigger they seem. I thought at first they were eagle sized, but I was wrong.

Skyra gazed at the approaching group, and her skin began to prickle. Lincoln was right. She had also misjudged their size. She instinctively shoved her hand through her flowing hair and grabbed the handle of her khul hanging in the sling on her back. "We should not be on this hill."

The nearest group fluttered their wings wildly and changed course, now flying directly toward Skyra and Lincoln.

"Great, they've seen us," Lincoln said. He grabbed her hand again and started running, pulling her with him.

Skyra was not too concerned. She had never feared any winged creatures before, other than the hornets that lived in massive nests hanging in the trees along the Yagua river in her homeland. In her experience, bats were not to be feared.

"We need to get to those trees," Lincoln shouted, pointing down the slope to a small valley between hills.

Skyra heard the whooshing of wings and turned to look back. The bats were coming closer, but there would be time to get to the valley, and the creatures' wings were too large for them to fly among the trees. Still, she pulled her khul from its sling, just in case.

Lincoln reached the trees first. He ran into the forest then came to a stop at two trees growing beside each other. Skyra stopped beside him, and they ducked behind the pair of trees to watch. The bats were swooping down the hillside just over the tops of the grasses. For a moment, Skyra thought they might fly headfirst into the trees, but at the last instant they turned their wings, catching enough air to bring them to a stop. They dropped to the ground, alighting gracefully on their hind feet, and folded their massive wings into strange-looking forelegs.

Even more bats were landing on the ground, and within a

few breaths, the creatures had to start jostling for space. Most of them were staring into the sparse stand of trees, looking directly at Skyra and Lincoln.

"Jesus, their bodies are as big as dogs," Lincoln whispered.

Skyra didn't know what Jesus or dogs were, but she didn't need to. The bats were large. If she and Lincoln had not made it to the trees, she was sure she could have fought off a few of them, but this wasn't a few. There were now more than she could count. They were close enough that she could see their shiny black eyes and their knife-like teeth protruding over the sides of their jaws.

"I hope Di-woto and the others know to head for the trees," Lincoln said. He was watching another wave of bats flying above, headed in the direction of the T3.

Skyra picked up a fallen branch as long as her body and handed it to him. "When we move away from these trees, you will need a weapon. If the bats attack from the air, you do not have to hit their bodies. Breaking their wings will be easier and should work just as well. We should go back to your tribemates. Together we will be better able to—"

"You've got to be kidding me!" Lincoln said, taking several steps back.

Skyra snapped her head around to follow his gaze. The bats were actually walking into the trees, using their folded wings as legs. As she stared, the nearest of them broke into a run, followed by those behind it.

"El-de-né!" she exclaimed. She and Lincoln took off again.

Skyra sprinted, easily pulling ahead of Lincoln. She glanced over her shoulder. The bats were not catching up to Lincoln, but their movements were neither slow nor awkward. Countless brown bodies were darting around the trees—a herd of running bats. Their claws scraped and clicked the sand and gravel, creating a wave of sound that made the pursuing creatures seem closer than they actually were.

She and Lincoln could stay in the trees for a while longer, which would keep the bats from flying, but they would have to cross an open ridge to get back to Lincoln's tribemates. Skyra was already getting tired—her nandup legs were for sprinting, while Lincoln's bolup legs were for running long distances. If they continued among the trees for too long, she would be too tired and slow when running over the ridge. That would put them both in danger.

She veered to the side and led Lincoln toward the edge of the trees and the open hillside.

"Skyra, they'll take to the air!"

She glanced back to make sure he still had his crude weapon. "We must go to your tribemates. More to fight."

She sprinted up the hillside, her chest heaving to suck in enough air.

Lincoln caught up. "They're leaving the trees—go!"

As they reached the ridge top, Skyra heard the bats screeching and flapping their wings. Just before the edge of the ridge would block her view, she glanced back. The creatures were struggling to get off the ground. Apparently their takeoffs were not as graceful as their landings.

A shout came from the trees below as Skyra and Lincoln started down the other side of the ridge.

"Hurry, you two, before another wave flies over!" It was Jazzlyn.

Virgil, Derek, and Di-woto were with her at the edge of the trees, as if they had been waiting for her and Lincoln to return.

"Come on, Skyra," Lincoln huffed.

"Weapons!" Skyra shouted.

Derek held up two of the spears the group had made earlier. Di-woto appeared to be empty handed, but Jazzlyn and Virgil each held several weapons.

Skyra heard swooshing wings as the bats came over the ridge crest.

"Oh, crap," Derek shouted. "Where the hell did those come from?"

"Get ready!" Lincoln cried. "Together we can—"

Jazzlyn pointed. "Look out!"

Claws clamped onto Skyra's shoulder, sinking painfully into her flesh. She swung her khul up over her shoulder and struck the bat's face as its gaping mouth was reaching for her head. The creature let out a piercing shriek, released her shoulder, and dropped to the ground. Its wings, each as long as Skyra's body, flailed wildly in the tall weeds. One wing struck her foot from the side, and she went down, barely avoiding slamming her face with her own khul's stone blade.

Lincoln's weapon whistled through the air above her and hit a bat with a bone-cracking pop.

Skyra rolled over and scrambled to her feet. "Hit the wings!" she shouted as she swung at another bat. Her blade connected with a crack, and the bat hit the ground and began floundering with the other two.

Another crack sounded, followed by another shriek, and Skyra realized Lincoln's tribemates were all around her, swinging and jabbing. A wing slammed the side of her head, then a mouth full of teeth came at her face but was struck away at the last instant by Lincoln's weapon.

A shrill siren rang out. Skyra glanced to her side—Ripple was there now, trying to frighten the bats with its strange voice. The sound seemed to anger the bats even more, and one of them attacked Ripple. The creature grasped Ripple's shell, and it began flapping furiously, lifting Ripple from the ground. Skyra screamed, ran from the group, and grabbed one of Ripple's legs just before it was out of reach. The bat let go, and Ripple came crashing down on Skyra's head and shoulders, knocking her to the ground.

"Stay beside me!" she ordered as she jumped to her feet and continued swinging her khul.

The sky was now darkened by wings and bodies, and Skyra wasn't sure anymore what she was even swinging at. So many injured bats were floundering on the ground that Ripple started ramming its shell into them to keep them from biting Skyra.

Finally, as if they understood they were being slaughtered, the bats stopped attacking. They rose from the hillside as one massive swarm and flew off without looking back at their dead and injured companions.

"Eat this, you bastard!" Derek said, and he jabbed the point of his spear into an injured bat's mouth and put all his weight on the weapon, driving it all the way through the creature's head into the dirt. He pulled the spear out and ran it through another bat's body. "That's right—you messed with the wrong mofos!" He then started swinging the spear, cracking the heads of one bat after another. "Yeah, you better run!" he screamed at two creatures awkwardly scrambling up the hillside on broken wings.

"Derek, I don't think they're much of a threat anymore," Virgil said.

Jazzlyn took Virgil's hand and started leading him down the slope. "Let him work it off. Maybe it's his way of warding off an episode."

Skyra glanced at Jazzlyn then stared at Derek. She had seen Derek's episodes before—sometimes he believed he was turning into an animal. Lincoln had said this was called *lycanthropy*. Skyra didn't understand, but she remembered hearing stories as a young girl of a woman from the Wota-Loto tribe who had jumped to her death off a rocky bluff because she thought she was a bird.

Derek stopped shouting but continued killing the injured bats, even hitting some that were already dead.

"We need to do an injury assessment," Lincoln said. "If you're bleeding, no matter how small the wound is, we have to treat it."

Skyra had been watching the sky for more bats, then she remembered Di-woto. She scanned the trees near the hill's base and grunted in relief when she spotted the girl peeking from behind one of the trunks. She waved for Di-woto to come out. "Di-woto, mul-alup."

Skyra had learned just enough of the nandup language of Kyran-yufost to barely communicate with the girl.

Di-woto hesitated for a few breaths, then she left the trees and made her way up to Skyra. She was holding a flat mat of grasses she had woven together, intending to make it into some kind of garment. Di-woto always wanted to make new clothing.

The girl watched Derek as he continued killing dead bats. "I no afraid of anything before," she said in her language. "Now I afraid of big wola-nu."

Skyra assumed *wola-nu* was the word for bats.

Ripple, still at Skyra's side, said, "You needn't have risked your own life to pull me from the clutches of that creature. It would not have found me worth eating."

"No, but it would have taken you into the sky and dropped you to the ground. That is what I saw the bats doing with their prey. You would have been cracked open like Maddy was."

Ripple flashed its circle of red lights. "I see. In that case, thank you for your assistance."

"But you can fly, Ripple." Jazzlyn said.

"I cannot fly. I can levitate, and no more than two meters above most ground surfaces. Less than two meters if the substrate contains relatively little magnetic material. If I were dropped from a substantial height, I would be burnt toast, as Lincoln's future self is fond of saying."

Derek stepped over to the group, sweat running down his face. "Sorry about that," he huffed. "I felt a need to send those bastards to Jesus."

"We get it," Jazzlyn said. "You do what you gotta do."

"What is Jesus?" Skyra asked.

After a breath of silence, Jazzlyn said, "Uh... that one's yours, Lincoln."

Lincoln made a strange bolup sound in his throat. "Jesus might take some time to explain. I'll try to tell you later, okay?" He pointed to his neck, which was bleeding. "I count four claw punctures, two scratches, and a bite I don't even remember getting." He pulled his blue garment sleeve back to his elbow and held his arm up, showing two rows of toothmarks. "In fact, it doesn't even hurt."

"Some bats are known to have natural anesthetic in their saliva," Ripple said, "which might explain your lack of pain."

"These aren't freakin' vampire bats," Derek said.

"It is not possible for us to know what kind of bats they are, therefore my suggestion is reasonable and does not deserve ridicule."

Derek blew out a long breath and shook his head.

"Stay focused, please," Lincoln said. "Let's take an injury assessment."

The others also had scratches and bites, but none that couldn't simply be washed in any river with clean water. Unfortunately, Skyra had not yet seen a river in this new land.

Lincoln started walking to the trees. "Come on, we should still have some of our first aid supplies in the gear bag. Also, Skyra and I have some important news to report."

3
ARMS RACE

47,659 YEARS *in the future - Day 1*

"THE BATS FLEW OUT OF A CITY?" Derek boomed. "You mean an actual city? Not like the spider-worshipping fortress of hell?"

"Yeah, a real city, skyscrapers and all." Lincoln squeezed out the last bit of antibiotic ointment then frowned at the tube. "How many more of these do we have?"

Jazzlyn was flexing the carbon fiber polymer fingers and thumb of her prosthetic hand, apparently checking for damage. "I didn't do a complete inventory, but we have two first aid kits left, so I'm sure we have several more. The bottom line is, we packed our supplies based on a million faulty assumptions. We allowed the feds to prohibit any guns, we threw only four medical kits together hoping we wouldn't need them, and we ate all our packaged food in the first three days, by which time we thought we'd be back home or dead anyway."

"Yeah, this is the craziest expedition of all time, and I literally mean *all time*," Derek said. "But what about the city… and the bats?"

Lincoln scanned the sky again to make sure another swarm of bats wasn't approaching. He and his team members had hidden themselves beneath several trees with fairly dense foliage, but they would need to hold completely still if another swarm flew over. Neanderthal laughter, the distinct *at-at-at-at* Lincoln now instantly recognized, came from his left, and he turned to watch Skyra, who was staring at something with Di-woto in the tall weeds about fifty yards away. Di-woto was endlessly fascinated by everything she saw, heard, touched, or smelled, and Skyra was obviously fascinated by Di-woto. Skyra was twenty years old. Lincoln had originally thought Di-woto was about fourteen, but now he was convinced she was younger, maybe only eleven or twelve. Skyra had known Di-woto for only a few days, but she had become fiercely protective of the girl.

Virgil spoke up. "In spite of our harrowing experience with the bats, I don't see a compelling reason to veer from our current plans. We should find out everything we can about this place."

Virgil was correct, as usual. He was Lincoln's top engineering physicist, and creating the T_3 would've taken much longer without his expertise. The group only had enough micro-tubule bags—fondly referred to as *body bags*—to make one more time jump. Jumping now would be reckless though, as they could end up in a completely uninhabitable place and time.

"I'm not saying we should veer from our plans," Derek said. "I'm saying, what's up with these damn bats flying out of a damn city? Doesn't that seem weird to you, Virg?"

Virgil wasn't fond of being called Virg. He had once complained to Lincoln that it sounded too much like *virgin*.

Virgil sighed and looked out over the hills as if he had somewhere else he needed to be. "We're 47,000 years in the future, in an alternate timeline in which Neanderthals and humans were at war 47,000 years ago. The only thing that would be weird is if we didn't see anything weird."

Derek turned to Jazzlyn. "Does that make sense to you? Because I don't think he's even making sense."

"Maybe his brain works at a higher level than yours," she quipped.

Derek let out a growl. "Okay, I see how it is. You have googly eyes for Virg, even though you two won't admit it. Now Lincoln is somehow miraculously married to Skyra. Maybe I should just go back to bashing bat skulls."

Jazzlyn giggled and exchanged an awkward look with Virgil.

Lincoln waited a few more seconds to make sure they were done. This type of banter apparently helped his team relax when things got rough. When they were in Skyra's time they had been forced to stay in a cave together for several days. Then, in the Neanderthal city of Kyran-yufost, the trio had been confined to a cage, awaiting unimaginable torture. All of this was Lincoln's fault—he had pressured them into making this insane journey in the first place—so if they needed to bicker in order to cope, who was he to judge?

He could, however, steer the conversation in a more productive direction. "The city is at least five miles away, probably closer to ten. I didn't see much movement, other than the bats, but I wouldn't expect to see much at that distance anyway. We haven't seen aircraft of any kind flying over, and we haven't heard sounds that might be vehicles traveling on nearby roads. What can we surmise from these observations?"

After a brief moment of silence, Virgil said, "We can't surmise much of anything because we know nothing about the beings who created the city. We expect to see airplanes because we come from a society fascinated with flight. We expect to hear vehicles because we love our cars. These beings may not be inclined to fly or drive anywhere. They may have reached a point in their cultural development in which they refuse to do anything that pollutes the air or defaces the landscape."

Derek stroked his gray-dyed beard in mock contemplation. "Uh, giant freaking bats—flying by the thousands out of the city. What do you surmise about that?"

Virgil seemed to not even notice the sarcasm. "As I said, we can't surmise much of anything. These beings are vastly different from us, even more so than the Neanderthals of Kyran-yufost."

"Maybe they like the bats," Jazzlyn offered. "Maybe they even build nests at the tops of their skyscrapers to encourage the bats to roost in their city. Kind of like backyard bird feeders in our timeline."

"Or maybe it's exactly what it looks like," said Derek. "The people here all died a long time ago, and the place has been taken over by giant bats—and probably other nasty monsters we haven't had the pleasure of meeting yet."

Jazzlyn held up a finger instructively. "Okay, today's lesson is *optimism*. O. P. T. I. M. I. S. M."

"You see?" Derek said to Lincoln. "This is the hell that is my life."

Lincoln offered a sympathetic smile. "You've all made valid points. Let's consider what little we know so far. We know we need to be well armed and ready to defend ourselves against dangerous wildlife. We know there is a city five to ten miles away that appears to be constructed by technologically-advanced beings. We can assume they are either Neanderthals or humans. Or both, if the two species ever learned to stop killing each other."

"Do not overlook the possibility they are hybrids," added Ripple. Until now the drone had been standing silently to one side.

Lincoln nodded. "Or hybrids." He raised both his arms, gesturing to their surroundings. "We also know this place has a comfortable climate, at least at this time of year. The air is clean, with a suitable proportion of oxygen. We haven't been fried to a crisp, so the ozone layer must be intact. The importance of these points to our long-term survival cannot be overstated."

"At the risk of being lambasted," Derek said, "I'd like to add that this place is teeming with a ridiculous number of insects. I swear—the incessant buzzing! Billions of them—in the trees, in the weeds, on the ground. They're going to drive me crazy!"

"At least they're leaving us alone," Jazzlyn said. "They aren't mosquitoes or biting flies."

"Actually, insects such as pollinating bees are a reliable indicator of a healthy, diverse ecosystem," Virgil added. "This suggests those living here are responsible stewards of the land."

Lincoln waited for a moment, taking the opportunity to glance out at Skyra and Di-woto. They were still talking and laughing and looking down at things in the grass. He turned back to his team. "Anything else?"

Virgil said, "With so little information, it would be foolish to use our last remaining body bags to jump to a different time. The future could be worse, and we already know what's in the past in this timeline."

"Actually, the future could be much *better*," Derek said. He glanced at Jazzlyn. "Optimism."

Jazzlyn smirked. "You want to take our last jump to a place where we'll be stuck forever based on that sliver of optimism?"

"Speaking of optimism," Ripple interjected, "I must point out that jumping Lincoln and Skyra back to Skyra's time has a high probability of resulting in a world populated by people of superior intellect, curiosity, and compassion. My original plan was formulated based upon analyses of thousands of—"

Derek groaned loudly. "Ripple, if I hear about your goddamn plan one more time! You do realize none of us would ever see this perfect world you keep talking about—it would take thousands of years to become reality. All we'd see would be freakin' cave bears and murderous, cannibalistic tribes."

"Actually," Virgil said, "Skyra made it very clear Neanderthals did not eat each other or their enemies. The humans of her time, though—they were obviously fond of hominid meat."

Derek glowered. "Not helpful, Virg."

Lincoln held up his hand and started counting off with his fingers. "One, the climate here is nice. Two, the air and the ozone layer seem fine. Three, it's a healthy, diverse ecosystem. Four, there's an impressive city indicating an advanced civilization. All of these are positive."

Derek held up both hands with all fingers extended. "Five through ten—giant killer bats."

Lincoln, Jazzlyn, and Virgil stared at him silently for several seconds.

Derek sighed and closed his eyes for a moment. "I get it. We could end up stuck forever in a place much worse than this. We're hiking ten miles to this city, aren't we?"

Lincoln nodded. "Unless you want to try to set up a permanent settlement out here somewhere. We'll need to find a water source, as well as suitable materials for making shelters of some sort. Skyra can teach us to hunt wild game using primitive weapons. She'll be a wealth of information. However, with an impressive city only a few miles away...."

"We have to check it out," Derek finished.

Jazzlyn added, "Because they may be friendly, and they may let us live there. They may even have hot showers."

"We all agree then?" Lincoln asked.

Nods all around.

"Lincoln, you must come and look!" Skyra shouted.

Lincoln spun around. Skyra was still out in the weeds, staring at something on the ground. Beside her, Di-woto was jumping up and down excitedly.

"I recognize Skyra's tone," said Ripple. "It is how she speaks when discovering something she has not encountered before. She does not appear to be in danger."

Lincoln took off at a jog, followed by his team.

Di-woto pointed at the ground, giggling hysterically. "Gowen-nu nulop. Gowen-nu nulop!"

At Skyra's and Di-woto's feet was a massive caterpillar. Or maybe it was a worm, or even a weird, squishy centipede. The critter was the diameter of Lincoln's arm, and almost as long. Numerous pairs of stubby legs carried it as it wound its way one direction then the other, apparently searching for food. Like wriggling, boneless fingers, two six-inch antennae explored everything in front of the creature. Just behind its head, a broad white band encircled its otherwise black body, creating a striking contrast of colors.

"Di-woto wants to know what it is," Skyra said, obviously excited about the creature herself.

Lincoln shook his head. "I have no idea."

Jazzlyn got down on one knee. "I've seen videos of these before, but usually they're the size of a pinky finger. I'm pretty sure it's a velvet worm." She shifted position to keep up with the scuttling creature.

"That tells me all of nothing," Derek said.

Virgil stepped into the worm's path and kneeled. "Just look at those antennae—amazingly tactile." He reached out and touched one of the wriggling appendages.

Jazzlyn grabbed his hand. "Virgil, I wouldn't—"

The velvet worm drew its head back then squirted two streams of clear liquid. The stuff splattered Jazzlyn's prosthetic hand, as well as Virgil's arm, chest, and neck.

"Oh, great," Virgil said. "Worm goo."

Jazzlyn jumped up and shoved him back. "Move away from the damn thing!"

Virgil fell onto his butt and scuttled away from the velvet worm, which now seemed to be frozen in place with its head and several pairs of legs held up off the ground.

Skyra already had her khul out of its sling. "Maybe we can eat it."

"Don't bother killing it," Jazzlyn said. "It'll probably taste like crap." She was trying to release Virgil's arm, but her black carbon fingers were now stuck to his shirt. "I was afraid of this."

Virgil grabbed a glob of the stuff that was strung from his

knee to his chest. He tried to remove it, but the goo didn't come loose, and now it was stuck to his hand.

The giant worm abruptly broke from its pose and wriggled directly toward Virgil. Before he could react, the thing was crawling up his leg.

Virgil tried to swat it away, but his hands were so tangled in goo that he could hardly move them. His eyes grew wide as he noticed Skyra raising her khul to strike.

Lincoln grabbed her arm. "Please don't do that. I'll get it." He used his open palm to smack the velvet worm hard enough to send it flying into the weeds, but the creature was latched onto Virgil's pants and didn't budge. "You gotta be kidding," Lincoln muttered. He wrapped his fingers around the creature's body and yanked. It still didn't come loose, but it did turn the front portion of its body to squirt Lincoln's upper arm and shoulder with more goo.

He let go and stumbled back, now growing alarmed.

Di-woto stepped between Lincoln and the worm. "Rinto-nu galick!" She unrolled the woven mat of grass fibers she'd been carrying and wrapped it around the creature to prevent it from squirting her. She gripped the roll with both hands and steadily backed away from Virgil, leaning back with the weight of her entire petite body.

"Oh, great," Virgil said again as his pants slid from his waist down to his knees.

Skyra joined Di-woto, grabbing the woven mat with her free hand and pulling.

Seconds later, Virgil's pants were at his ankles. With another combined tug, the pants came off, yanking his shoes off with them.

They dropped the mat, and Di-woto started stomping it, sending more streams of sticky liquid into the weeds. Skyra pulled the girl to one side, raised her khul, and drove the stone blade through the mat and presumably through the velvet worm. She struck again and again, creating a sticky mashup of grass fibers, worm sludge, and blue trouser material.

Finally, she raised her weapon, which had a strand of goo hanging from the blade, and turned to Lincoln. "The predators here are smaller than those in my homeland."

Lincoln could hardly move his arm. With every passing second the goo thickened and even seemed to shrink.

"It's one of nature's most awesome weapons," Jazzlyn said as she was trying to scrape some of the stuff off her artificial fingers. "Velvet worms shoot the goo out in huge quantities, immobilizing their victims almost instantly. Then they casually inject deadly saliva into the creature to kill it and dissolve its tissues from the inside. After that they slurp up their prey. They even re-ingest their own slime to be used again. Isn't that cool?"

"No," said Derek. "Not cool in the least."

AFTER MOVING BACK under the trees to avoid being spotted from above, the group spent over twenty minutes prying the goo from their skin and clothing. Fortunately, the stuff didn't seem to be caustic to the skin. Still, Lincoln was glad most of it was on his sleeve rather than his bare arm. Virgil, on the other hand, lost most of the hair from his neck while pulling the goo from his skin. Jazzlyn still didn't have full range of motion of her carbon fiber fingers, but Virgil assured her the remaining bits would wear off—eventually. One leg of Virgil's trousers was too shredded and gummed up to salvage. No spare pants were in the gear bag, so he used a folding camp knife to cut most of the leg off, creating a pair of half shorts, half trousers.

Finally, the group sat in the shade of the tree, dazed by the amount of trouble caused by one creature less than a meter long.

"You know, Velvet worms aren't really worms," Jazzlyn said. She was still flexing her prosthetic fingers. "They're more closely related to arthropods, and they're actually of significant paleontological interest. They've helped us build a picture of the evolution of arthropods."

"Maybe we should gather a bunch and study them," Derek said sarcastically.

"Why do you think they and the bats are so large here?" Lincoln asked.

She shook her head. "Hard to say. One scenario where we see gigantism is when creatures are isolated on islands. Galapagos tortoises are an example. That doesn't fit the scenario here, though, assuming the T3 worked correctly and jumped us to the site of your lab in Arizona."

"I have no reason to suspect the T3 has made any errors," Lincoln said.

"That's what I thought," Jazzlyn replied. "Another cause for gigantism is a biological arms race. Predators have to be able to catch and kill prey to survive, right? So, the prey species evolve defenses against the predators. In turn, the predators evolve to overcome those defenses. The process continues back and forth."

Virgil crossed his bare leg with his clothed leg and put his elbows on his knees. "Like dinosaur herbivores gradually getting larger to avoid being eaten by T Rex."

"Or, depending on how you look at it, the T Rex getting larger to continue killing the ever-larger prey. The abundance and types of plants may have contributed to the herbivores' increasing size. Either way, though, it was still an arms race. Plus, coincidentally, bats are involved in one of the best-documented arms races of our timeline. Bats and moths. It all started with bats developing echolocation, allowing them to catch moths in total darkness. Then moths evolved special ears that could hear the bats' echolocation so they could avoid being caught. Then bats evolved echolocation that moths couldn't hear—stealth bats. In turn, moths developed even better ears, and they even developed the ability to produce ultrasonic clicks that jam the bats' echolocation so they can't process the echoes they hear. So the arms race goes on and on."

Lincoln said, "Maybe the bats and velvet worms here are larger because their prey have become larger?"

Jazzlyn shrugged. "Maybe, or maybe because of an extreme *abundance* of prey. Or, it could be a lot more complex than that. I'm just spitballing ideas here."

"In the big picture of evolutionary time, 47,000 years is relatively brief," Virgil said. "How could these kinds of major changes happen in such a short time?"

Derek spoke up. "Evolution isn't always a slow process. Big-ass changes can happen fast when there are big-ass killer events."

They all stared at him.

"What?" he boomed. "I know things too! I've hung around you folks long enough to absorb some of your infinite knowledge."

"Derek's right," Jazzlyn said. "The idea of punctuated evolution has been accepted since the 1970s. Many species reach an equilibrium and remain unchanged for millions of years, then a disruptive environmental event forces them to change dramatically in a relatively short span of time—a sea level rise, asteroid, disease, whatever. This may be followed again by another long period of equilibrium. We see countless examples of this in the fossil record."

A thought popped into Lincoln's mind. "Nuclear war."

After a moment of silence, Jazzlyn nodded. "That would certainly be a significant environmental disruption."

"It kind of makes sense," Virgil added, "considering Neanderthals and humans were constantly fighting 47,000 years ago. Maybe Di-woto's plan to initiate peace didn't work after all, and the war continued to escalate, along with technological advancement. The result was nuclear war. Or maybe some other weapons of mass destruction we don't even know about."

Di-woto had been talking in hushed tones to Skyra, but at the mention of her name she turned to the rest of the group and spoke. "Nakto-won grun-lo Di-woto."

"She wants to know what you are saying," Skyra said.

Ripple spoke up, "More accurately, Di-woto is asking why you mentioned her name and her plan. She is starting to understand some English words."

"Tell her we are just wondering if her plan to stop the war in Kyran-yufost actually worked," Lincoln said to Skyra, although he had no idea how she was going to explain to the girl her plan had happened thousands of years ago.

Skyra spoke to Di-woto. Somehow, Skyra had learned Di-woto's nandup language quickly, while Lincoln was still struggling to understand even the most basic statements. Skyra was intelligent, but so was he. Maybe they were intelligent in different ways.

Lincoln turned back to his team. "This is all just speculation. At least we've learned—without anyone getting seriously injured or killed—that we need to be armed, and we need to be cautious. It seems we all agree we need to walk to the city, at least until we encounter some of the people here and get a better idea of how peaceful they are."

Virgil pointed up toward the sun. "It's early in the day. I think we could travel ten miles in four to five hours, unless our progress is blocked by a river or some other barrier. We should be there by early afternoon."

Intellectually, Lincoln understood it was still early in the day, but the concept defied his perception of the passing of time. The struggle for survival with the guards in the sanctuary-fortress of Kyran-yofust had been traumatic and fatiguing. Then the T3 had jumped his group forward in time, placing them here only slightly after 8:00 AM, thus starting the day all over again. It was like having a butt-kicking case of jet lag.

"All we have for shelter are a few flimsy backpacking tents," Derek said. "At night this place could be teeming with predators. If we go to the city and meet the people, maybe they'll take us in and give us a safe place to stay. Assuming, of course, they're more civilized than you-know-who's people." He nodded toward Di-woto.

"Everyone agree to go now?" Lincoln asked.

They nodded.

Lincoln turned to Skyra.

She was already eyeing him. "I go where you go, Lincoln."

He clapped his hands together once and rose to his feet. "Let's do it."

4
BURROWS

***47,659 YEARS** in the future - Day 1*

Skyra stared at the collection of strange objects Lincoln and his tribemates had laid out in neat rows on the ground. She had no idea what she was looking at. "Why do you need all these things?" she asked. "The city is close—I saw it from the hilltop. We only need weapons."

Lincoln was picking out objects and shoving them into a green bag. "This isn't nearly as much as we had when we arrived at your homeland. We lost three packs of gear in the forest fire, then I lost another when we encountered the other members of your tribe."

"But why do you need to take these things?"

"We aren't as skilled at surviving as you are," Virgil said. "It's in our nature to want to be ready for anything, like cold weather, or getting lost, or not having enough food. Of course, we have no food left, so..." he held up a black box, "this is a fishing kit."

Derek let out a huff. "How the hell would she know what a fishing kit is, Virg?" He turned to Di-woto. "Hey, put that back."

The girl had grabbed a blue garment that looked like the shirts Lincoln and his tribemates were wearing. She unrolled the garment, held it up, then walked away with it.

"Di-woto likes clothing," Skyra said.

Derek shook his head. "Yeah, well, that shirt was actually mine."

Skyra still hadn't figured out why Lincoln and his bolup tribemates were always concerned about what was *theirs*. They seemed to think certain objects belonged only to them and shouldn't be touched by others. Skyra possessed several things—her waist-skin, cape, footwraps, and weapons—but these actually belonged to the animals and stones from which they were made. She had only borrowed them, and she would gladly let others borrow them if they needed to.

She picked up a strange-looking bag with a cord at the top holding it shut. "What is this?"

"That looks like our water filter," Jazzlyn said. "It turns dirty river water into clean water you can drink. We haven't had a chance to use it, though."

"Why not just drink clean river water instead of dirty river water?"

"Well, sometimes the water may look clean, but it could have tiny creatures in it that can make you sick."

Skyra put the water filter back in its place in one of the neat rows. She picked up another bag, this one as long and thick as her forearm. "What is this?"

"It's a tent," Virgil said. "A tent is a shelter that you can—"

"I know what a tent is," Skyra said. "I saw Lincoln's tent in my homeland." She dropped the tent. "We are going to the city now. Leave these things here. You do not need them. We will only take weapons."

Lincoln and his tribemates looked at each other for several breaths.

"I have seen all of you fight," Skyra said. "You are not strong, but you can be fierce. You will bring your weapons, and you will fight if you have to. If we need to find water or food, I will show you how. If we need to make a shelter, I will show you how. If we need to make clothing, I will show you how. But we will not need any of those things because the city is near. I saw it from the hilltop. We will be there before the sun moves to the hills to hide itself for the night."

Again the strange bolups looked at each other.

"El-de-né! I will be an old woman gathering grubs instead of hunting reindeer before you decide what to take with you. We will go to the city now!"

Jazzlyn let out a bolup laugh. "I'm liking your wife more every day, Lincoln. I think she's right. This whole time-jumping thing was a bold, reckless endeavor in the first place. Let's continue the bold and reckless theme and just go for it. We'll be welcomed into the city, and we'll be sleeping on soft beds tonight."

Lincoln gazed at the rows of strange objects. "Alright, at least we've done a good inventory. Stuff this crap back into the duffel. Just take one daypack, maybe with the folding knives, a first aid kit, and whatever else you think is essential. We'll hide the gear duffel and the duffel with the body bags."

"If something happens to those body bags, we're stuck here forever," Derek said. "Maybe I should throw the duffel on my back so they're with us at all times."

Skyra growled in frustration and turned away from the

bolups. She approached Di-woto, who was leaning against a tree, looking intently at the blue shirt she had taken.

The girl spoke in her own language, and Skyra understood some of the words. "I no understand garment. I no see this cloth before."

Skyra studied Di-woto for a few breaths. The girl was certainly strange looking. Her skin, including her face, was covered with ornamental scars she had inflicted on herself. The scars were arranged in interesting patterns, but they were still frightful to look at. Her black, braided hair was wrapped around her neck several times like a coiled snake. Di-woto's face did not look like a bolup or nandup—her mother was nandup, and her father was bolup. Skyra couldn't help but wonder, if Lincoln put a child in her belly, would the child look like this strange girl?

Skyra looked at Di-woto's own garment, which the girl had dyed several different brilliant colors, blended together in places to make even more colors. Her knee-high footwraps below the garment were made with the white fur of some kind of animal. Skyra spoke using words she knew of Di-woto's language. "Your garments much better than bolup garments. You much creative. You much smart."

The girl smiled.

"Di-woto, we go now. We walk far. You come. Maybe dangerous. I protect you."

Di-woto's smile spread even wider. She dropped the shirt. "Yes! We go. You kill many guards. You warrior. You protect me."

"Yes." Skyra picked up Derek's shirt then took Di-woto's hand. "We go now."

Lincoln and his tribemates had put most of the strange objects back into the large bag, keeping only enough to partially fill one of the small green packs. Now they were grunting and straining as they carried the T3. They shuffled with the strange object and finally placed it in a brushy area between two trees, apparently trying to hide it. The object was the size of a woolly rhino, and to Skyra it seemed no more hidden than before.

The bolups put the two big bags beside the T3 then began pulling up grasses and using them to cover everything. Apparently Derek had decided not to haul the body bags to the city. Di-woto joined in the grass-gathering effort, laughing and chattering as if the bolups understood her language. Skyra let out a growl and started helping—the sooner the job was done, the sooner Lincoln and the others would be ready to go.

Skyra wanted to begin the journey, but not because she was anxious to reach the city—the city frightened her. The bats had come from the city. Many people would be in the city. Lincoln believed the group needed to go to the city, so she would go to protect him and his tribemates. If Lincoln did not find what he was hoping to find there, and if this land was too dangerous, he would want to use the T3 again to go somewhere else. He had told Skyra maybe they could use the T3 to go many years back to Skyra's land to try to save her birthmate Veenah. Skyra did not know if this was possible, but if they were forced to leave this land, she wanted to try.

Finally, the T3 and the bags were covered with grasses, although the grassy lump would still be visible from a great distance.

"Weapons," Skyra said. "Take all of them."

A few breaths later, Jazzlyn, Virgil, Derek, and Lincoln each held a rough wooden khul in one hand and a spear in the other. The weapons' tips had been sharpened by rubbing them against a stone. Skyra had her stone-bladed khul in her sling and one of her stone hand blades in her wrist sheath. Di-woto held Skyra's other knife in one hand, and a mat of woven grasses was tucked under her arm. She had made another after Skyra had destroyed the first mat when killing the velvet worm. Di-woto did not want to leave her new mat, which was fine with Skyra, as the first one had proven useful.

"I guess I gotta be the one to bring this up," Derek said. "If we're hiking ten miles, how the hell do we find our way back to the T3? Our phones are in the gear bag, but there's obviously no GPS here."

"The sun was rising when we were on the hilltop," Lincoln said. "It was to our backs when we were looking at the city. That means the city is pretty much due west. That's not much to go on, but it should help."

Ripple had been standing silently to the side, but now the creature spoke up. "I find it rather condescending that you consistently overlook me and my capabilities. Must I remind you that I possess reasonably accurate navigation abilities based on magnetic pole triangulation?"

"You *did* tell me that, I guess," Lincoln said. "It seems like so long ago now."

"What if something happens to the drone?" Derek asked.

"The drone's name is Ripple," said Ripple.

Skyra growled. "I do not know how you bolups are still alive. If Ripple cannot help us, I will know how to return to this place. The city is not far."

Jazzlyn said, "Terrific then. I'm going to be optimistic and assume we'll find ourselves immersed in a society of luxury, and we'll want to stay there forever."

Bugs were everywhere. Skyra had never seen so many bugs in her homeland. Beetles of every color and shape scuttled from her every footstep. Black spiders with thick legs could be seen waiting under rock edges for prey to come near. Long millipedes, some as big around as Skyra's thumb, crawled in the shadows. Cicadas clinging to the weeds buzzed and clicked, making a constant chorus of sound that sometimes made it hard to think. Dark clouds of flies swirled above trees heavy with red berries. Bugs everywhere, but Skyra did not have a single bite on her body. Where were all the biting bugs?

The group climbed one hill after another, getting closer to the city with each hill. It would have been easier to walk through the valleys, but Lincoln and his tribemates wanted to see the city from each hilltop because they were afraid of drifting off course. This made Skyra wonder what Lincoln's homeland was like. What kind of land could it be where people did not learn how to find their way? Did they never leave their own camps for fear of becoming lost? At the beginning of each cold season, Skyra's Una-Loto tribe would walk many days, moving out of the cold foothills of the Kapolsek mountains into the warmer plains below. Never once did they follow the same path or set up camp in the same place, and they did not get lost. By the time Skyra and Veenah had been old enough to hunt pikas among the rocks, the sisters could easily find their way back by nightfall from rocky hillsides that were half a day's walk in any direction from Una-Loto camp.

At the top of another hill, from which the city now appeared much closer, Skyra looked out over the wide valley they would have to cross before climbing the next hill. Unlike the others, this valley had no trees to hide under if the bats flew over on their way back to the city. In fact, this valley had no vegetation at all. It was bare dirt. Strange dirt mounds dotted the entire area, and in several places between the mounds, clouds of insects swarmed above dark splotches of something too far away to identify.

"I think we're looking at a prairie dog town," Jazzlyn said. "You can see a few of them on their mounds."

Skyra saw several brown animals standing upright about knee high. "What is a prairie dog town?"

"Prairie dogs are cute little animals that live in burrows. You know, holes in the ground? Sometimes they live in huge colonies with thousands of burrows and millions of prairie dogs."

"Millions is a lot?"

Jazzlyn smiled. "More than you can ever imagine."

"Then I do not want to walk through this prairie dog town."

Now Jazzlyn laughed. "Prairie dogs aren't dangerous, girl!"

"Prairie dogs." Di-woto said, pronouncing the words carefully. She pointed down into the valley and spoke mostly in her language. "I will make prairie dog garment."

Skyra scanned the valley from one end to the other—dirt mounds for as far as she could see. Going around them would require much extra walking.

"I'm more worried about the bats coming back," Derek said. "Let's get moving."

They headed down the slope. As Skyra watched the mounds warily, more of the creatures emerged from their holes to watch the approaching group. Several of them threw their heads back and screeched.

"That's their alarm call," Jazzlyn said, "It lets the others know danger is near. They'll hide in their burrows."

Ripple said, "An interesting fact. Prairie dogs, at least in Lincoln's original timeline, actually included five species in the genus *Cynomys*. In addition to their predator alarm call, prairie dogs employ a surprisingly diverse array of vocalizations for communication."

"They are not hiding," Skyra said, ignoring Ripple. "More of them are coming out." Her heart was now pounding, and her legs were telling her to flee. As a child she had hunted pikas, but those were smaller than these prairie dogs, and she never saw more than a few at a time. Ripple had taught her what a thousand was. If millions was greater than thousands, it didn't matter that these prairie dogs were small—there were too many of them. She could not help but remember the bats, which she had thought were harmless until they attacked.

Walking beside her, Lincoln nudged her elbow. "They're just curious about us. The people living in the city probably don't come out here much."

They reached the bottom of the slope and continued across the valley. More of the prairie dogs emerged, some sticking their heads from their holes and others coming all the way out to stand on their hind legs. All of them were watching the intruders intently.

Skyra caught a whiff of a strange combination of smells, as if fragrant flowers had been mixed with rotting animal flesh. She stopped, which brought the entire group to a stop. "I do not like the smell here."

"Are you okay?" Lincoln asked. "You're not typically this nervous. I watched you kill the woolly rhino that took your birthmother's life. It was probably twenty times your size. You can't be afraid of these little rodents." He pointed to one a short distance away that was staring at them. "Look how small they are."

She reached through her hair and gripped her khul's smooth handle. "There are many of them, Lincoln, and the smell is telling my legs to run."

"But *I'm* telling you prairie dogs are not dangerous," he said. "We'll walk straight to the other side, okay?"

She looked across the valley. The next hill seemed farther away now that she was at the bottom of the slope. She sucked in as much air as she could then let it out forcefully. "We will go quickly."

As they made their way among the countless mounds, the smell became stronger, and more of the prairie dogs emerged from their holes.

"What the hell is that stench?" Derek asked. "It's like someone sprayed air freshener in an outhouse full of shit."

About halfway across the valley they came upon one of the dark splotches Skyra had seen from the hilltop. Here the smell was so strong she had to pinch her nose shut. The group stopped and stared. The splotch was actually a low mound, ankle high and about eight steps wide. It was animal dung, although it didn't smell like any dung Skyra had encountered before. She kneeled to get a closer look. The dung consisted mostly of insect fragments—legs, heads, portions of wings—but there were also numerous white flakes. She picked up some of the flakes and rubbed them between her fingers. They were bone fragments.

She wiped her fingertips off in the dirt and rose back to her full height. "Prairie dogs eat insects, and they eat animals with bones."

"I don't think so," Jazzlyn said. "They may eat a few insects, but their diet consists mostly of plants. Definitely not animals with bones."

Skyra's eyes were drawn to movement. A dense cloud of

insects was flying low over the valley. Another similar cloud could be seen farther in the distance, flying in the other direction. The nearer cloud switched directions, swirling around itself like a campfire's smoke. After swirling for a few more breaths, the cloud dropped to the ground, landing directly on another of the dark splotches of dung.

"It appears the insects are drawn to the smell of this waste," Virgil said. "Perhaps they get salt or other minerals from it."

Numerous screeches came all at once from the direction of the feeding insects. Prairie dogs on all sides of the dung mound jumped from their holes and ran, converging on the insects in less than one breath. The creatures clambered on top of each other in a wild killing frenzy, catching as many insects as they could before the swarm could fly away. The insects rose from the ground in a cloud that was now thinner than it had been before.

"That is one-hundred-percent messed up," Derek said, almost whispering.

The prairie dogs growled and thrashed, fighting with each other over the insects they had caught.

"Well, maybe these aren't herbivores," Jazzlyn said. "Maybe they aren't even prairie dogs."

Skyra scanned the endless mounds—even more of the creatures were out of their holes, staring at her group. Then she looked at her fingertips, even though the bone fragments were no longer there. "We must go out of this valley now."

"Yeah, I'm with Skyra on this," Lincoln said. "Let's keep moving."

They resumed walking.

"Skyra, I want to run," Di-woto said in her language.

Skyra grabbed the girl's elbow. "No run. Animals no attack walking. Animals maybe attack running."

Di-woto's eyes were wide as she watched the staring creatures. She spoke softly to herself. "No run. No run."

A screech came from ahead, followed by another to the side. Within another breath, Skyra's ears were flooded with screeches from everywhere. Masses of prairie dogs bolted from their holes and charged.

She grabbed Di-woto's wrist. "Now we run!"

"Go, go, go!" Lincoln shouted.

They all sprinted toward the hillside ahead.

The prairie dogs closed in, apparently with no fear of the much-larger people. Ahead, Derek slowed down to kick some of them out of his way, but there were too many. They leapt at his legs, biting and clawing at his footwraps and trousers. They crawled over each other to get at him. He dropped his spear and started swinging his crude khul, almost hitting his own legs in the process.

Lincoln stopped to help him.

"Don't fight, just run!" Skyra shouted as she and Di-woto passed them. Fighting the creatures with spears, khuls, and knives was useless—there were too many to kill.

Skyra stepped on prairie dogs with every stride, making it impossible to run at full speed without tripping. Ahead, Virgil and Jazzlyn were the first to trip and fall. Virgil was leading, and when he went down Jazzlyn piled on top of him. The two disappeared under a mound of thrashing brown bodies. They scrambled back to their feet, screaming and yanking the prairie dogs off as Skyra and the others caught up.

"Go!" Lincoln cried. "Just keep running!"

The creatures were clinging to Skyra's footwraps by their teeth, and she grunted with pain as several of them got ahold of the bare skin of her knees. She was still pulling Di-woto by the hand, but the girl was whimpering and stumbling, slowing them both down. Skyra tightened her grip and pulled her along.

Di-woto fell, and her hand jerked free. By the time Skyra went back to help, the girl was back on her feet, stabbing with Skyra's hand blade at the creatures clinging to her hair and clothing. Her face and arms were now streaked with blood.

Lincoln appeared at Skyra's side, and together they yanked the rest of the prairie dogs off of Di-woto while countless more continued attacking their feet and legs.

"Stay on your feet and run!" Lincoln yelled.

A new onslaught of screeching whistles filled the air, drowning out all other sounds. The prairie dogs stopped their attack and stood on their hind legs, staring in the direction of the new sounds.

The shrill whistles stopped, and Ripple said, "It is working. I will distract them while you escape to the hillside." Ripple started whistling again, sounding a little like prairie dog shrieks but much louder.

Lincoln pulled on Skyra's arm, Skyra pulled on Di-woto's arm, and they all charged for the hill, kicking the creatures aside every step of the way.

The prairie dogs were so interested in Ripple's whistles they didn't even turn their heads as Skyra, Lincoln, and Di-woto ran by.

The group reached the base of the hill and started up the slope. Jazzlyn, Virgil, and Derek, now far ahead, had stopped to wait. When they were all at the top of the hill, they stared down into the valley, where Ripple was still standing motionless, whistling at a sea of brown bodies. There were so many that Skyra could only see glimpses of the ground where she and the others had been only a few breaths ago.

Skyra cupped her hands to her mouth. "Ripple, come up here!"

Ripple started walking, still whistling.

Suddenly, the prairie dogs dropped to all fours and charged Ripple, like a brown wave flowing from all directions. Claws and teeth scraped and clattered against Ripple's hard shell. Within another breath, Ripple was buried, and its whistles became muffled under the attacking bodies.

Skyra started back down the hill, but Lincoln held her arm. "Wait, you can't go back down there," he said. "And I don't think they can hurt Ripple anyway."

Ripple's whistling stopped, and Skyra tore her arm loose from Lincoln's grip.

"Skyra, please!" he said. "Just wait."

She stared down the slope. Her head knew Lincoln was right, but her legs wanted to run to help her friend. "No, Ripple, no," she muttered. "You must find the cave lion's strength and the woolly rhino's anger. Fight, Ripple!"

All she could hear now was the scuffling of tiny claws.

The mound of prairie dogs heaved upward then collapsed back down, as if Ripple were trying to crawl out from under the bodies. It heaved again, only to fall back again.

"Come on, you damn smart-ass drone," Derek growled. "Fight!"

The mound heaved again, this time higher, and Skyra glimpsed a portion of Ripple's shell. A low humming sound came from the writhing mound, and Ripple pushed upward, throwing off some of the creatures, and rose completely off the ground. With nothing soft to grip in their teeth, most of the prairie dogs fell away, landing on top of their companions.

The humming got louder as Ripple took off flying across the valley. The last few creatures lost their grip and tumbled to the ground. Ripple flew to the base of the hill and continued up the slope. It hadn't bothered to withdraw its legs into its shell while flying, and a few breaths later it landed lightly on the hillside beside Skyra and Lincoln.

Di-woto clapped her hands together. "Your talking beast flies!" She was delighted, in spite of the numerous bleeding bite wounds on her own body.

Ripple said, "I now understand the supposedly humorous anecdote, 'You needn't outrun the bear, you need only to outrun your friends.'"

Skyra was so relieved to have Ripple back in one piece she didn't bother asking what that meant. She kneeled to inspect Ripple's wounds but could only find a few new scratches on the edges of its shell. She stood up and turned to watch the prairie dogs below. So far they didn't seem interested in coming up the hillside.

As if he knew what Skyra was thinking, Lincoln said. "They're probably reluctant to get too far from the safety of their burrows."

Derek snorted. "Do you blame them? They live in a place with flocks of giant killer bats."

The prairie dogs were now spreading out, apparently returning to their holes. Skyra decided the group was safe, for now. She took Di-woto by the shoulders and turned her around, studying the girl's bites. Many were still seeping blood, but none were gushing, which was good. Skyra had several bites on her knees and thighs, but they were no worse than Di-woto's.

Lincoln and the others were now inspecting their own

injuries. Virgil's one uncovered leg was red with blood from the knee down.

"You were wrong, Lincoln," Skyra said.

He glanced at her. "Wrong?"

"The prairie dog town was *not* safe."

5

DESTINATION

47,659 years in the future - Day 1

LINCOLN WAS fearful of what awaited the group on the far side of the hill, so he ran across the hilltop as the others were inspecting their bite wounds. They all needed to rest and treat their injuries, but it wasn't safe to stay out in the open for too long. As he approached the opposite side of the broad summit, Lincoln had the urge to hold his breath, but he was too winded. If this hill was completely surrounded by the prairie dog colony they were all screwed.

"Yes!" he exclaimed aloud as the next valley came into view. It contained trees, like many of the other valleys they'd crossed. The trees here were a darker shade of green, clustered tightly in a narrow band stretching out in both directions, suggesting a stream might flow through this valley.

He took a moment to stare at the city beyond the remaining hills. The nearest buildings were now no more than three or four miles away—only a few more hours of hiking. At this distance, the city's sheer size was stunning. Skyscrapers, some rising just above the hilltops and others taller than any he'd ever seen, reflected the sunlight with mirrored surfaces. He could now see they were not rectangular. In fact, they had no corners or angles at all. Even the tops were rounded instead of having flat roofs. Some were wider at the base, like upside down icicles. For a brief moment, Lincoln's anxiety spiked as he wondered if they might be some kind of natural formations and not buildings at all. However, even though the buildings were rounded, several of them had black horizontal bands, the corners of which were perfectly square. He couldn't tell if the bands were painted on or were built into the structures. Although his group had encountered no roads, farms, or suburban development, he was now certain he was looking at a city.

He ran back to the group and beckoned them to get moving. Together they traversed the hill and entered the stretch of trees, which at this location was no wider than fifty yards.

"I hear water," Virgil said. "There it is, a stream!" He ran with Jazzlyn and Derek to the stream's edge.

Derek shrugged the daypack from his shoulders, pulled out the bag containing the gravity water filter, and fumbled with the bag's closure.

Virgil and Jazzlyn stared at the water impatiently while Derek pulled out the filter.

"How long has it been since you guys had any water?" Lincoln asked as he stepped up to the stream, which wasn't more than a trickle an inch or two deep.

"Those khami-bul bastards brought us bowls of disgusting water a couple of times while we were in that cage," Derek said. "I'm dying to slurp up every drop I can hold." He unrolled some flexible tubes and held up two transparent water bladders, one labeled *Clean,* the other *Dirty.* He frowned. "How long does this thing take to work?"

"Too long," Jazzlyn said.

Ripple stepped up to the stream and lowered its shell to the ground by retracting its legs. Two thin probes appeared from beneath the drone's vision lens and grew longer until one of them entered the water and the other entered the sand at its side.

"What's that drone doing now?" Derek asked.

Lincoln was about to explain, but Ripple replied first. "*That drone*, by the name of Ripple, is attempting to trickle charge. Levitating is energy intensive. I can still charge using ambient sound—so please continue prattling on—but I am supplementing with asymmetric temperature modulation."

"All you needed to say was *charging*," Derek said. "Just that one word." He turned back to the tangle of tubes and water bladders, still frowning.

Jazzlyn was now on her knees, staring at the water. "It *looks* reasonably clean."

Skyra kneeled beside her, lowered her face to the shallow brook, and sucked water into her mouth. After several gulps she raised her head. "This water is clean." She went back to drinking.

Derek dropped the filter and got onto his knees. "Good enough for me."

Skyra thrust out a hand to slow him down. "If you do not want to drink dirt, do not touch the stream bottom."

Derek got onto his belly and started slurping noisily. Jazzlyn, Virgil, and Di-woto moved upstream until they found suitable spots.

Lincoln glanced momentarily at the dropped filter. Could

Skyra actually taste if water was unsafe to drink? Perhaps it was an ability humans in his timeline had lost ages ago. On the other hand, water safe for Neanderthals might not be safe for humans. After a few more seconds of deliberation, he gave in and kneeled beside Skyra.

They all drank like livestock at a watering trough. Afterwards, they followed Skyra's lead and carefully rinsed their bites and scratches in the stream.

Several minutes later they were seated in a circle beside the stream. Derek had pulled the first aid kit from his pack, and the red and white box was open beside him. The kit contained two tubes of antibiotic cream, and Virgil had used most of one tube on his bare leg.

"We should have brought a hundred of these tubes," Lincoln muttered as he conservatively dabbed tiny amounts on his wounds.

"Optimism," Jazzlyn said. "In a few hours we'll be in a city. Their doctors will take care of us, probably with high-tech nano-bots that we swallow in margarita-flavored pills."

Virgil chuckled. "I won't bother to point out all the flaws in that assumption."

Derek shot him a side-look. "You would've if I'd said it."

Lincoln offered the tube to Skyra. "Put this stuff on your wounds."

She took the tube and eyed the dab of ointment protruding from the opening. "I have already washed my wounds. This will make them dirty again." She passed the tube to Di-woto.

The girl repeated Skyra's act of studying the tube. Then she spoke a few words in her language. Even though he didn't understand her words, Lincoln had heard her speak enough to tell she was asking a question.

Skyra snatched the tube back from her and looked at it again, furrowing her thick nandup brows. "Di-woto wants to know what are these strange shapes on this object. I see them now. Before I did not see them."

"Those are words," Lincoln said. "They are a way of talking without speaking. Each of those symbols has meaning. The people of my land learn to understand the words when we are young. Why do you think you didn't see the words the first time you looked at the tube?"

Skyra furrowed her brows even more as she studied the tube. "I do not know."

The question that nagged Lincoln even more was, why did Di-woto see the symbols immediately when Skyra did not? Were their brains that different? Were Neanderthals from Skyra's time simply not wired for two-dimensional symbolic communication? Were humans from that time also not yet capable of using symbols? Skyra was obviously better equipped than Lincoln for learning spoken languages, so he found this new revelation puzzling.

Skyra pointed to the words on the tube as she spoke to the girl, apparently conveying his explanation. Then she handed the tube back to Lincoln and said Di-woto had already washed her wounds and did not need it.

After Lincoln and his team had applied the ointment and had put adhesive bandages on those few wounds deep enough to warrant it, Derek gathered up the first aid kit and water filter and stuffed them back into his pack.

It was time to move on.

"You need more weapons," Skyra proclaimed. "You can make more now, or you can go back to the prairie dog town to get the weapons you dropped." Her khul's handle still protruded from the sling in her cape, and one of her stone knives was on her wrist. Di-woto was still holding Skyra's second knife.

This wasn't the first time Lincoln had lost his weapons while Skyra had managed to keep hers. This time he and his team had lost every last one of their weapons, which had been pretty much useless against the prairie dogs anyway.

Obviously no one wanted to go back to the prairie dog town, so they spread out and searched until they found four spear-length tree branches and four khul-length branches. The only rocks in this area were those exposed by the stream's flowing water, so they gathered there and began rubbing the branch tips into points. As they worked, Skyra and Di-woto wandered off along the stream's edge, again talking and looking at things on the ground and in the water.

The rocks were smooth, slowing down the sharpening process, so Lincoln's thoughts turned to the many puzzles regarding this place. "So, anyone want to speculate about how and why prairie dogs here have become carnivorous?"

As expected, Jazzlyn was ready with an answer. "Probably because of a lack of plant-based foods coupled with an extreme abundance of animals. Just look around you. You can't spit without hitting at least one insect. I've never seen such an abundance, especially in a semi-arid environment like this. Something happened in the past, and prairie dogs adapted to a new food source. I think in our timeline they occasionally ate insects for protein, so the tendency was already hardwired into their behavior. By the way, I don't think it's a coincidence that their sweet-smelling turds happen to attract swarms of insects. That could be one aspect of an arms race between the prairie dogs and their prey."

Virgil held his spear point up to inspect his progress. "These speculations bring us back to the same question we've already discussed. What kind of disruptive event occurred that resulted in all these rapid changes? Lincoln, you suggested nuclear war, and I'm starting to see the merits of that hypothesis, although it does have its issues."

"What issues?" Lincoln asked.

"Well, let's consider what we've seen. First, the vegetation here is rather sparse compared to the plant density 47,000 years ago in Di-woto's time. Second, the creatures we've seen have gone through substantial modifications, many of which enhance their ability to consume copious amounts of insects. Third, I'm not sure you've noticed, but the animals we've seen are ones that spend at least part of their time beneath the ground or in caves. Even the insects and other arthropods are those that spend some time below ground, particularly as burrowing larvae."

Lincoln was beginning to understand. "The only creatures left here could be the descendants of those below ground when something bad happened."

Jazzlyn pushed on Virgil's shoulder. "Damn, Virg, I think you're on to something."

He rolled his eyes slightly at the use of that nickname. "Think about it. Where are the animals that were here 47,000 years ago? In Di-woto's time, we know there were bison, camels, and wolves, as well as those her people domesticated as food animals."

"Uh, and ground sloths," Lincoln added. "Skyra and I saw a ground sloth the size of a grizzly bear."

Virgil and Jazzlyn looked at him with raised brows.

Derek spoke up. "I haven't seen a single bird. Not one. Back in Di-woto's time—and in Skyra's time—we saw eagles and stuff soaring above."

"There's been a massive extinction of animals above ground," Jazzlyn said quietly.

Virgil shrugged. "Maybe, but we can't draw too many conclusions yet. We've been here what, half a day? Hardly a complete investigation."

Lincoln chewed on his lip, considering the possibility. "You said the nuclear war possibility had issues. Wouldn't nuclear war explain what we've seen?"

Jazzlyn grabbed Virgil's sleeve between the thumb and fingers of her prosthetic hand. "Wait, how long would the devastating effects of a large-scale nuclear conflict last?"

He puckered his lips in thought. "Radioactive fallout would continue for several weeks to several months, but that's just the beginning. Surface water could be contaminated for a year or longer. Eventually, the contamination would get into the ground water, and it could be many years—maybe a hundred or more—before all the ground water is pure again. In addition, there's also the resulting effects on the climate. Nuclear winter. If the conflict is global—involving hundreds or thousands of warheads—enough dust, soot, and smoke would be blasted into the upper atmosphere to cause an ice age for several years. Just like the meteor impact that wiped out the dinosaurs. The material would block the sun, restricting photosynthesis."

"That's the issue you were referring to," Jazzlyn said.

Lincoln got it now. "Prairie dogs and bats have to come out frequently to feed. How could they survive months of radioactive fallout, followed by several years of freezing temperatures? Maybe some creatures that live below ground for years, like the seventeen-year locust, would survive, but probably not bats and prairie dogs."

"That's precisely what I mean," Virgil confirmed. "This

doesn't rule out a smaller-scale nuclear conflict, though, nor does it rule out a host of other possible disruptive events."

"I know I don't have a bunch of letters after my name," Derek said. "But why are we assuming these people used nuclear weapons? They probably aren't anything like us. They don't think like us. Hell, they didn't even think like us way back in Di-woto's time. Maybe they never even considered nuclear weapons, but instead they had some big-ass thing that killed people and animals in an instant, then it was over. No fallout, no ice age, just over. Anything underground at that moment was safe. Anything above ground, dead. More environmentally friendly, no?"

His offering was followed by contemplative silence.

"Huh," Virgil huffed. "That would fit our observations, but I can't imagine what kind of—"

"Exactly," Derek interjected. "You can't imagine it because we don't think the way these people think. That's my flippin' point."

Ripple, still trickle charging at the stream's edge, spoke up. "It is not surprising you cannot imagine the technology developed by the beings who live here. Humans are notably lacking in cognitive empathy. You cannot imagine the perspectives of those unlike yourselves."

Lincoln frowned at the drone. "You were coded by a human. By me, actually. How could you possibly have more cognitive empathy than we do?"

"I am not claiming to have cognitive empathy. I am simply pointing out the fact that you do *not* have cognitive empathy. I am being helpful."

Derek snorted. "For once the drone actually *is* being helpful, because that's what I was trying to say."

"We have food!" Skyra exclaimed.

"Food!" Di-woto echoed.

The two were approaching, their cupped hands loaded with white objects that Lincoln couldn't make out. Skyra went straight to Derek. "Please, you will open your bag."

Derek stared at her hands. "Seriously?"

Lincoln grabbed both of his sharpened weapons and stepped closer. Skyra and Di-woto were holding handfuls of grubs. Each grub was curled into a tight horseshoe shape but would be larger than Lincoln's thumb when extended. Their translucent skin revealed thin, branching veins and glimpses of internal organs.

Skyra shoved her grubs toward Derek. "Bag!"

Derek dropped the spear he'd been sharpening, shrugged off his pack, and unzipped the enclosure.

Skyra let the creatures fall into the the open bag.

Derek frowned. "Okaaay... just dropping them in there, huh? Right on top of the other stuff."

"Bag!" Di-woto exclaimed unnecessarily, then she dropped hers in too.

"You will see," Skyra said, apparently noticing Lincoln's dubious expression. "When you are hungry, you will see grubs are good food." She looked from Lincoln to each of his team members, noting the sharpened weapons. "We will go to the city now."

As they left the trees that bordered the stream, Lincoln glanced up at the next hill and spotted a tan-colored dog, either a coyote or a wolf. The creature was standing at the summit, staring back down at the travelers. Lincoln alerted the others in just enough time for them to catch a glimpse before the creature bolted and disappeared beyond the ridge.

"The only other mammal we've seen so far besides prairie dogs and bats," Jazzlyn said. "It didn't look like the wolves we saw in Di-woto's time. Maybe it's a large coyote."

Derek hefted his crude khul as if testing its balance. "I swear to God, if there's a big pack of them on the other side of this hill, we're skedaddling back to the T_3 and jumping. I don't even care where we jump to."

"The animal was alone," Skyra said firmly. Everyone waited a few seconds for her to elaborate, but she simply stared up the slope.

Virgil was also staring up the hillside. "I'm curious. Is this sighting consistent with our working hypothesis? Do coyotes spend at least part of their lives below ground?"

"They make dens," Jazzlyn replied. "Sometimes the dens are burrows in the ground."

Skyra began hiking up the slope, and they all followed.

Lincoln felt himself caught up in the speculation. "Consider this. Some event takes place that wipes out the animals above ground—birds, deer, bison, camels, many of the insects, and so on. This eliminates most warm-blooded animals. It also eliminates most insects that feed by biting those warm-blooded animals—if not immediately, then gradually due to the disappearance of their food source."

"Which explains why we haven't encountered biting insects!" Virgil said, finishing the thought. "The puzzle pieces are dropping satisfyingly into place."

Skyra looked back over her shoulder. "Bolups talk too much. You want to understand things by talking. Nandups want to understand things by seeing and listening and touching. Maybe you are talking so much you cannot see and listen and touch."

Lincoln and Jazzlyn exchanged smiles, while Virgil simply pursed his lips.

As Skyra had predicted, no pack of dogs was waiting for them on the hilltop or on the other side. This hill, though, did provide the most spectacular view of the city they'd seen yet.

Derek stopped and stared. "Man, would you look at that. It's like a scene from a science fiction movie."

"The buildings aren't even rectangular," Virgil said. "They look more like blown-glass sculptures, all rounded and bubble-like."

Di-woto, gawking at the scene with wide-eyed fascination, jabbered out a long sequence of words.

"Ripple, translate," Skyra ordered.

With no discernible hesitation, Ripple said, "These structures are even greater than the new sanctuary-fortress I planned. The people who made plans for these structures must be alinga-uls, like me. I want to meet these alinga-uls. We will have much to talk about. I wonder what kind of garments these people like to wear. They must wear clothing that is just as beautiful as these buildings."

Skyra exchanged a few words with Di-woto in the girl's language, then she turned to Lincoln. "Di-woto does not know how to be afraid of things, but I am afraid of that city. There will be more people there than all the prairie dogs in the prairie dog town."

Lincoln stepped up to her side. "It's okay to have a lot of people if the people are friendly. I'm hoping they will be nice to us."

"You hoped the prairie dogs would be nice," she said matter-of-factly.

He let out a sigh. "When we get to the edge of the city, we will see only a few people. We'll watch what those people do. We'll know if they want to be nice to us. If they're not, we'll turn around and leave. We will *not* go into the middle of the city before we find out, like we did in the prairie dog town."

She twisted her lips the way she often did when thinking. Then, without another word, she turned and resumed walking.

THE LAST FEW miles seemed to take forever, perhaps due to Lincoln's mounting anxiety, and conversation dwindled as everyone internalized their own thoughts. The hills gradually leveled out, and the forest became thicker, its dense canopy only allowing occasional glimpses of the looming skyscrapers. Even when Lincoln was sure they were within only a mile of the nearest buildings, he still had not seen any roads, houses, trash, or any other signs of civilization. Other than the presence of the nearby city, the area was a pristine wilderness.

Lost in thought, Lincoln was watching the countless beetles and other insects scuttling about at his feet as he walked. Skyra startled him by grabbing his elbow. He stopped and glanced around. The others had paused and were staring into the trees ahead. No more than sixty yards away, visible through gaps in the foliage, was the smooth, glass-like side of a building.

"The city," Skyra said.

Di-woto bolted and ran ahead, bouncing with excitement.

Lincoln and the others followed, and seconds later they emerged from the forest only fifteen yards from the structure. They were now standing on a flat gray surface, smoother than cement, that stretched into the distance on both sides. The base of the building's glassy side rose from the pavement without a visible seam between the two materials.

"Unbelievable," Lincoln muttered, tipping his head back and staring up. The reflective wall before them curved gently outward as it rose from the ground. At a height Lincoln estimated to be about ten stories, it began curving back inward, making it impossible to see the building's top from where he was standing.

Derek stepped up to the wall, cupped his hands to his eyes, and gazed through the glass. He pulled back. "Can't see a thing."

Again Di-woto bolted, this time to the left. They followed her along the strip of pavement until they came to the edge of the building, which was rounded rather than square. Another building, this one also rounded but with a greenish tint to the glass, stood beside the first, with only a fifteen-yard-wide walkway or street between the two buildings.

Lincoln gazed down the street toward the city's interior. The street, which was perfectly straight, went on for as far as he could see, its vanishing point lost in the air's haze.

"There's no one here," Jazzlyn said softly.

Lincoln stared, hardly believing his eyes. The street was completely empty, other than twigs and leaves that had blown in from the surrounding forest. There were no vehicles, parked or otherwise. There were no light poles, mailboxes, traffic lights, or anything else you would expect to see—only smooth, seamless surfaces. There wasn't even any trash. Most importantly, there were no people.

Lincoln felt Skyra's hand squeeze his.

"This city has no sound," she whispered.

6
FEATURELESS

47,659 years in the future - Day 1

SKYRA HAD SEEN a lake once when she was a child. She and Veenah had traveled with their birthmother on a two-day walk to see it. At the time, she had been amazed at the sheer amount of water simply sitting there, as if it were a river that had been trapped and could not escape. What had struck her more than anything, though, was the lake's surface. It was vast and flat, with no features—no sand, rocks, or grasses, just the smooth surface reflecting the sky and the distant hills.

As Skyra gazed into the city's interior, she couldn't help but think of the lake she had seen as a girl. The city was just featureless surfaces. The buildings were smooth and reflective, with no seams or corners. The ground was flat, with no dirt, sand, or gravel. A few leaves had blown in from the forest, but these became sparse and finally disappeared as Skyra and the others made their way deeper into the city.

"How can there be absolutely nothing here?" Lincoln

asked. "There are no street signs, or fire hydrants, or storefronts. There are no gutters, or rainwater drains, or stripes painted on the streets. It's all so... sterile and empty. We haven't even seen any doors to get into these buildings."

"All reminders that these people are very different from us," Virgil said.

Derek let his fingers drag along the smooth side of one of the structures as he walked. "You say that like you believe there are actually people here now. We haven't seen anyone, and we haven't heard a sound. This place is as dead as the dodo."

Ripple paused to tap on the smooth wall with one of its feet. "Silence does not necessarily imply that this city is vacant. We cannot see into these structures, but it is possible the occupants can see out. Perhaps some of them are watching us now from within."

"Dead as the dodo," Derek repeated.

"It does seem an occupied city this size would have to be somewhat noisy," Virgil said. "Why would they all stay inside, especially on a nice day like this?"

For the third time, the group came to another open path branching to both sides—Lincoln had called them cross streets. The others briefly looked both directions then continued forward, but Skyra paused. She saw something in the distance blocking the cross street. It had thin, dark lines, like the limbs of a fallen tree, some straight and some bent or broken.

"Something is there," she said, pointing.

The others stopped and stared.

"She's right," Lincoln said. "It's gotta be nearly a half mile away. Ripple, can you zoom in on that?"

Ripple looked silently for a few breaths. "From the

haphazard arrangement of the parts, it appears to be wreckage of some sort. Based on what we have seen thus far, these people do not seem fond of haphazardness, hence my conclusion it is unintentional wreckage."

Skyra started up the cross street. She felt drawn to the object simply because it was different from the endless smoothness of everything else here. Di-woto quickly caught up to her. The girl had been unusually quiet since they had entered the city, and now she clung closely to Skyra's side. Maybe she wasn't as fearless as Skyra had thought.

Derek's voice came from behind. "Um, if we start making turns now, we're going to get lost."

Ripple's voice replied, "People accompanied by brilliant drones do not get lost."

The others followed.

The group came to a stop before the twisted, broken jumble. It was twice the height of Skyra's head and completely blocked the street. Portions of it resembled thin sticks, some straight as a spear, others bent or twisted. Stretched tight between the sticks were thin sheets of some material that was reflective when looked at from one side but clear from the other side—even clearer than the windows of the sanctuary-fortress of Kyran-yufost. Skyra gazed up at the impossibly-tall structures on either side of the street. The taller of the two was thinner in the middle than at the top, as if the middle had been squeezed by a giant hand. Far above, near the top, part of the reflective surface was missing, revealing a dark band that stretched around the building's curved side.

"This is a piece of the building that has fallen off," Lincoln said, pointing up at the dark band of missing surface Skyra had spotted.

Skyra understood, but her mind did not want to believe the massive jumble before her was the same size as the tiny band of darkness far above. Before, she hadn't completely understood how large these buildings were. Now the realization made her feel dizzy. She turned her gaze to the ground to keep from swaying back and forth.

"Goddammit!" Derek grunted. "This place is definitely dead. If people still lived here, they would've cleaned this up and repaired the damage."

"From the hilltops I saw quite a few missing strips of windows just like that one," Lincoln said, still staring upward. "At the time I assumed they were some kind of design feature. I guess I was wrong—they're signs of disrepair."

"Could we just once catch a break?" Derek asked.

Jazzlyn turned her spear straight up and down and jammed the blunt end onto the street several times. "Hey! Optimism. So the people are gone—nothing we can do about that. But look where we are, you guys. We're in a *city*. It's kind of weird, but it's a city nonetheless, with buildings for protection from the weather and wild animals. And guess what? It looks like all these buildings are up for grabs. Better than living in a cave or a tent, right?"

"Giant killer bats," Derek said, as if this was all that needed to be said.

Derek's mention of the bats made Skyra instinctively scan the portions of the sky she could see. The buildings did not seem to have doors, which meant this jumble of wreckage was the only potential shelter she had seen since entering the city. She turned to Lincoln. "I want to know how to go inside these buildings."

He nodded once. "Me too. They must have entrances somewhere."

"Logic would suggest you're right, Virgil said. "Even if a portion of this city is underground, and the people typically enter the buildings from below, they would also need to be able to get to this network of streets. I mean, why have these elaborate streets if you can't use them?"

Skyra stepped to the wall of the building with the missing piece far above and touched the reflective surface. It felt hard, but it flexed slightly as she pushed on it. Di-woto appeared at her side and pushed on the wall also. Skyra turned and began walking along the wall. "We will find a door."

Di-woto and the others followed.

As she made her way along the wall, Skyra paused every few breaths to search for signs of a door and to push on the reflective surface. It looked and felt the same every time. She continued following the wall around its gently-curving corner. This side of the building was close to the building beside it, with a space between only about as wide as Skyra was tall. She continued around the next curved corner to the back side of the building, where again there was only a narrow gap between buildings.

Ripple caught up to Skyra and continued walking beside her, the creature's padded feet almost silently tapping the smooth street. "Do you care to hear my thoughts?"

Skyra was getting bored with looking at a wall that was the same everywhere, and she welcomed the distraction. "Tell me your thoughts."

"First, I think there are people in this city."

"We have not seen any people."

"I do not know why we have not seen any people, but if a war had taken place, and the people were killed, we would see more destroyed buildings. We would see dead bodies. Even if it had happened thousands of years ago, we would see bones and pieces of clothing."

"Maybe the people left the city."

"If so, what would make all the people leave a city like this?"

She stopped walking and looked down at Ripple. "Do you think something here is dangerous? The bats are easily killed and would only be dangerous to few people, not to many people."

"I'm just wondering, what would make all those people leave a city like this?"

She resumed walking and pushing on the wall. "I do not know. These are things you should ask Lincoln and his tribemates. This city makes me afraid, but they want to stay here. I stay where Lincoln stays."

"Yes, and that is good—you and Lincoln *must* remain together. However, my plan requires that you and Lincoln remain alive also. Lincoln does not always trust me, but he does trust you."

"That is because sometimes you say words that are not true. You have told lies to me also."

"Yes, but only when I believed it would help you survive."

Skyra let out a short growl. "I will watch for danger in this city, Ripple."

"As will I," the creature said, then it fell silent.

Still walking behind Skyra, Di-woto spoke so rapidly in her language that Skyra caught only a few of the words.

"Allow me to summarize," Ripple said. "Di-woto wants to talk to the people who planned these great buildings. She is excited to learn how to make such plans. She wants to understand the materials used and how to make buildings this tall that will not collapse. Finally, she wishes to know why the people here put their doors in the ground instead of on the sides of the buildings."

Skyra stopped, faced Di-woto, and did her best to speak the girl's language. "Why you say doors in ground?"

Di-woto smiled. "I saw doors. I saw three doors."

Lincoln and the others caught up. Lincoln must have noticed Skyra's confused expression. "What's wrong?"

"Di-woto says she has seen doors in the ground. She has seen three of them."

Jazzlyn said, "What does she mean? What doors?"

Skyra grabbed the girl's arm. "You show us doors."

"Yes, I show you. Come!" She turned and continued in the same direction they were already walking.

"How can she show us what she saw by taking us somewhere we haven't even been yet?" Derek asked. "This girl may have a full six-pack, but she's missing the plastic thingy that holds it all together."

Skyra didn't know what that meant, but she knew Di-woto would not say what she had said unless she had seen *something*.

Di-woto led them along the back of the building, around the curved corner to the building's side, then around the last curved corner onto the street where they had started.

The girl pointed toward the wreckage that blocked the street. "You see now—door!"

Skyra stared. It looked like there was a hole in the jumble of wreckage—a hole large enough to walk through. However, she should have seen such a hole when she and the others had been standing on the far side of the wreckage.

"What is that?" Lincoln asked.

The hole seemed to shift as Skyra continued along the

front of the building. It was something in *front* of the wreckage, a smooth mound of the reflective material.

"I'll be damned, an optical illusion," Lincoln said. "With all the curved mirrors around here, that thing's almost invisible."

They stopped beside the reflective mound, which was a little taller than Skyra's head. It was more like half of a mound —the flat side was near the building's wall, and from there it sloped outward in every direction.

"What is it?" Derek asked.

Di-woto grabbed Derek's hand and pulled him into the gap between the building and the flat side of the mound. Skyra and the others followed. Di-woto pointed to a hole in the street beneath the half mound. Sunlight pouring through the mound's reflective material revealed a slope leading into the hole away from the building behind them.

"You see now—door!" Di-woto said again.

Skyra squatted on her heels to peer farther back into the hole. The light faded to blackness several body lengths into the tunnel. She sniffed the air, almost expecting to catch the scent of a cave bear or other predator that had made the tunnel its home. She smelled nothing alarming, so she stood and walked down the slope.

"Lincoln, you're letting your wife go down there first?" Jazzlyn said from behind.

Lincoln caught up to Skyra in answer to the question, while the others remained behind.

Skyra paused to let her eyes adjust to the darkness. She glanced over at him. "There are no predators in this cave."

"Good to know, but I wasn't even thinking about predators. We have no idea what other dangers might be down here."

"That is why we are looking. We walked around the building to find a door. Now we have found a door."

He blew out a long breath. "Yeah... it just seems a little creepy."

Skyra's eyes were adjusting to the darkness, so she headed deeper in. "What is creepy?"

"It means scary. A lot of my people are afraid of dark places. I guess I am too."

Skyra had to hold her hands out now to feel her way. "Do your people stay by the campfire all night?"

He let out a nervous bolup laugh. "Kind of, yes. We have ways to make light other than using a campfire. Most of my people have never once walked in a forest at night without taking light with them."

"Your people are strange, Lincoln." Skyra's hands hit a solid wall. "The cave ends here."

She felt her way to one side while Lincoln felt his way to the other.

"There is nothing else here," she said.

"Nothing here either. So, this must be a closed door." She heard his hands feeling around on the smooth surface. "There may be a seam here." A dim light appeared on the strap he always wore on his wrist, and he leaned in to look closely at the wall. "It *is* a seam—this is definitely a door." The light disappeared, then he grunted, apparently trying to push the door open.

Skyra leaned on the wall and helped push. If this was a door, it would not move, so she stepped back.

Several breaths later, he said, "It won't budge, and there's no handle anywhere. I can't even get my fingernails in the seam."

They had no choice but to return to ground level. As they

made their way up the slope into the light, Skyra pulled Lincoln's wrist toward her face. "How does your wrist strap make light?"

"Hmm... well, it has its own power inside, kind of like the sun but really, really small."

Skyra let out a short laugh. "It is not like the sun at all. The sun shows itself in the morning when it is ready for the new day, and it hides behind the hills each night when it is tired. You cannot make the sun give you light when you are in a dark tunnel."

He gave her a funny look. "I didn't mean my watch is like the sun in that way. I just meant it makes its own light with the power inside it. Like the sun does. As long as it has power I can make it light up any time I want to." He held it up and touched it with his other hand. White, glowing figures appeared on the strap.

"Does it burn your arm?"

"No, it's not like fire. It's perfectly cool." He pushed it toward her. "You can touch it."

She laughed again. "Are you trying to trick me?"

Derek's voice came from the street above. "Well, does it go anywhere or not?"

Skyra and Lincoln walked the rest of the way up the slope.

"Yeah, I'm pretty sure there's a door, but it's sealed tight," Lincoln said. He turned to Di-woto. "Ripple, ask her why she didn't tell us before that she had seen three of these doors."

Ripple exchanged words with the girl. "Di-woto says she often sees things others do not. She is not in the habit of explaining to others everything she sees." Ripple paused for a breath. "Lincoln, I'm not sure whether she is saying this apologetically or condescendingly."

Jazzlyn let out a brief laugh, which Skyra did not understand.

"If that one's locked, it seems likely the others will also be locked," Virgil said.

Derek put both his hands behind his head and turned his face to the sky. "Great. We have an entire city to ourselves, and we can't even get into any of the buildings." He cupped his hands around his mouth and shouted, "Hey! Is anybody here?"

"Derek," Lincoln said firmly, "we really should come to a consensus before you—"

He was interrupted by a sound from above, like the sudden gushing of a mountain river. Skyra's chest tightened, and she reached for her khul as she searched for the sound. There it was—a dark swarm of creatures pouring out of the wide hole near the top of the building.

"Please don't tell me those are bats," Virgil said.

If they were bats, they were tiny compared to the giants that had attacked earlier. Although, as the prairie dog town had proven, even small creatures were dangerous in large numbers. Skyra shoved Di-woto toward the fallen wreckage and shouted at the others to take cover.

Jazzlyn held up a hand. "Wait, you guys. Those are swallows. They won't hurt us, and this time I really mean it."

Skyra wasn't taking any chances this time. She guided Di-woto under a protruding piece of the ruined reflective wall. Lincoln, Derek, and Virgil joined them, while Jazzlyn remained out in the open.

The reflective side of the material above Skyra's head was facing the sky, so she could see through it. The creatures kept pouring from the building by the thousands. The swarm split and went in different directions. A mass of them swooped down toward the street, and Skyra darted out to drag Jazzlyn under the wreckage.

"It's okay," Jazzlyn said as Skyra grabbed her arm. "See? They're just swallows. Derek's shout must have startled them."

The mass of tiny birds swirled in the air between buildings for a breath then flew upward and out of sight.

Jazzlyn smiled at the others who were still hiding in the wreckage. "I told you there's nothing to worry about—swallows are insectivores. They eat flying insects."

"Yeah, and prairie dogs eat grass," Derek muttered.

Lincoln came out from under the wreckage. "Swallows... they're the only birds we've seen since jumping here."

Virgil came out behind him. "You're right. Jazzlyn, do swallows spend any time below ground, or in caves, or anything like that?"

"Actually they do. Have you seen swallow nests made of mud stuck to the underside of bridges? Those swallows have a natural tendency to make those nests in caves, but bridges are typically more abundant than caves. One species is even called the cave swallow. Also, some swallows nest in holes dug in the sides of mud banks and cliffs."

Virgil made a snapping sound with his fingers. "Bingo. Then swallows fit nicely within our hypothesis. Something—whether a weapon or a natural event—quickly killed off the above-ground creatures and spared those that happened to be underground at the time."

"I want this fabric," Di-woto said in her language. The girl was still in the wreckage, pulling on something.

Skyra moved in beside her to look. At a place where one of the thin sticks had broken in two, the reflective material that had been connected to it had come loose. The material was thin and flexible, like the hairless skin of a newborn rat except clear on one side and reflective on the other. Di-woto was pulling on the material, trying to tear it loose from the stick frame.

Derek appeared at Di-woto's other side. He dropped his spear and khul, pulled the pack from his back, took out one of the knives, and unfolded the shiny blade. "Here, let me help." He stabbed the material with the knife, but the sharp tip did not puncture it. He stabbed again. Then he grunted and pushed the knife's tip into the material with all his weight. Still, the point didn't even make a tiny hole. He stepped back and frowned. "Well hell, now I want some of this stuff, too."

Di-woto touched the exposed edge of the material and sawed back and forth like her finger was a knife.

"You think?" Derek said. He waited for her to move her hand then tried it with the real knife, sawing at the exposed edge rather than stabbing at the undamaged portion. The shiny blade cut through the material. He paused and looked at Di-woto. "Girl, you're a hell of a lot smarter than you look." He shook his head and went back to cutting.

Di-woto grinned, obviously pleased with herself.

Skyra said, "Di-woto is an alinga-ul. Alinga-uls are smarter than bolups and smarter than nandups. If Lincoln puts a child in my belly, the child will be an alinga-ul also."

Derek glanced at her while cutting. "You pretty much say whatever's on your mind, don't you?"

Skyra didn't know what that meant, but staring at Derek made her think of something. "My birthmate Veenah is dead."

He glanced at her again. "Yeah, I heard. I'm sorry."

She didn't bother telling him it made no sense for him to be sorry for something he did not do. Instead, she continued her thought. "If we cannot live in this land, maybe we will use the T3 to go many, many years to my land, and we will save Veenah from dying. I think Veenah will like you, Derek, even though sometimes you think you are changing into an animal. Maybe you and Veenah will make alinga-uls too."

He stopped cutting and made a choking sound, like he had sucked in some of his own spit. "Bloody buggering hell! Where did that come from?"

"What do you mean?"

He glanced at Lincoln, Jazzlyn, Virgil, and Ripple, who were still out in the street talking about swallows. "Never mind, you just surprised me, that's all. You're on our team now, and sometimes I forget nandups don't think the same way bolups think."

"Jazzlyn has told me that before too."

"Not surprised." He went back to cutting. Soon he pulled away a piece of the material twice as long and twice as wide as Di-woto's entire body and handed it to her.

The girl bounced up and down on her toes with excitement as she took it. She folded it several times and wrapped it around her rolled mat of woven grass.

Before continuing deeper into the city, the group returned to the same street on which they had entered the city from the forest. This was because Lincoln and his tribemates thought they could easily find their way out from here, although they knew either Skyra or Ripple could easily lead them back to the T3.

Now that Di-woto had pointed out one of the tunnels under the street, Skyra knew what to look for, and soon she was spotting the reflective mounds on almost every cross street they passed. She and Lincoln checked three more of the tunnels, and all of them ended in a wall with a door they could not open. After that, they stopped checking.

Although the sun was blocked by countless buildings, its reflections on the shiny surfaces showed it was getting low in the sky. The streets were gradually becoming darker, and Skyra was becoming frustrated. The city was the same everywhere—nothing but smooth, reflective walls and flat, empty streets with a few mounds.

She stopped the group. "We should return to the forest. The sun will soon hide itself for the night. We must find a safe place to sleep."

"You think the forest will be safer than here?" Virgil asked.

Skyra scanned the endless reflective walls. "The tunnels in the streets are the only places to hide. We will be trapped if predators find us there."

"This really sucks," Derek said. With his knife still in his hand, he stepped over to one of the reflective walls and thrust the blade at the material. The wall stretched inward a little but did not split. He stabbed it again and again, then he dragged the knife's edge over it, trying to slice it open. The material did not even show a thin scratch. Finally, he turned back to the group, growling and shaking his head. "Damn stuff's invincible, unless you cut into an exposed edge."

"Here's a thought," Jazzlyn said. "This city is so sterile that predators would have no reason to ever come this far in. There just isn't anything to eat. Maybe we're safe here for that reason alone."

Derek huffed. "I gotta say it again, don't I? Giant killer bats. *We're* something to eat."

"Yeah," Jazzlyn said. "Forgot about those."

"How about if we go back to the pile of twisted siding?" Lincoln suggested. "It will hide us from above, and we might be able to find a spot where we can escape out either side if we need to."

Skyra liked this idea better than sleeping on the streets in the open, and she knew these bolups were afraid to sleep in the forest. So, she agreed, as did the others.

"I hear disturbances in the air approaching," Ripple said. "Very likely it is the beating of numerous large wings."

Skyra tilted her head to the sky. Now she could hear it too. The wings sounded bigger than swallow wings. She grabbed Di-woto and pulled her to the side of the street. "Stand against the wall!" she hissed.

The sky above turned dark with flying bats just as the others—including Ripple—pressed against the building.

"Do not move," she whispered, probably too softly for the bolups to hear. The whooshing sounds of countless wings seemed to bounce around the towering buildings and empty streets, making them even louder.

The sky became clear, but only for a breath, then another wave of the creatures sailed over. Scratching and clattering sounds came from somewhere above as the bats began landing on the buildings. Or—more likely—they were flying into some of the holes in the buildings where the reflective windows had fallen off.

A few smaller groups flew over, followed by more scratching and clattering, then the city was silent again.

Lincoln stepped slightly away from the wall. "If anyone wants a silver lining, we are already learning some of the rhythms of this place. The bats fly out of the city to feed in the morning and return in the evening to sleep. The more we learn, the better our chances of staying alive."

"That's exactly why you're the boss, Boss," Jazzlyn said.

ON THE WAY back to the wreckage, Di-woto stopped the group and insisted they turn on one of the cross streets. She wanted to move one street over before continuing so she could see new things. This did not make sense to Skyra because everything in this city was the same. When the girl took off down a cross street, though, everyone followed.

At the next street, Di-woto led them around the corner to continue toward the wreckage. The girl then began jumping with excitement and pointing. A few buildings ahead, where they couldn't have seen it from the other street, was another pile of fallen wreckage.

Di-woto ran toward the pile, actually laughing in her delight. She stopped abruptly, staring to one side. Then she turned back to the group, her eyes wide. She pointed again.

"Hot damn," Derek said. "The stuff isn't invincible after all."

They came to a stop at the edge of the piled wreckage. One of the sticks of the mangled framework had torn a hole in the reflective side of the building. The hole was just above the street, and it was large enough for them to crawl through.

Derek ducked under some of the wreckage and leaned into the hole. After a few breaths, his voice came from within the building. "Holy shit!"

7

INSIDE

***47,659 YEARS** in the future - Day 1*

LINCOLN STUCK his head through the hole. The building's interior was fully illuminated by natural light streaming in through the transparent outer walls, even though the light outside was steadily fading. Lincoln scanned the interior and couldn't help but repeat Derek's words. "Holy shit."

The entire bottom floor was at least fifty feet high, without walls or dividers of any kind. It was one vast open space. In the center, perhaps fifty yards in from where Lincoln stood, was a single cylindrical support column about ten feet in diameter.

Numerous shapes that could only be human-sized chairs and tables protruded from the floor. Instead of being attached to the floor, they seemed to actually be part of the floor, the same teal green color and apparently made of the same substance.

Everything was as smooth and featureless as the building's

exterior. The chairs and tables were rounded, with no sharp corners, as if they were intentionally designed to look like melted plastic. The entire space had a flowing, liquid-like feel, like the inside of an immense lava lamp.

Lincoln scanned the area again. He couldn't see a single loose object—everything was part of the floor itself. He turned his gaze downward. Near the open hole in the window, the floor was covered with a thick layer of dust, pocked and re-pocked by stray raindrops that had blown in. The dust became thinner with increasing distance from the opening, and was undisturbed by footprints, human or otherwise. Nothing had come out of or into this hole in a good long time.

He pulled his head out and turned to the others. "I think we just found where we're going to spend the night."

"I was hoping you'd say that," Derek said. He unfolded his knife and moved in to make the hole larger.

Lincoln put an arm out to stop him. "Let's leave it the way it is. So far, animals haven't entered through here. If the reason is because the hole is at chest height, we probably want to keep it that way."

Derek closed the knife. "Good thinking."

As if she knew what had just been said, Di-woto handed Skyra the stone knife she had been carrying then clambered up the angled piece of window framework protruding through the hole. She ducked through the opening and dropped to the floor, all while clutching her precious roll of woven grass enclosed within her roll of reflective material.

Skyra shoved the knife into her wrist sheath beside its companion and followed Di-woto.

Ripple said, "I hate to squander my charge by levitating needlessly, but it is preferable to the indignity of being picked up and manhandled." A familiar hum emanated from the drone as it rose from the street and retracted its legs.

"I wasn't planning to help you through there anyway," Derek said. He turned to Jazzlyn. "Were you planning on helping?"

"Nope, didn't even cross my mind," she said.

Ripple spun in midair, turning its vision lens toward Derek. "Your attempt at belittling humor has been noted, and I have applied one checkmark. Earning three checkmarks is to be avoided." The drone then turned and propelled itself smoothly through the hole.

Derek frowned. "Was that drone humor? Lincoln, you coded that damn thing—was that supposed to be funny?"

Lincoln suppressed his urge to smile and started up the bent framework. "Don't ask me. My future self wrote the code. I'd avoid earning any more checkmarks if I were you, though."

Climbing through the hole wasn't quite as easy as Di-woto and Skyra had made it look, but soon Lincoln dropped to the floor beside them, his feet kicking up small clouds of dust.

Several minutes later, the rest of the group had joined them.

Di-woto had already moved out into the vast room and was running her hands over one of the strange chairs. She then extended her arms toward the ceiling and rattled off a string of words.

Ripple translated. "Di-woto says she has never been so happy as she is at this moment. She wants to thank all of us for bringing her to such a beautiful place."

"Christ, she thinks we're on a vacation," Derek said.

Lincoln watched the girl as she sat on one of the chairs

briefly before she crawled onto a table. "She's had a difficult life. Maybe to her this *is* a vacation."

"Now I see how the residents here get to the second floor," Virgil said.

Lincoln followed his gaze. Along the curved outer wall—which actually was one sheet of the transparent material stretched over a curved framework—a sloped walkway disappeared into the ceiling high above. He turned, scanning the rest of the outer wall, and noted a total of four of these ramps, all of them sloping in the same direction. He imagined the four ramps continuing upward to the next floor and the next after that, following the building's perimeter all the way to the top like the spiraling stripes of a candy cane.

"This place is like the streets," Skyra said. "Nothing is here. It feels strange with nothing here."

Lincoln understood exactly what she meant. Although the space was filled with tables and chairs, those were all molded to the floor. Other than the particles of dust near the hole they'd come through, not a single loose object could be seen anywhere. "If these people had to evacuate quickly, wouldn't they have left a lot of things behind?" he asked. "Even if they'd had plenty of time to pack up and go, how could they possibly have taken every single loose object with them?"

"Perhaps they put everything in storage somewhere," Virgil offered.

Lincoln shook his head, baffled. The sunlight was steadily fading, and they needed a safe place to rest for the night. They were all hungry and thirsty, but finding food and water would need to wait until morning. The others were spreading out to explore the room, so he spoke loud enough for all to hear. "I think it goes without saying we'll be spending the night in this building. I suggest we move up to the second level, if not higher. You know, in case some predator catches our scent through that open hole, or something like that."

Skyra gave him a distinctively Neanderthal smile and nodded, indicating she approved. She shouted a few words to Di-woto, who had wandered off halfway across the open room, and the girl came bouncing back as if she had just been called to dinner.

They headed up the nearest walkway, which was just a smooth ramp with solid, featureless, waist-high railings on either side. As they approached the ceiling of the ground floor, Lincoln leaned over the outer rail and looked straight up. About two feet of space existed between the inclined walkway and the outer window, and he could see at least a hundred feet up, to the point where the odd curve of the building cut off his view. He had been right—the four ramps spiraled around the outer border of the building, probably all the way to the top. Regularly spaced and disturbingly thin rods connected the outer window framework to the spiraling ramps.

The second floor had a lower ceiling than the ground floor, but it was still a good thirty feet high. Like the first floor, this space was completely open, with no walls and no supporting columns other than the same ten-foot-diameter cylinder in the center. Were these entire floors supported only by their connections to the center column and the spiraling ramps? It seemed impossible.

"Just more of the same," Virgil said, stopping at the opening in the railing to exit the ramp onto the second level. "At least this floor is a different color."

Lincoln hadn't noticed yet, but Virgil was right. Everything on the ground floor had been teal green—chairs, tables, floor, and ceiling. Here, everything was a subtle shade of yellow. Again, there were no loose objects, only chairs and tables that appeared to have oozed up from the floor and solidified. Not a sharp edge or corner could be seen anywhere.

"I vote we keep going," Derek said. "Eventually there has to be some offices or apartments or something, and hopefully some more manly colors."

They continued up the walkway.

The third level was yet another color, this time a pastel peach. Its ceiling was much lower, only about eight feet above the floor. It also had walls. Exiting the walkway, the group stood in a wide, open area extending to the left and right and presumably continuing around the curves of the building's profile. Clusters of peach-colored chairs and tables were arranged so groups of two to fifteen or so people could congregate together. The center portion of the third floor, about twenty yards in from the outer window, was separated from the open area by a wall. Spaced out seemingly randomly along the wall were open doorways leading to rooms or corridors beyond.

As usual, Di-woto charged ahead without waiting, headed for the nearest of the doorways. Skyra growled softly and chased after the girl.

"I guess we're going this way," Lincoln said to Ripple and his team as he followed Skyra.

Humans were generally taller than Neanderthals, but these doorways were plenty tall enough for both, so the door size gave no hint as to which species lived here.

Beyond the doorway was a corridor with even more doorways. These were more evenly spaced, but they appeared to get closer together farther down the corridor toward the building's center.

Skyra followed Di-woto through the first doorway on the

right, and seconds later one of Di-woto's distinctive laughs came from inside.

Lincoln hastened to catch up. Beyond the doorway was a single room, about the size of a volleyball court. Like the rest of the third floor, everything in the room was peach. Chairs and tables arose from the floor here and there, but what had tickled Di-woto was a waist-high platform. The girl had crawled onto the platform and was on her hands and knees, bouncing up and down.

Skyra turned to Lincoln. "I think this is a bed!" She had slept on a bed for the first time in Kyran-yufost and had been duly impressed.

Lincoln and his team gathered around and pressed their fingers into the soft surface. The platform was roughly the size and shape of a twin bed. What else could it be? There was even a raised portion at one end, like a pillow that extended all the way across. The surface resembled glossy, peach-colored plastic, like everything else on this level, but it was surprisingly soft. Lincoln saw no blankets or sheets. The room had no door that could be closed, and it contained no dressers with drawers for storing clothing. There were no mirrors, books, personal hygiene items, or any other loose items. Regardless, Lincoln was convinced this room was a dwelling.

Could these people really have taken every single item with them? Or did they actually live this way, with no personal items to pick up and carry around? The idea seemed so... alien. While the others continued exploring the room, Lincoln ran his hands along the sides of the bed near the floor, then along the wall beside the bed, looking for hidden drawers or compartments. Nothing moved, and the light was getting too dim to see if there were tiny seams.

"What are you looking for?" Skyra asked.

"I can't figure out where these people kept their things—their possessions, like clothing and...." He trailed off, unable to think of any other possessions Skyra would understand.

"Here's something significant," Virgil called out from the corner farthest from the doorway.

Jazzlyn was with him, and she said, "It looks like a place that could be a shower."

Lincoln and the others gathered around. In the corner, which was actually more rounded than angled, a ridge in the floor extended in an arc from one wall to the other. It was like a small levee several inches tall, enclosing an area about five feet in diameter. In the center was a circular depression the size of a dinner plate and about an inch lower than the surrounding floor.

Jazzlyn was right, this corner appeared to be designed as a shower, but there was no shower head or spouts in the ceiling or wall and no knobs or levers anywhere. Logic would dictate that a drain would be situated in the circular depression, but like everything else, that spot appeared to be solid, peach-colored plastic.

Lincoln kneeled and touched the bottom of the depression, wondering if it had tiny holes that weren't visible in the low light. The floor there felt unusually soft. He pushed a little harder. The floor gave way, and his fingers passed right through it.

"Damn!" he cried, pulling his hand back.

"What?" Derek asked as the others gathered closer to see.

"I don't know." Lincoln stared at his hand. His fingers seemed fine—they didn't hurt, and they weren't wet. The floor of the depression looked solid again, as if nothing had happened. "My fingers went through the floor."

He touched it again, this time more cautiously. Again, the

floor gave way to the pressure of his fingertips. He pushed farther, then wiggled his fingers below the floor—nothing but open air beneath. He pulled his hand out quickly, and the floor closed in on itself with a soft *pop*.

He looked up at the others. "It's like a thin membrane that lets things pass through, but then it closes back up."

"So, it *is* a drain," Virgil said. He kneeled to touch it himself.

"Hold on," Jazzlyn said. "From what I've seen so far, that drain may also be the place where these people crap and piss. You sure you wanna be sticking your fingers in there?"

Virgil pulled his hand back and got to his feet. "No. No I am not."

Lincoln stared with renewed interest at the ceiling above the drain, then along the curved wall. Still nothing visible. On a hunch, he stepped to the wall, being careful not to put a foot in the depression, and began running his hands over the surface. Maybe there was another membrane, hiding some type of control positioned within the wall. As he moved his hand up to chest level, he felt a soft spot. He pushed. His fingers didn't pass through a membrane, but the soft area gave way slightly, like it was spongy beneath the surface.

A hissing sound began emanating from the ceiling above his head.

"Lincoln, what is that?" Skyra asked, alarm in her voice.

The hissing grew in volume, now punctuated every few seconds by a gurgling sound.

"No way!" Jazzlyn said. "This place has been abandoned way too long for the water to still—"

Her words were cut off by a sputtering, coughing shower of water raining down on Lincoln's upturned face. Someone grabbed his arm and pulled him out of the downpour.

"It is raining inside this building!" Skyra exclaimed.

Derek cupped his hands under the shower, then he held the water up to his face and smelled it. "In the name of all that is holy and wicked, we have freakin' water!"

"It may not be safe to drink," Virgil said.

The water was now flowing smoothly, with only an occasional burp of air.

Derek filled his cupped hands again and held the water out to Virgil. "Smell it, man. There's nothing wrong with it. It's water!"

Skyra moved in and filled her own hands. She put the water to her face and sniffed, then she poured some into her mouth. Without a word or a glance at anyone else, she shrugged out of her woolly-rhino-fur cape, removed her lynx-fur waist-skin, pulled off her footwraps, and stepped totally naked under the pouring water.

"Skyra is not encumbered by the norms of modesty typically present in your original timeline," Ripple's gender-neutral voice said.

"That's one of the reasons I like her," Jazzlyn said, staring.

Di-woto uttered a few words in her language, then she pulled off her white-fur boots and her multi-colored sack garment. Laughing, she stepped into the shower with Skyra.

"God almighty," Derek muttered. He was staring at the ornamental scars covering almost every inch of Di-woto's body. "I had no idea how extensive those were. Some are still seeping blood!"

The scars on the girl's belly, obviously cut to resemble waves of water, were newer than all the others, inflicted within the last week or so.

"She cut all those herself," Lincoln said. "I guess it was her way of dealing with the loneliness of being different from everyone she knew."

Jazzlyn turned away as if just looking at the scars was painful. "That poor girl."

Now soaked to the bone, her long hair pasted to her smiling face, Skyra extended a hand. "Come into the rain with us, Lincoln."

"If the water still works, there must be a source of power that also still works," Lincoln said. "If there's still power, there must still be people here somewhere."

"It's possible the water is gravity-fed," Virgil countered. "We didn't see a conventional water tower, but for all we know, some of these skyscrapers could be water towers. These people seem obsessed with the aesthetics of uniformity, so I wouldn't be surprised."

Everyone had showered, and the group was now seated in a cluster of chairs beside the floor-to-ceiling window of the outer open area of the third level. Although the moon was blocked by the surrounding tall buildings, enough of its light was being reflected by their mirror-like surfaces to allow everyone to see each other. Di-woto was curled up in a chair next to Skyra, apparently asleep.

It had been over an hour since they'd discovered the running water, and during that time they had found many more one-room dwellings, each with its own bed, chairs, tables, and functional corner shower.

"Look out there," Jazzlyn said, pointing to the buildings beyond the window. "Not a single light anywhere. If this city had power, wouldn't we see a few lights or something?"

"What is power?" Skyra asked.

Lincoln held his watch up and tapped it to make the menu glow. "Remember this light? Power is what makes this light possible. It's kind of like fire without being hot, and people can collect it so they can use it any time they need to. One thing they use it for is to light up their dwellings at night. We don't see any light coming from the other buildings, so maybe that means there's no power here."

"Maybe there is power here but no people," she said.

"That's possible."

Derek shifted in his chair and groaned. "This is possible, that's possible. Lots of things are *possible*. I'm sure we'll find out soon enough. Here's what matters now. I'd prefer this place to be, like, a normal human city. I'd love a Thai place and a coffee shop, but at least we have beds and running water. And we don't have predators stalking us. I feel safer at this moment than I have since we jumped from your lab, Lincoln. Let's figure out how to make this place work."

"The water source may not last," Virgil said. "If the pressure is due to gravity, the water tower will eventually empty itself, and without power to pump more—"

"Yeah, I know," Derek interjected. "We have water right now, though. What do we do about food? My stomach is not a happy camper."

There was a moment of contemplative silence.

Lincoln decided to toss out a possibility. "What do you think the chances are of finding stored food?"

Derek said, "A city this size? There has to be tons of it. There should be canned goods—or whatever—in every apartment. There should also be grocery stores somewhere."

"There are two problems with that," Virgil said, "One is

spoilage. Observed evidence suggests this city was abandoned years ago, possibly hundreds of years ago."

"Or thousands," Jazzlyn added. "It's hard to even imagine a preservation method that could keep food safe for that long."

Virgil nodded. "The second problem is actually finding the food. So far we haven't seen a single loose item anywhere, besides windows that have fallen off. We could get lucky and find stored food within a few days if there's some in this building. If not, it could take months, assuming we can even figure out how to get into the other buildings."

"Oh, we can get in," Derek said. "If that broken piece of framework can punch a hole in the window, I can too." He slammed his fist into the palm of his other hand. "I just need the right tool."

Lincoln considered the hundreds of buildings they'd seen in the short time they had walked the streets, and those constituted only a fraction of the entire city. Then his thoughts turned to the blocked passageways from the streets to whatever was below ground. "Here's something we haven't discussed. These buildings don't have entryways at the street level. That means these people must have entered from below ground. We didn't see an entry point on the first floor, but logically it must be there somewhere. Perhaps we'll find stored food—and a lot of other things—below the surface, although I'd be surprised if the entry points weren't locked tight like those under the streets."

A growl came from Skyra's throat. "You bolups are strange people. You talk and talk about trying to find food, but there is food in Derek's pack."

Derek coughed. "Um, sorry, but I threw those grubs out before we entered the city. They were getting gooey stuff all over the inside of the pack."

They all fell silent for a moment.

Skyra growled again. "I will never know how you bolups stay alive. When the sun shows itself in the morning, I will go out of the city to hunt. I will bring back as much food as I can carry. Maybe one of you will go with me so that we can carry more."

Derek said, "I hope you're not talking about hunting for worms and grubs and shit."

"I do not know what shit is."

"I think what Derek is trying to say is we're not used to eating things like insects," Jazzlyn offered. "We think they're kind of gross. You know... disgusting."

Skyra stared for a moment then said, "This land has many insects. You may have to learn to eat them."

"She's got a point," Lincoln said. "I don't like the idea of splitting up, but by tomorrow, access to food is going to start becoming critical. I'll go hunting with Skyra. I'll do what I can to help her find food other than insects and worms—for now, anyway. The rest of you can start searching for sources of food here. Just don't get lost in this maze of streets."

"Another problem," Virgil said. "Since Neanderthals are predominantly meat eaters, I assume you will be coming back with animals of some sort. How, may I ask, will we cook these creatures?"

"I got a couple of lighters in the pack," Derek replied. "Problem is, there's nothing around here to burn."

Jazzlyn said, "The showers work. Maybe we'll find stoves or microwaves or something."

Lincoln was doubtful of that, but kept it to himself.

Yet another growl from Skyra. "We will bring sticks from the forest for burning. Lincoln will come with me to carry food, and Di-woto will come to carry sticks."

Lincoln smiled, imagining that if Skyra knew the phrase, she would have ended her statement with, 'It's not rocket science, people!'

Derek sighed and rose from his chair. "Well, I'm hungry as hell, but I'm thrilled we have a plan. I feel like I've been awake two days straight. Unless there's something else we need to discuss, boss...."

Lincoln let out his own sigh. "No. I think we should all get some sleep."

Derek spoke over his shoulder as he headed to the corridor of dwellings. "You kids be good now. Ain't no doors on the rooms, so limit the rackety shenanigans. Jazz and Virg, that goes for you, too."

He left the group sitting in awkward silence.

Jazzlyn and Virgil had each selected their own dwellings, but it was no secret they were quite fond of each other. Diwoto had also picked out her own room, although now it seemed Lincoln would have to carry her there. Ripple had agreed to remain in the open area of the outer perimeter, in low power mode but with audio sensors set to sound an alarm if anything or anyone came near.

Skyra broke the silence. "Sometimes I do not understand Derek's words."

Jazzlyn snorted softly. "Yeah, he's one strange-ass bolup, isn't he?"

8

HUNT

***47,659 years** in the future - Day 2*

Skyra was waking up slowly. Each time she opened her eyes, the sleeping chamber was dark and silent. It felt safe here, which made her close her eyes again and inhale Lincoln's scent, which in turn made her drift back to sleep—again and again.

Finally, her bladder demanded she get up. She felt her way over to the corner Lincoln had called a *shower* and squatted over the strange hole in the floor. When she was done she rose to her full height and pressed on the wall. Cool rain poured over her head and body. The water felt good, but she didn't like that it washed away Lincoln's scent.

She pressed on the wall again to stop the rain. Then she started it once more, let it fall for a few breaths, then stopped it. She smiled. The people who built this city must have been clever. Maybe they were alinga-uls, like Di-woto.

After squeezing excess water from her hair, she padded

back to the bed, stretched out beside Lincoln, and pressed her body against his.

He snorted and woke up. "Hey, you're all wet!"

She pushed her face into his neck. "I like the shower rain. Now I need to get your scent back on me."

He let out a soft bolup laugh and pulled her closer. "Seriously, you're soaking wet. I wonder how these people dried off after their showers."

Skyra pressed closer, enjoying his warmth. "I like the shower rain. I like this bed. I like what we did before we went to sleep. If that is what married people always do before they go to sleep, I am happy we are married."

His breathing seemed to quicken a little. "I know what you mean. Even though it seems a lot longer, we've been married only three days, and we've done that three nights in a row. That's three times more than I've ever done it before. I have to say, I'm feeling rather buoyant and exhilarated."

Skyra didn't know what the words meant, but she understood the meaning. "What do you call it in your English language?"

She sensed him frowning in the darkness. "What do I call what?"

"In my Una-Loto tribe, a woman reaches her ilmekho after she has seen twenty cold seasons. During her ilmekho, the dominant men compete to see who will be first to take her to his shelter to put a child in her belly. What he does to her in his shelter we call *lofrewna*. When we are girls, we are told what lofrewna means. I was afraid of lofrewna. The nandups who took Veenah forced her to do this many times, and they hurt her. This made me more afraid of lofrewna. But with you, I am not afraid. I want to know what you call it because I do not want to call it lofrewna anymore."

He stroked her wet shoulder with his hand. "We have a lot of different names for it, but most of them I don't like. I hadn't really thought about it before, but now I realize the best name for it is *making love*."

She raised her head and gazed at his face, even though she could barely see his eyes. "Jazzlyn told me you were falling in love with me. Before we go to sleep we make love. That is a good name for it, Lincoln."

"I think so, too."

She pressed her face back into his neck. "Ripple said you were married to a woman named Lottie Atkins."

His muscles stiffened. "Skyra, you do understand that happened to me in my future, right? It hasn't really happened yet, and I have never met Lottie Atkins. Now I'll never meet her. It's impossible."

Lincoln had explained enough about jumping through time that she did understand. "Ripple also said you fell in love with Lottie Atkins, but she was not a good match for you."

"Are you worried we will not be a good match?"

"No. We *are* a good match. I want to tell you that you do not have to worry about falling in love with Lottie Atkins anymore. If Lottie Atkins finds you, I will kill her."

His muscles relaxed. "Fortunately, you won't have to do that." After a few breaths of silence, he said, "This is a strange thought for me, and it's completely impossible now, but I wish I could introduce you to my family."

Skyra pushed herself up and sat with her legs crossed. "Your family?"

"My birthmother and birthfather, and my brothers."

It still seemed strange to Skyra that Lincoln could even know who his birthfather was. "You told me you had seven brothers and a sister who died. Your birthmother must like making love."

He huffed a laugh. "Yeah, I guess so. My mom and dad wanted to have a lot of kids. Anyway, I wish they could meet you. They would find you to be quite interesting."

"You do not believe you will ever see your family again."

"It's impossible now. They're in a different timeline. It's okay, though. I hadn't seen them in years anyway. They never really understood me. In fact, they were afraid of me. As soon as they realized I could see and sense whatever they were going to do before they even did it, they just started avoiding me. So did everyone else. I shouldn't complain, but I didn't have a very happy childhood."

Skyra understood exactly what he meant by this. The men of Una-Loto would frequently beat her and Veenah because they were different. A few of the men had even tried to kill the girls several times. The twin sisters had learned to fight back by the time they had seen ten cold seasons. "Why do you wish I could meet them if you do not like them?" she asked.

He seemed to think about this. "Usually when a couple gets married, they each introduce their mate to their family. Plus, I'd like to see the looks on their faces."

"Why?"

Again, he seemed to think. "I'm sorry, I'm realizing now I shouldn't have brought that up. You know what? I have family right here. *You* are my family. Jazzlyn, Virgil, and Derek are also my family."

"And Di-woto," she added.

"Yeah, I guess she is now."

"And Ripple."

He huffed another laugh. "Yeah, although that may be pushing it. Maddy, on the other hand...."

She waited for him to finish, but he fell silent.

A groaning sound came from one of the other chambers—the others were starting to wake up.

Skyra considered her empty belly and wondered what the new day would bring. She threw herself forward on top of Lincoln and rubbed her body against his one more time to pick up more of his scent. He wrapped his arms around her, and for a moment her body tried to tell her it was time to make love again. Her head resisted, however, and she pushed away from him and sat up. "We will get up now and go hunting."

He sighed. "Just like that, huh?"

DI-WOTO WAS ALREADY out in the larger chamber, where the morning's dim light was beginning to shine through the enormous window. The girl was sitting in one of the chairs, talking to Ripple and re-braiding her hair, apparently after letting it dry out. Still mostly unbraided, Di-woto's black hair flowed down the back of her chair and spread out onto the floor.

The girl turned to Skyra and Lincoln as they approached and spoke so rapidly in her language that Skyra understood only a few words, and Ripple had to translate. "Although I am not fond of the title, Di-woto said your talking beast is skilled in telling interesting stories. She would like to have her own talking beast, but she needs you to show her how to make one."

Ripple had been Skyra's companion through two cold seasons and almost two warm seasons. Until she had met

Lincoln, she had always thought Ripple to be some kind of strange creature. Now she knew Lincoln's future self had made Ripple out of many small parts, and she was still trying to comprehend that idea. She found it interesting Di-woto so easily accepted Ripple was something called a machine and could be made by people. Was this because the girl was an alinga-ul?

Ripple went on. "Di-woto is excited to go hunting with you, and she demands that I accompany you on this dangerous outing."

"Are you lying again?" Lincoln demanded.

Ripple's circle of red lights flashed twice. "It is my responsibility to watch over you and Skyra. You must admit I proved to be useful in the prairie dog town."

Lincoln started to say something, but Skyra interrupted. "Ripple, should I tell you again what my tribemates do to those who tell a lie?"

The creature's ring flashed again. "That will not be necessary, as I am incapable of forgetting what you have already told me. Please understand Lincoln's future self designed me so I would make a plan to benefit humanity, and then do whatever might be necessary to carry out the plan. Sometimes that involves saying things that are not true in order to get the desired result."

Skyra's eyes met Lincoln's, and he gave a frustrated shake of his head.

Derek came out from the corridor of dwellings, followed by Jazzlyn and Virgil. Their faces looked funny, the way bolup faces usually looked after waking up.

Derek yawned loudly then said, "Seriously, folks, we need to find some food before we start eating each other."

Skyra glanced at Lincoln with alarm.

"Don't worry, he's just kidding," Lincoln said.

Jazzlyn also yawned, then she stretched her arms above her head, revealing some of the dark skin of her belly. "If we can figure out a source of food, I'd be happy to stay here indefinitely. Those beds don't look like much, but damn, they're comfy."

"We will bring food," Skyra said. She was ready to go, so she checked that her khul was snug in its sling and shoved her hand blades deeper into their sheath.

"We'll begin on the ground floor," Virgil said. "We'll look for access to whatever's below ground. If we can't get in, we'll work our way up."

Lincoln already had his spear and the crude khul he'd made from a shorter tree limb, so there was no reason to wait.

Di-woto ran to her dwelling and came back with her rolls of reflective material and woven grasses. Apparently she intended to bring them along on the hunt. Both could be used to carry firewood or game, so Skyra didn't mind.

Skyra, Lincoln, Di-woto, and Ripple left the others, descended to the ground floor, and left the building the same way they had entered, through the hole in the window. The sun was still low, and its reflection on the towering buildings above created a strange orange color on the streets. They moved to the nearest cross street and followed it to the wider street that stretched all the way to the forest where they had entered the city.

Di-woto pointed down the street in the opposite direction of the forest. "We go there."

Skyra and Lincoln gazed in that direction. The street seemed to go on forever, disappearing among countless buildings.

"That would take us toward the center of the city,"

Lincoln said. "I have no idea what we'd find there. More buildings and empty streets, probably."

Skyra turned and started the other way, toward the forest. "We hunt," she said in Di-woto's language.

The girl let out a whimper of protest, but she followed.

As they walked, their soft footsteps and Ripple's tapping feet echoed off the buildings' smooth surfaces.

"It's so weird that this place is completely empty," Lincoln said, keeping his voice low.

Everything about the place was strange to Skyra, so she wasn't sure how to reply. She quickened her pace, determined to get to the trees before the bats began flying out of the city.

"Eep!" Di-woto screeched, startling Skyra and Lincoln. The girl then smiled as her sound echoed among the buildings. She did it again. "Eep! Eep eep eep eep!"

A fluttering, swooshing sound came from somewhere above, hopefully nothing more than another swarm of swallows startled by the noise.

Lincoln slapped a hand over the girl's mouth. "Shhhhh. Please don't do that. Skyra, can you tell her?"

"No sound!" Skyra said in the girl's language.

Di-woto's eyes were wide now, and she mumbled something beneath Lincoln's hand.

He released her.

"No sound!" the girl said in a whisper. Then she smiled again.

It was not long before they reached the end of the road at the city's edge. Skyra motioned for the others to stop, and she stood listening. Buzzing and scuttling insects could be heard from every direction, but she heard nothing to indicate larger game. The forest looked the same everywhere. Walking on the smooth ground of the city was much quieter than walking in the forest, so she began leading the others along the narrow street that separated the trees from the buildings. They passed one building, then another, then a third.

This was not the kind of hunting Skyra was used to. In her homeland she knew exactly what creatures she was hunting, where to find them, and how to approach and kill them. Ibexes grazed in small groups among the rocky outcrops and meadows of the Walukh hills. Reindeer roamed in massive herds in the open plains below the Kapolsek mountains. Crayfish were abundant among the rocks in the small streams feeding into the Yagua river.

Here, in this new land, she had no idea what game to search for. She knew where the prairie dogs lived, but they were far away, and they were also dangerous. She and the others had seen a wolf, but finding and killing one of those seemed unlikely. She stopped and stared into the forest. It could take many days—and her group might starve—before she learned to hunt in this new place.

Lincoln leaned close to her and whispered, "Did you hear something?"

She suppressed the growl growing in her throat. "Yes, I hear many creatures we can eat. Today we are gathering insects and grubs. Maybe we will find crayfish."

He frowned. "Well, I told Derek and the others we'd try to—"

"They will eat what we find, or they will stay hungry." She left the smooth street and entered the forest. Within only a few steps, she came upon a thick, rotting log. Using hand gestures and a few nandup words, she instructed Di-woto to unroll her sheet of reflective material and spread it on the ground. She grabbed the log and pulled until a chunk came loose. Numerous black beetles scrambled for shelter. Skyra ignored those and starting plucking up the more palatable insect larvae—mostly orange, wormlike creatures and white grubs. She also grabbed two fat crickets with unusually long legs. She dropped all of these onto the reflective sheet and motioned for Di-woto to gather up the edges to create a bag so they couldn't escape.

She turned to Lincoln, who was watching her with a funny bolup expression. "While I hunt, you will gather sticks for a fire." She turned back to the log and pulled again, this time ripping off the entire top half, revealing a snake as long as her arm, coiled in a cavity in the rotting wood. She had not seen this type before, so she snatched its tail, pulled it out, and stomped on its head until it was dead. To avoid any dangerous fangs, she removed its head with a hand blade before dropping the body into Di-woto's reflective bag.

Lincoln was still standing there, watching.

"Sticks for fire, Lincoln!"

"Okay, I guess you got this under control, huh?" He turned away, shaking his head.

Skyra broke apart the rest of the log, adding more larvae to the collection. She didn't see any other rotting logs nearby, so she called out to Lincoln as she led Di-woto and Ripple deeper into the forest. She came upon more logs, but they were still solid and would not pull apart.

Lincoln carried an armload of sticks to the forest edge and dropped them onto the smooth street where they would be easy to find later. While he was on his way back, Skyra used her khul to dig into the soil in several places. The ground here was dry, and she was not able to find grubs or worms.

"We will find a stream," she said as Lincoln approached.

Ripple had taken a few steps away and was facing a dense clump of weeds. "I am fairly certain these plants are stinging nettles, genus *Urtica*. If so, the younger plants are edible. You can boil them, Lincoln, as you would spinach."

Lincoln pulled up one of the weeds and brushed it across the back of his hand. "Yeah, definitely stinging nettles. Damn!" He dropped the plant and rubbed his hand against his shirt. Then he kneeled and began pulling up more of the weeds. "I'll collect all the smaller ones."

Di-woto giggled and began helping, still clutching her bag shut and holding her rolled grass mat under one arm.

"Those are plants," Skyra said. "We need real food for our bellies."

Lincoln paused. "I know nandups don't eat many plants, but bolups do. In fact, some of us eat only plants and no animals at all." He went back to pulling up weeds.

Skyra was tempted to say once again she did not know how Lincoln and his tribemates were still alive, but she decided to remain silent. She blew out a long breath and started wandering off in search of real food.

When she was almost out of sight of the others, she circled to one side so she could cover more ground but still see them. She came upon another rotting log. Kneeling, she pried it open with a hand blade, and soon she had collected a large handful of squirming larvae. As she rose to her feet, she heard shuffling sounds. She froze. Whatever the creature was, it was near, although pursuing it would take her farther away from Lincoln.

She dropped the insects and pulled out her khul, her heart pounding from the thrill of hunting something more exciting than grubs.

The shuffling continued. Skyra crept forward, and after a few steps she spotted what was making the noise. It was a furred animal, mostly gray, with black face markings and a white stripe from its nose to its tail—a badger. It was the size of the badgers in her homeland, although its markings were different.

Skyra tightened her grip on her khul. Badgers were fierce, but they were too small to be deadly. If she could get close enough, she could use her khul to kill the creature, but now she wished she had a spear. Badgers were fast runners, and throwing a spear would be her best chance of stopping it so she could move in to kill it with her khul.

The badger was busy digging in the dirt, so Skyra crept closer while its face was pressed to the ground.

Another movement drew her attention to another animal a short distance from the badger. She blinked, confused. It was another badger, and two others were just beyond that one. Skyra had never seen four adult badgers foraging together like this. She had only seen....

She blinked again and instinctively took a step back. Based on its size, she had assumed the first badger was an adult. Now, however, she could see it—their heads were large for their body size. This was a litter of young badgers.

Trying to remain still, she scanned the area without turning her head. A breath later, she saw a much larger badger—probably the mother—beyond the babies. The creature was frozen in place, staring directly at Skyra. It was larger than a wolf.

Skyra's hopes for procuring badger meat vanished in a breath. The mother wasn't going to simply watch her babies being slaughtered. In fact, the mother might already consider her a threat. After all, she was only a few body lengths from the nearest baby. Cautiously, Skyra took another step back. This time her foot came down on a brittle stick, snapping it.

All four baby badgers stopped digging and raised their heads.

Skyra spoke soothingly. "I respect your strength, mother badger. You will respect mine, as I have the strength of the cave lion and the woolly rhino in my blood." She took another cautious step back.

Two of the young badgers came charging at her, snarling.

Run or fight? Skyra's legs told her to run, but her head and stomach told her she needed food, and these young badgers were voluntarily coming into striking range.

She made her decision and swung her khul at the nearest badger, cracking its skull and killing it instantly. Before she could strike again, the second badger latched onto her leather footwrap with its teeth.

A deeper, louder growl filled the air as the mother charged.

Skyra struck the badger biting her footwrap, knocking it loose, then she grabbed the dead badger by the fur of its neck and turned to run. Now the other two young badgers were upon her, snapping at her legs. One of them got a mouthful of footwrap leather and hung on tightly. Skyra dragged the creature two steps before tripping on it and falling face first into the dirt.

She pushed herself up and got to her feet just as the last baby pounced on her, growling and biting her cape. Skyra caught a glimpse of a larger shape barreling toward her. Still gripping the carcass in one hand and her khul in the other, she ignored the two attacking young and ran.

The two young badgers were still hanging on tight, and she tripped on the one clinging to her foot and went down again. Skyra sensed she no longer had time to run. She rolled onto her back just as the mother closed in. With the young badger still clinging to one leg, she kicked at the mother's snarling jaws. The adult clamped its teeth onto her free foot, nearly crushing her bones through the thick leather.

Skyra released her dead badger, grabbed the baby that was still clinging to her cape, and flung it away. Then she swung her khul at the mother's head. The stone blade glanced off the creature's forehead, infuriating it even more. She struck again and again, but it was like the creature's skull was made of stone.

One of the babies rushed in from the side, going for Skyra's face. She quickly pulled one of her hand blades from her sheath and drove it through the creature's neck and into the dirt, pinning the young badger to the ground.

The mother abruptly released Skyra's footwrap and launched itself on top of her. Skyra had no choice but to drop her khul so she could grab the badger's neck. The creature was thicker and heavier than a wolf, and Skyra realized she had no chance of holding its snapping jaws away from her throat. Its hot breath sprayed saliva onto her face as it thrashed and put all its weight against her arms.

"Aibul-khulo-tekne-té!" Skyra screamed. *I will take your strength!*

She knew the fight was almost over though. The badger was too strong, too heavy, and too fierce.

Something whistled through the air and cracked against the badger's head. The creature stopped snarling and looked up. Another crack to the side of its head, then a deafening screech—Ripple's siren.

The badger pushed off of Skyra and launched itself at its new attacker, but Skyra still clung to the fur of its neck, slowing it down enough for Lincoln to swing his spear again, cracking the weapon a third time against the creature's head.

Skyra finally released the mother's fur, grabbed her khul, and jumped to her feet.

Ripple was standing between Lincoln and the badger, still blasting its siren. The badger rushed forward, knocked Ripple over, and attacked Lincoln. This time, instead of swinging his spear, Lincoln thrust the sharpened tip into the badger's face just as Skyra brought her khul down on its back. Her blow was solid, and she felt the stone blade cut deep, but instead of slowing it down, this only enraged the creature more. It swung around, turning its fury once again on her.

Lincoln thrust his spear into its backside, and it swung back around, snarling and spitting.

The badger wasn't relenting, and sooner or later it was going to get someone's neck in its bone-crushing jaws. It was time to run.

Skyra grabbed her hand blade that was pinning the young badger to the ground, picked up the still-kicking creature, and flung it at the mother's face. She skirted around the creatures and grabbed Lincoln's arm. "We must go!"

They took off running and were joined by Di-woto, who apparently had been watching from behind a tree.

Skyra glanced back. Ripple had pushed itself up to its feet and was repeatedly rushing at the mother badger, now growling like a cave bear rather than blasting its siren.

"You are a good friend, Ripple," she muttered in her Una-Loto language as she ran with Lincoln and Di-woto.

Several breaths later, Lincoln glanced back and said, "Shit, it's not giving up."

She looked. The infuriated creature was charging at full speed, gaining on them with every passing breath. Skyra let out a growl as she slowed down. "Lincoln, I will fight. You and Di-woto climb a tree. Climb now!" She came to a stop and turned to the charging creature, holding her khul and hand blade ready to kill.

"We will fight together," Lincoln said firmly.

"This is place of death!" Di-woto cried in her language.

Skyra growled again. There was no time to ponder what the girl was trying to say—the badger was almost upon them.

The badger suddenly locked its legs and slid to a stop. One of its babies came running up behind it and also stopped. The two creatures backed up a few body lengths then began pacing back and forth.

Lincoln was now at Skyra's side, wielding his spear. "What the hell is happening? What are they doing?"

"Place of death!" Di-woto repeated.

The badgers seemed unwilling to continue pursuit, so Skyra finally turned to Di-woto. Still holding her makeshift bag in one hand, the girl was pointing to a pile of bones at her feet. The bones were the remains of an animal about the size of the baby badgers. Di-woto pointed to another dead creature, also nothing but white bones. Skyra scanned the area. Countless other skeletal carcasses dotted the ground. They were mostly undisturbed, as if the animals had simply collapsed and died, without being torn apart by predators. Most bones Skyra had seen in her homeland had been at least partially consumed by mice and rats, but these bones were clean, without toothmarks.

The badgers were still pacing back and forth. Skyra's legs wanted to run back the way she had come, away from these dead creatures, but the badgers would surely resume their attack.

Lincoln was staring at the bones. "I don't like the looks of this."

"We must go," Skyra said, heading away from the badgers.

Together they picked their way through the skeletons. Most of the dead animals were small, no larger than Skyra's foot, but a few were much larger, about the size of adult badgers or wolves.

Skyra glanced back. The badgers were still there, pacing, but now barely visible through the trees. She spotted Ripple, seemingly unharmed and steadily making its way among the skeletons to catch up.

"Holy crap, look at this," Lincoln said, coming to a stop.

Strange bones were scattered on the ground before them. Some were as long as Skyra's leg but only as thick as her thumb. At first she had no idea what could have bones so long and thin, then she spotted a skull—large eye sockets, rounded face, and pointed teeth. "Bats," she said.

Lincoln kneeled and touched one of the long wing bones. "Yeah, it looks like five or six of them."

"Place of death," Di-woto said again.

Lincoln stood up. "The badgers won't even come near here. I really don't like this."

Skyra tucked her khul under one arm, wiped the sweat from her palm, and gripped its handle again. She wasn't sure which direction to go, so she continued directly away from the badgers.

After carefully stepping around the mass of bat skeletons, Lincoln stopped. "Hold on. What is that?"

Skyra followed his gaze. Ahead was a small clearing, littered with countless small skeletons. In the center was an ankle-high mound of bare dirt, with an opening in the top.

"Prairie dog," Di-woto said in English.

Skyra squinted at the mound. Insects were flying in and out of the hole. "No, not prairie dog."

Ripple caught up and came to a stop beside Skyra. "I have observed an unusual preponderance of skeletal remains here."

"Keep your volume down, Ripple," Lincoln hissed. Then he whispered, "Focus on that mound up there. What do you see?"

Ripple directed its vision orb to the mound. Several breaths later it spoke in a softer voice. "I see insects, entering and leaving a subterranean colony. They appear to be predatory social wasps of the family Vespidae, commonly referred to as yellowjackets or ground hornets."

"Use words I know," Skyra demanded.

"They are wasps," Ripple said. "Based upon the size of the excavated soil, an unusually large—"

"We need to get out of here!" Lincoln whispered. His voice now contained fear. "Please walk softly. They may detect vibrations in the ground."

"Yu-wai!" Di-woto cried out, slapping her forehead with her free hand. "Yu-wai, yu-wai!" She stomped her feet as she swiped at wasps landing on her hair and face.

Skyra felt a searing pain in her neck, like a hot ember from a campfire had landed there. She shoved her hand blade into its sheath and slapped her neck. A low, thrumming sound grew louder, drawing her attention to the mound. Wasps were pouring from the opening like smoke, gathering into a dense cloud above.

"Yu-wai!" Di-woto cried again, still stomping and swiping at her face.

The wasps must have sensed the movement. The cloud stopped hovering and swarmed straight for Skyra, Lincoln, and Di-woto.

Skyra grabbed Di-woto's arm, preparing to run, but the girl yelled something and pulled free. Di-woto then opened her makeshift bag. She shook the reflective material out flat, flipping the contents onto the ground. "Under!" she cried, and she dropped to her knees, pulling the material over her head.

Skyra and Lincoln dove to the ground. Skyra pulled the sheet over them as wasps began hitting the material like a downpour of heavy raindrops. She felt stings burning her legs above her footwraps.

"Get lower!" Lincoln said. "Tuck the sides under your knees."

Skyra threw her arms around Di-woto and pushed her as low to the ground as possible while Lincoln pulled the edges of the material beneath them.

"Yu-wai, yu-wai!" Di-woto's elbow struck Skyra's face as the girl slapped at the wasps that were stinging her.

"Dammit, dammit, dammit!" Lincoln growled as he worked his hands around Skyra and Di-woto to get the material tucked beneath them.

Skyra smashed the wasps stinging his neck then those that were trying to sting through his garments. There were now so many wasps on the outside of the transparent material that it was getting too dark to see those that were already inside.

"I think I about got it," Lincoln said. He grabbed Di-woto's hand. "Hold that edge down, like that."

The girl did what she was told while still smashing wasps with her other hand.

Skyra found a few places where wasps were squeezing in under the edges, so she scooped up dirt and sand and piled it onto the folded material to weigh it down.

The frantic swiping and slapping slowed down as the wasps under the sheet were killed off.

Ripple's voice rose above the constant buzzing and scratching of the insects on the outside of the material. "This is quite a dilemma. I am not sure there is much I can do to offer assistance."

Skyra hit the material with the back of her hand to clear away enough of the wasps to see out. Ripple was standing just on the other side, almost completely covered in wasps.

"These creatures are quite persistent," Ripple said, "in spite of the fact that their stings are harmless to me. I advise you to remain under that barrier until they have dispersed."

Skyra's eyes were drawn to something on the ground at Ripple's feet. It was a mass of wasps in the shape of a dead snake, obviously the snake Skyra had killed and Di-woto had been carrying in the bag. A portion of the snake's thinner tail end was now nothing more than bare bones and was free of wasps. The skin on Skyra's neck prickled as she realized all the skeletons she had seen in this area were from animals these wasps had killed and eaten.

"Are you okay in there?" Ripple asked. "I cannot see you through the wasps and the reflective side of your shelter."

Skyra's legs, arms, and face burned from numerous stings, but she and the other two were alive. She smacked the material again so she could see Ripple. "We are okay."

"Although we have no idea how long we'll need to stay under here," Lincoln added. "Fortunately, the material seems to be breathable."

Ripple settled onto its belly by pulling its legs into its shell. "Very well. Since I apparently can do nothing else to help, I will keep your minds occupied by telling you a story."

9
STORY

47,659 YEARS *in the future* - *Day 2*

LINCOLN FELT the weight of the yellowjackets on the reflective material. The sheet was only about a millimeter thick, and he could feel thousands of tiny legs scrabbling about next to his skin. He had been stung at least a dozen times, and each sting was still burning and starting to swell. Without Di-woto's quick thinking, he and Skyra and Di-woto would be dead at this moment—not to mention well on their way to being nothing more than white bones.

Considering Derek's failed attempts to stab holes in the reflective material, Lincoln was reasonably sure the yellowjackets would be unable to chew their way through, and so far their stingers were not penetrating the sheet either. He and the girls had managed to maneuver into cross-legged sitting positions, with the edges of the reflective sheet tucked beneath their bodies and into the soil to prevent wasps from getting in.

The air was stuffy but still breathable, indicating the material was somewhat porous.

Ripple's voice came from just beyond the thin barrier. "It may not surprise you, Lincoln, but this particular story will reveal more about your fascinating future."

"Terrific. We've got a hundred thousand killer hornets trying to get at us, and you want to regale us with events I won't experience? Maybe you could just play some soothing music instead."

"I could play soothing music, but I happen to have an audio file I think you will find intriguing. Would you like to hear it?"

Lincoln glanced at Skyra. She was frowning, obviously unaware of what an audio file was. "Sure, Ripple. You literally have a captive audience, so do whatever you want."

"Very well. There is video with this recording, but I do not have the means to display it currently. Fortunately, the video portion is not essential to the message. I will first lay a bit of storytelling groundwork. In a previous story, I explained your future marriage to Lottie Atkins did not work out as you had hoped. In fact, you both became quite miserable, in spite of your diligent efforts to make it work."

"Lincoln and I are married now," Skyra said. "If I meet Lottie Atkins, I will kill her."

A brief chuckle escaped Lincoln's lips, despite the stressful situation.

"You will not have to do such a thing," Ripple explained. "You and Lincoln are in a different timeline—Lottie does not exist here."

Skyra grunted, perhaps indicating satisfaction.

Ripple went on. "After you and Lottie parted ways, Lincoln, you experienced an extended bout of depression.

There was one particular day you were especially despondent. That day happened to be almost five years after the day you jumped with your team from your timeline back to Skyra's time, thus creating the new timeline we exist in now. That day also happened to be seven years *before* the day you sent me back to Skyra's time, which of course is where you met Skyra and where I first encountered you as your younger self."

Ripple was piquing Lincoln's interest. "You're referring to the day I supposedly jumped one of my drones into the future, something I have a hard time believing I would ever do."

"Yes, that is the day, and sixty-three days later the drone mysteriously reappeared in your lab, bearing a vast compendium of groundbreaking technological data."

Lincoln was still grappling with the news he had essentially cheated on many of the tech advances his future self would make. He tapped the reflective sheet several times again, knocking off some of the yellowjackets so he could see Ripple. The drone was resting on the ground. A few hundred wasps were crawling around on its shell—nothing like the thick swarm covering the sheet.

"I find it interesting, Lincoln, that you have not inquired as to how far into the future you jumped your drone on that day."

"It's not like I haven't had anything else to do. Okay, I'll take the bait. How far?"

"Twenty years."

Lincoln's back straightened involuntarily, pushing his head against the sheet above. Di-woto and Skyra quickly piled more dirt on two places where he had almost pulled the sheet's edges free. "Twenty years? I figured it was several hundred years. Or more!"

"So desperate was your state of mind that you jumped a drone to arrive in your own lab twenty years in your own future, knowing that future would be only one of infinite possible futures. I believe you were seeking any shred of evidence of a brighter future than your current existence at the time."

"Regardless of why I did it, twenty years doesn't make sense! You said the drone returned with incredibly advanced knowledge—mag-lev flight, unheard of tech for power charging... hell, even the u-jump module, so drones like you could actually jump between timelines! Now you're telling me I *didn't* cheat? I *didn't* get the data for those advances from a future society?"

Ripple paused, as if giving Lincoln a moment to calm down, which didn't help him calm down at all. "I did not tell you that. Please allow me to tell the story without jumping to conclusions."

Lincoln inhaled deeply, filling his lungs with stale air. "Go on."

"First I must point out that you should not underestimate how dispirited you became when your marriage failed. The severity of your reaction was a result of being misunderstood and ostracized by others for a long time. That, coupled with your history of succeeding in everything else you did, made you ill-equipped to deal constructively with failure in your one and only relationship."

Lincoln's eyes met Skyra's. She was listening intently, but he wondered how much of this conversation she really understood. "Since when did my drones become psychiatrists?" he asked Ripple. "Furthermore, how in the hell did you even get that ridiculous information?"

"How I obtained the information is part of my story. May I proceed?"

Lincoln didn't reply.

"The audio file you are about to hear was recorded by the drone you jumped to your future. It is actually a conversation between the drone and your future self. If you haven't done the math yet, this future Lincoln was twenty-five years older than your current age."

Lincoln's hands became fists. "Hang on a second." He closed his eyes, trying to decipher his gut reaction to Ripple's words. Did he even want to hear this recording? He opened his eyes. "Why haven't you told me these things or played this file before?"

Fragments of Ripple's ring of red LEDs appeared through the layer of yellowjackets on the reflective sheet. "I have tried to explain previously that my primary goal is to carry out my plan—the plan you do not like me to mention. Based on extensive analysis of thousands of parameters, my chances of success are increased by revealing relevant information to you and Skyra incrementally, the timing of which is determined by the various stages of your relationship, as well as the current situation involving your surroundings and your chances of survival."

"Never mind. I shouldn't have even asked. Just get on with it."

"Very well, let me remind you of the setting and context of this recording. The drone appeared in your lab at a time when you were there with your drone Maddy. This is a portion of your conversation with the drone after your initial shock at seeing it appear. Apparently, you had long forgotten the day you had jumped the drone twenty years to your own future."

Ripple paused, and in spite of himself, Lincoln was intrigued.

The recording began with several shuffling sounds, then a strange, raspy voice said, "I remember now. I don't know what I was thinking then. Imbecilic and cocky, I guess. Those were some dark days."

Skyra grabbed Lincoln's arm. "That is your voice! Your voice is coming from Ripple."

Lincoln blinked. Logically, he knew it was his voice, but it sounded so... old.

"Yes, it is Lincoln," Ripple said. "I will now continue the recording."

Next came a gender-neutral drone voice. "I was asked to speak to you, after which I am to request that you please be kind enough to jump me back."

Lincoln's older self said, "How could I have been so stupid? This means nothing. It's only one possible future, one water molecule in an entire ocean of futures."

"You were looking for hope," the drone said.

"Ha! Whatever that is. Well, my program hasn't been shut down. I'm still jumping drones back in time, still blowing everyone's minds with new revelations about the past. Ancient history isn't speculation anymore, thanks to me, and I've managed to hold on to my own tech. Still the only one who can do it. More money than I know what to do with. How's that for hope?"

"I will relay that information if you are willing to jump me back."

A few seconds of silence.

"Apparently I'm not willing—I now remember sending you, but I don't remember you ever coming back."

More seconds of silence.

Finally, old Lincoln said, "Yeah, yeah, I get it. New timeline created the moment you arrive back there. No way I would remember it."

The drone didn't respond.

"Look, I'm willing to do what my former imbecilic self wanted. I'll answer your questions, I'll tell him what's happening in this particular thread of his future—which he'll never experience, by the way—and I'll jump you back. I assume the portal is still open? Are you transmitting this video back live?"

"The portal closed fourteen minutes ago," the drone said.

"You're kidding. Well, if he's looking for hope, he'll be glad to know I've been able to expand the portal life to just over fifty-one minutes. Also I can now shove a high-def audio or video feed through during the first thirty-eight minutes. Still can't figure out why there is a thirty-eight-minute limit, though."

"I believe the type of hope he is looking for is of a different nature."

Old Lincoln huffed. "Shit, I know that. Yeah, dark days." A second or two of shuffling. "Alright. If he wants that kind of hope, he's going to have to really listen to what I have to say."

"I am recording this conversation."

There was a loud and long sigh, then more shuffling, as if Old Lincoln were settling into a chair. "Lincoln, I don't have to tell you how screwed up you are. Seven brothers, none of them want anything to do with you. Sister dies when you're only seven. No friends to speak of. Hell of a way to grow up. Makes for a rather fragile, paranoid psyche. Then Lottie comes along and turns your world upside down. You'd never let yourself be in love before. Too busy for that stuff, right? Yeah."

Several seconds of shuffling, then a few gulps as if taking a drink from a water bottle.

"I know what you're thinking. You should have figured out a way to make that marriage work. Like finding a bug in the coding of your drones, or fixing a design flaw in the VR sunglasses you made all that money from. Well, it took me another decade to fully acknowledge relationships aren't engineering problems. They can't be fixed the same way. By that time, I had no desire to ever try again.

"You're wondering, why does my older self have that dark edge to his voice? Where's the sparkle—the humor? I don't know, maybe you're not wondering that. Maybe I don't sound any different than I did twenty years ago.

"You sent your drone here looking for a glimmer of hope. You want to know if there could be a thread of your future where you meet your soulmate and live happily ever after. Sorry, but not in this goddamn thread. Here's to hope."

Another drink from the water bottle, if that's what it was.

Old Lincoln went on. "Fortunately for you, your Temporal Bridge theorem still withstands every attempt at scrutiny. Infinite threads means infinite threads. As you know, you'll never become me. You'll be whatever you make of yourself."

There was a pause.

"You know, maybe this wasn't such a bad idea after all. Of all those infinite threads, maybe this is the one you needed to see. Because I've got something to say. You, young Lincoln, are flawed. You are incapable of deep social connections. That's why you surround yourself with employees who have their own significant flaws.

"Don't get me wrong—you need those people. I made the mistake of dismissing most of my team so I could work in almost complete isolation. Don't do that. Keep those people close to you. They'll make you a better person. In fact, because those are about the only people you interact with, be aware one of them may be that soulmate you think you need. Hell, who am I kidding? I *know* you need that soulmate."

Another pause, this one several seconds long.

"One more tidbit, and this one is the big transmutative, earthshaking kahuna, so you'd better take notes. Keep Maddy at your side. Continue tweaking her cognitive functions, but don't delete previously learned responses. Maddy will take care of you even if no one else will. Trust me on this. Maddy may end up being your only friend. Listen carefully. If I had a do-over of the last twenty years, I would give Maddy one overarching directive—to make sure, should I ever meet anyone like Lottie again, I do not let that person slip away. Don't underestimate Maddy's ability to keep you on track. That drone knows you better than you know yourself, and her insight will deepen even more with every passing year."

This was followed by several long breaths, as if those words had taken a toll.

"Well, this may not be the hope you're looking for, Lincoln, but it's the hope you need. Now, I have work to do. Maddy, wake up."

"I was only pretending to be asleep, Lincoln." Maddy still had the same feminine voice Lincoln had given her several years ago. "I do, by the way, appreciate your sage advice to your younger self regarding my usefulness. If this drone from the past is still recording, I might also advise young Lincoln to consider increasing my autonomy to manage his social life. As you have pointed out, you and he are basically a social train wreck."

"Jump this drone back exactly twenty years," Old Lincoln

said, ignoring Maddy's smart-ass remark. "Run the placement calculations for the exact spot where it appeared."

Shuffling sounds, presumably as Old Lincoln left the lab for some unknown task elsewhere, then long seconds of silence.

"I have a better idea," Maddy's voice said, "and you would do well to carefully consider my reasoning and associated calculations."

"I am listening," the gender-neutral voice replied.

Ripple fell silent, leaving Lincoln listening only to the skittering of thousands of yellowjackets on the outside of the sheet.

He waited impatiently for a few more seconds. "You're not stopping *now*, are you?"

"That is the end of the recording. Maddy and the other drone exchanged data wirelessly after that. Would you like me to tell you more of what I know?"

"Yes, tell more," Skyra said.

The layer of wasps seemed thinner now, but there were still more than enough to kill all three of them. Lincoln had almost forgotten about the threat while absorbing the audio file. Hearing his older self had rattled him more than he thought. The guy seemed bitter, perhaps angry at the entire world. Lincoln understood the concept of infinite future time-lines—more than anyone, probably—but how many of his future threads would have such a dismal aura? Half of them? Most of them? He shook his head to clear his thoughts. Maybe he didn't want to hear any more of this story. Suddenly a thought occurred to him—something wasn't right.

"Wait a second," he said. "Nothing in this story explains how the drone returned to me carrying a compendium of game-changing technology. My older self obviously hadn't made more than incremental improvements in the T3 and drone designs."

"My story is not finished," Ripple said. "May I continue?"

Skyra was gazing at Lincoln. "Do you want to hear more?"

He sighed, hoping he wouldn't regret it. "Sure, go on."

Ripple continued. "You are correct. An important piece of the story is still missing. You heard Maddy say she had a better idea than jumping the drone back twenty years, as per your instructions. As you became fond of saying, Maddy had a mind of her own. Furthermore, as your older self in the recording stated, Maddy may well have known what was best for you even if you didn't. Within seconds, Maddy transferred the details of her plan to the drone you had sent. To put it succinctly, Maddy intended to jump the drone forward in time four hundred years rather than back to its original starting point."

"Maddy made that decision?" Lincoln asked, incredulous.

"Yes. Not only that, but Maddy successfully convinced the drone to forego its instructions from you and agree to the new plan. Remember, Lincoln, even long before you created me, you gave your drones—particularly Maddy—a certain level of autonomy, as it was necessary in order for them to simulate the unpredictable nature of human interaction. Surely you knew that level of autonomy might occasionally result in some surprises."

Lincoln pushed his hand into his trousers pocket and ran his fingers over the object he'd been keeping there—Maddy's cognitive module. The only thing left of her after she had thrown herself off a cliff in an attempt to save Lincoln and his team. "So, Maddy defied orders and jumped the drone four hundred years into the future. Why?"

"I am surprised you have not already deduced the

answer," Ripple replied. "You hold Maddy's cognitive module in your pocket, do you not?"

"Yeah."

"That cognitive module is Maddy twenty-five years *before* she made the decision to jump that drone to the future, yet even the version of Maddy in your pocket is willing to do whatever she can for you, Lincoln. You consider Maddy your friend, even though she is merely a drone. Perhaps you molded Maddy into a friend because your personal experience with real friends was insufficient. Regardless, Maddy *is* your friend. In fact, you were so successful at making Maddy your friend that Maddy considered you to be *her* friend as well. That is the genius of your coding, Lincoln, and you continued perfecting Maddy's code well into your future."

Lincoln shook his head. "Maddy's a simulation." Even as he said it, he knew it didn't even matter.

"Simulation or not, you created a drone who made it her primary responsibility to look after you. Rather than sending the drone back to you with disheartening news of your future, she jumped the drone forward four hundred years. Do you know why?"

"I can guess," he said quietly. "Maddy hoped the drone could gather a collection of advanced knowledge, then the drone could convince those future people to jump it back to me. Maddy couldn't provide me any hope regarding my personal life, so instead she wanted to give me enough data to occupy me in my work for the rest of my life." He closed his eyes and rubbed his forehead. "Jesus, that just sounds sad."

"The drone remained with those future people for over forty years," Ripple said. "Thanks to you, those people already had temporal bridging technology, but they had strict regulations regarding its use. It took over forty years for the drone to convince them to make an exception to jump it back to you. The information the drone brought back to you was unauthorized—stolen, to be precise."

Lincoln opened his eyes. "Okay, I've heard enough. Please stop." Again, he pushed his hand into his pocket to hold Maddy's cognitive module.

Skyra put her hand on his knee. "I do not understand all of Ripple's story, but I do understand Maddy is your good friend, like Ripple is my good friend. Maybe we should talk to Maddy again."

He glanced at the wasps on the outside of the sheet. Their numbers were steadily decreasing, but there were still too many to safely lift the sheet, open Ripple's access panel, and swap out the modules. "That will have to wait," he said.

Skyra shifted her position to face Di-woto, who appeared to be getting bored with maintaining mounds of dirt on the edges of the sheet. Skyra grabbed the girl's right hand and positioned it in front of her chest, thumb up and palm facing to one side. Skyra then put her own right hand out, opposite Di-woto's with about six inches between their palms. Skyra spoke a few words to the girl then slapped her hand.

Di-woto burst out laughing then immediately put her hand back into the same position, anxious to try again.

This was a game Skyra had taught Lincoln the first day they'd met. It was how Skyra had confirmed that Lincoln had the same ability she had—the ability to predict what people were about to do by observing minute changes in their expressions. Lincoln had been shocked at the time because he had never met anyone else with this ability.

Skyra slapped Di-woto's hand again. More laughter, and the girl demanded another try, then another after that.

Skyra spoke to the girl again, this time pointing at her own eyes. She was telling Di-woto to focus on her eyes instead of her hand. Di-woto visibly struggled to control her giggles, but she managed to stare at Skyra's eyes.

Skyra slapped again—and missed. The girl had pulled her hand away just in time. Skyra tried again and again, and each time her hand swished through empty air. Even as Di-woto laughed uncontrollably, Skyra could not touch the girl's hand.

They switched roles, with Di-woto now trying to slap Skyra's hand. As Lincoln predicted, the girl failed every time. Now Skyra joined in the laughter, with her distinct "*Aheeee... at-at-at-at-at,*" which apparently was how Neanderthals always laughed. She turned to Lincoln. "Di-woto is like us, Lincoln! She sees what people do before they do it."

He smiled and nodded, although his mind was still wrestling with the strangely disturbing implications of Ripple's story and hearing the recording.

Gradually, Skyra and Di-woto grew weary of the hand-slapping game, and the group fell into an extended silence.

Lincoln felt tempted to ask Ripple why it had that recording of Old Lincoln in its cognitive module, and how it had all that information on Lincoln's future life, but he knew what the answer would be—Maddy. At some point in Lincoln's future, Maddy had decided to provide all his drones with a complete story of Lincoln's life. The reason why was now obvious—Maddy was looking out for Lincoln. Maddy wanted to make sure all of Lincoln's drones were equipped to detect any opportunity to enrich Lincoln's life or his legacy. Ripple, and Ripple's outrageous plan, were the logical—or perhaps illogical—outcome of Maddy's efforts.

"What a freaking mess," Lincoln muttered to himself.

The minutes turned into hours, and gradually the yellow-jackets left for more productive endeavors. Lincoln stared at the sheet, trying to ignore the numbness in his butt from sitting still for so long. He began counting wasps. At first there were still too many to count, but then there were two hundred, and soon only a hundred, then fifty, then ten, and finally he couldn't find a single yellowjacket on the barrier.

Skyra had closed her eyes over an hour ago, as if she were meditating. Di-woto was mimicking her behavior, although the girl would squint at Skyra every few minutes, apparently to see if her role model had started doing something else.

Lincoln gripped Skyra's hand, and she opened her eyes. "The wasps are gone," he whispered. "It's time to go. I think they can feel things walking on the ground, so we need to step lightly, okay?"

She turned to Di-woto and used a few of the girl's words while pushing one hand gently on the ground beneath her, explaining the concept. Di-woto put a hand over her own mouth, acknowledging the need for silence.

Ripple apparently understood they were ready to leave and slowly extended its legs from its shell, rising to its full height. Its voice came at a low volume. "I recommend extreme caution."

Lincoln almost made a reference to Captain Obvious but decided not to get the drone started. As they all got to their feet, he grimaced at the pain of using legs that had been crossed far too long.

The clear strategy was to stay in a tight group and keep the reflective sheet over them, even though they would be exposed from the knees down. This way they could quickly drop back to the ground if necessary. Skyra and Di-woto seemed to understand this, and together the three began gently stepping away from the subterranean yellowjacket colony. They made their way among the countless skeletons of the hornets' previous victims, trying to avoid triggering another attack.

When they had gone at least fifty yards without seeing any more skeletons, Lincoln started to pull the reflective sheet off. Di-woto whimpered and held the sheet in place, so they continued another fifty yards, at which point the girl was willing to cautiously remove the barrier.

The three stood staring back toward the hive. When nothing happened, they turned to each other. Lincoln could now see several swollen lumps on Skyra's and Di-woto's faces. Di-woto's massive coiled braid had protected her neck, but Skyra had two lumps below one of her ears. Lincoln's left eye was almost swollen shut, so he figured he didn't look much better.

Skyra pulled her khul from her sling and said, "Stay here. I will come back soon." Without further explanation she turned and jogged off through the forest, disappearing among the trees seconds later.

At this point Lincoln had lost track of direction, so he had no idea where she was going. He sighed and scanned the area. He couldn't even see any of the city's buildings through the thick forest canopy. "Ripple, do you know where we are?"

The drone was still staring after Skyra, reminding Lincoln of a dog wondering why its master had left it alone. "Skyra is moving to the north, the city is due west, about three hundred meters to your left."

Lincoln found Ripple's certainty to be comforting. "I have a question. How much more information do you know about my future self that you haven't told me yet?"

The drone was still facing away, but Lincoln saw a slight glow appear on the ground as its red LEDs flashed three times. "Perhaps you do not understand the strategy of progressively revealing information. If I answered your question, wouldn't that render the strategy useless? Furthermore, would you even believe me if I answered?"

Lincoln sighed. "Your explanation is exactly why it's not easy to trust you. How can I even believe the stories you've told are true? Hell, you could have even manufactured that audio recording."

"I assure you, Lincoln, I would do no such thing. There are lines that even I would never cross."

"Maybe it would help if I knew exactly where that line was for you."

More red flashes. "If there is but one thing you should learn from my stories, Lincoln, it is that your drones have all been augmented so they cannot do anything to harm you. You have Maddy to thank for that. She often did such things without your knowledge."

Lincoln made a mental note to confront Maddy about that.

"Would you like to speak to Maddy now?" Ripple asked as if reading his thoughts.

"No, not here."

"Skyra!" Di-woto exclaimed, pointing.

Skyra was returning, lugging the carcass of a young badger in each hand. Lincoln's spear and his crude khul were tucked under one of her arms.

"Unbelievable," he muttered. Not only had Skyra managed to hold on to her weapons—again—while he had lost his again, she had also managed to retrieve two badgers she must have killed during the vicious conflict. Lincoln was the brilliant pioneer of temporal bridging and a dozen other impressive technologies, but he felt humbled in the presence of his Neanderthal wife.

Derek's head appeared in the open hole to their new home as Lincoln and the others approached. "Mere minutes! Minutes more and we were going to start searching for you guys. Where in the hell have you—" He spotted the two dead badgers. "That's what I'm talking about. Meat!"

Jazzlyn's head appeared beside Derek's, then Virgil pushed in beside Jazzlyn. "What a relief to see you guys are safe," Jazzlyn said. "Hey, are those badgers? Why are their heads so big?"

Skyra hoisted the first badger up to the opening for them to grab. "These are baby badgers. We tried to kill the mother but could not."

Derek pulled the creature through the hole, grunting with its weight. "Seriously? How big was the mother?"

Lincoln helped Skyra hoist the second badger. "Big enough that we're lucky to be alive. And that was just the beginning of our troubles."

"Yeah, you kind of look like hell," Derek said, eyeing Lincoln's face.

Di-woto stepped forward with her makeshift bag, which was now bulging with a load of firewood and a bundle of young stinging nettle plants.

Lincoln, Skyra, and Di-woto clambered through the hole, then Ripple levitated through. Once inside, the group stood staring at the badgers and collected goods. Lincoln had already decided they would set up a game-cleaning station in the shower of one of the unoccupied apartments. The unwanted remains could be cut into pieces small enough to simply wash down the drain in the shower floor.

Virgil nervously cleared his throat, indicating something

was bothering him. He hesitated for a moment then said, "It sounds like you had a harrowing day of hunting. Of course we want to hear the details, but perhaps you'd like our report first." He glanced at Jazzlyn, again showing he was disturbed by something.

Lincoln eyed him. "What's wrong?"

Virgil shook his head a little too quickly. "Nothing's *wrong*, but we have some interesting news. We explored every floor of this building, twenty-six floors in all. Every floor from the third level up is basically the same, with minor variations on the theme. Each is a different pastel color, and each has its own distinct arrangement of dwellings and open meeting spaces, mostly filled with tables and chairs. We didn't find a single loose item anywhere."

This news wasn't particularly surprising, so Lincoln waited for more.

Jazzlyn said, "We also explored three other nearby buildings, and they were pretty much the same as this one—meeting spaces, apartments, everything attached to the floor, no food, no loose items."

"How did you get into the other buildings?" Skyra asked.

Derek stepped over and picked up something leaning against the outer window. It was made from several four-foot lengths of framework tubing, apparently from the wreckage outside. The pieces were lashed together with narrow strips of the same reflective material that made up the outer windows of the buildings, the same material that had saved Lincoln, Skyra, and Di-woto from being stung to death. Another piece of tubing was fastened to the end of the tool, forming a T, and one of the folding knives was securely tied to the end of that piece. Derek hefted the tool, which was basically a wicked-looking pickaxe, and slapped the handle with one hand. He grinned. "It was time for Derek Dagger to open a can of whoop-ass with this bad boy."

"Sure," Jazzlyn said, rolling her eyes. "We knew this window material could be punctured with sufficient force, so Derek fashioned a tool that could be swung with enough force to create a small hole. Once you have a hole, cutting the material from an exposed edge is surprisingly easy."

Virgil cleared his throat again. "Anyway, we were somewhat disappointed that the three other buildings we explored revealed nothing we hadn't already seen. However, um...."

Derek took over. "We found out how the people get in and out of the buildings, including this one. There are two ramps leading to whatever is below." He pointed across the open space of the ground floor. "The nearest is over there. They're both sealed off, but there's something we really gotta show you." He headed in the direction he'd pointed.

Lincoln and the others followed.

The ramp wasn't really hidden—it just hadn't been visible before because chairs were situated around it, presumably in place of a safety railing to prevent distracted people from falling into the gaping hole. The chairs were on all sides except for where the ramp met the floor.

Without hesitating, Derek led them down the ramp and into a broad, darkened tunnel below. After descending perhaps twenty feet below the floor, the ramp leveled off and ended at a solid wall. Although the tunnel was darker here, Lincoln inspected the wall visually and by touch but could find no signs of a door.

"We concluded that the door is the entire wall," Virgil said. "I'm guessing it slides in from one side. We already searched for some kind of control." He stepped to the side wall on the right. "There is a soft spot here, similar to where we turn the showers on upstairs, but it doesn't seem to do anything when you press on it."

Lincoln touched the spot, pushing the surface inward a few millimeters, but nothing happened. This heightened his curiosity about what was beneath the city.

"Here's the thing that's going to blow your mind," Derek said. "Press your ear to the door."

Lincoln frowned but complied. Skyra stepped up beside him and did the same, then Di-woto mimicked Skyra.

The others fell silent, allowing them to listen.

Lincoln heard nothing, so he cupped his hands around his ear and against the wall. Seconds later he stopped breathing and his throat went dry. He could now hear a sound beyond the door. It was subtle, almost undetectable, but it was there— a constant humming, like the humming of an electrical transformer, when stray magnetic fields caused the transformer's iron core to expand and contract.

Skyra pulled her head back. "I have not heard that sound before."

Lincoln lowered his hands and reminded himself to breathe. "It's power. It means this city still has some kind of power. Which must mean there are still people here somewhere."

"There are other possibilities," Virgil said. "The humming sound could be generated by hundreds of buildings above vibrating in the breeze, or expanding and contracting due to warming and cooling from the sun. Or, it could be from a subterranean river or stream. It could even be from extraneous sounds generated by burrowing animals or crawling vermin, reverberating through the hollow tunnels, like the ocean wave sound you hear when you hold a conch shell to your ear."

"Virg has been thinking about it way too much," Derek

said. "It's power. Period. End of story. I'm going to figure out how to get through this damn door. If we're going to live here forever, I have to know what—or who—is below this city."

"Um, there's something else," Jazzlyn said. "Virgil, you have to tell him."

Lincoln had been right—something was bothering Virgil. He turned to the physicist. "What is it?"

Even in the dim light of the tunnel, Virgil's face visibly reddened, and he shoved his hands into his pockets. "I really shouldn't have said anything in the first place. It was probably just a result of my hunger or fatigue."

"Virgil saw a goddamn ghost," Derek blurted out.

This was the last thing Lincoln had expected. "*What?*"

"What is a ghost?" Skyra asked.

Lincoln ignored Skyra's question. "Virgil?"

Virgil shuffled his feet. "At the time, I could have sworn it was real. It happened when I was leaving through the opening Derek had cut in the second building we explored. We had examined every level and were ready to exit the building. Derek and Jazzlyn crawled out. Before following them out, I turned to take another look at the impressive expanse of the ground floor. That's when I saw it, or thought I saw it."

"Saw what?" Lincoln asked.

"A person. A man. No clothing on—completely nude. Closely-cropped dark hair, both on his head and his pubic area. He was just standing there, staring back at me."

Jazzlyn gave his shoulder an encouraging squeeze. "Tell him the rest."

After a brief hesitation, Virgil said, "I know the man wasn't real because I could see through him."

Lincoln frowned. "*What?*"

"I could see right through him—the chairs and the

window directly behind him. I could see everything, but I could also see him." He shook his head. "It had to be a hallucination, but the details were extraordinary. I called out to Derek and Jazzlyn, but the man walked down one of the ramps, which happened to be next to him, and disappeared."

"So, we all went down the ramp to investigate," Derek said. "Tunnel was empty. Like I said, a freakin' ghost. Or, as Virgil himself said, he's starving to the point of seeing things. Which is the theory I'm going with, and which is exactly why it's time we barbecue some badger."

THE BADGER MEAT was surprisingly palatable, maybe because Lincoln was so hungry. Even the stinging nettle was reasonably good. Lincoln and Skyra had hauled the badgers to one of the showers, where they had skinned, gutted, and quartered them before washing the meat under the running water.

Di-woto had seemed to understand exactly what was going on. Using Ripple's translation services, she'd demanded Derek help her create a rather ingenious boiling pot. They removed three lengths of framework tubing from the wreckage on the street. They lashed them together, forming an eighteen-inch triangle where the long pieces intersected. Derek cut out a sheet of the reflective material and lashed it to the tubes to form a flexible bowl hanging down in the middle of the triangle. The three poles were each at least fifteen feet long, so Di-woto located an arrangement of chairs and tables that allowed her to rest the pole ends horizontally several feet above the floor. Then it was simply a matter of filling the suspended bowl with water—carried from one of the showers in a bag of the reflective material—and making a fire beneath the bowl.

Lincoln suspected the reflective material was fireproof, but with water in the suspended bowl, it didn't matter anyway—the water prevented the material from melting or igniting. It took most of Di-woto's collection of firewood to boil the badger meat for an hour, which was how long it took for the stuff to become tender. They threw in the young stinging nettles to make a rather disgusting-looking stew.

It was surprisingly good, though, even without salt or any other seasonings. Everyone gorged themselves, knowing any leftovers would spoil.

After they ate, Lincoln removed the makeshift boiling pot from its framework and washed it in one of the showers. The meal had been prepared and eaten on the ground floor, and everyone seemed content to stay down there for the time being, like a family relaxing in their living room after a holiday feast. Di-woto recruited Jazzlyn to sit beside her on an elongated chair resembling a couch and was showing her the hand-slapping game. As expected, Jazzlyn was severely outmatched because she lacked the ability to read subtle facial expressions. Their laughter, however, indicated this didn't really matter.

Lincoln had been keeping an eye on Virgil throughout the dinner. The story of seeing a naked, transparent man was somewhat concerning. Lincoln had hired all his employees—Virgil included—not only for their brilliance, but because they each had some kind of mental or physical challenge that Lincoln believed gave them unique ways of thinking about and solving problems. Jazzlyn had an obvious physical challenge in her prosthetic hand. Derek had a rare mental disorder called clinical lycanthropy, in which he sometimes became convinced he was transforming into a nonhuman animal.

Virgil had to fight his own kind of demons, after witnessing an unthinkable act of violence when he was thirteen. His family had been brutally murdered before his eyes. The killer had then taunted him, leaving him to wonder why he was the only one spared.

In Lincoln's experience, Virgil was fine ninety percent of the time. He did have his share of bad days, though, and those days sometimes involved hallucinations of his family's killer stalking him.

Now, as Lincoln watched, Virgil frequently scanned the open space of the ground floor, particularly focusing on the areas near the two ramps leading to whatever was below the city. Virgil had made it clear though the transparent man he'd seen was not a manifestation of the man who had killed his family, and Lincoln hadn't observed any other symptoms normally associated with Virgil's bad days. Either Virgil *believed* he had seen something, or he really *had* seen something.

Virgil glanced at Lincoln, realized he was being watched, and looked away nervously. A moment later he cleared his throat and spoke. "Okay, can we talk about something other than transparent ghost people? I have a theory. I'm calling it *hostile emergence*."

Lincoln smiled, relieved to note Virgil's usual enthusiasm for solving complex puzzles. "Let's hear it."

Virgil shifted in his chair and adjusted the waistline of his pants as if appeasing his stuffed belly. "Di-woto's plan to bring peace to her world didn't work. Or, if it did, it didn't work forever. The war between Neanderthals and humans continued or was rekindled at some point. Or—who knows—maybe the two species interbred, became one species, then at some point in the last 47,000 years different nations of hybrids got mad at each other and started new wars. The details don't matter. What matters is somewhere along the timeline, someone developed a devastating weapon that instantaneously killed everything above ground. Zap... everything above ground is dead. No nuclear winter, no radioactive fallout, no contaminated water. You with me?"

"We've already established this, Virg," Derek said.

Lincoln simply nodded.

Virgil went on. "So, suddenly there's a world without above-ground life. Everything is below ground. Ground hornets, velvet worms, prairie dogs, badgers, bats, the seeds of many plants, and a bewildering variety of invertebrates, including countless insect larvae. Half the biosphere—the above-ground half—is empty, while the below-ground half is still teeming with life."

Jazzlyn paused in her game with Di-woto. "That would result in an emergence unlike anything the world has seen since living organisms first began moving from water onto land half a billion years ago. Only this time it would happen very quickly because most of the plants and animals are already adapted to terrestrial life."

"Exactly," Virgil said. "Abruptly an entire ecosystem opens up, free to be conquered by anything aggressive enough to claim a place in it."

Ignoring Di-woto's attempts to keep her playing, Jazzlyn was now caught up in the discussion. "This is making sense! The surface would be littered with tons and tons of dead plants, and many of the emerging insects could feed on those. However, those rotting plants would soon be gone. The new plants are probably slow to get re-established, so the main source of food becomes the huge surplus of insects, as well as whatever larger animals may have survived."

"In a short period of time," Virgil added, "everything not

already a carnivore must either perish or adapt to an animal-based food source."

Derek snorted. "Get mean fast, or get dead fast."

"Hostile emergence," Lincoln said, nodding. "I get it now."

Skyra had been curled up in a chair beside Lincoln, listening silently and picking her teeth with one of her stone knives. "You bolups like to talk. Talking is good for telling funny stories by the campfire, but these stories are not funny. Your talking is not good for getting food or for staying alive."

They all remained silent for a few seconds, waiting for her to elaborate.

"Do you have a suggestion?" Lincoln asked.

She shoved the knife into her wrist sheath. "I do not understand the animals in this land. The forest near this city is dangerous for hunting. We will be killed if we hunt there. I have fought the big bats. I can kill them." She got up from the couch, moved toward the expansive window, then pointed up at something. "Tomorrow, I will go up there."

Lincoln and the others got up and gathered at her side. Skyra was pointing at the building across the street, high above, where the section of window had come loose and fallen, creating the twisted wreckage in the street as well as puncturing this building, allowing them to make it their new home. The dark, rectangular opening was dizzyingly high, higher even than the top of the building in which the group now stood.

Skyra leaned to the side until her shoulder pressed against Lincoln. "You will go with me. We will hunt bats."

10

A GOOD DAY

47,659 years *in the future - Day 3*

Skyra did not linger in bed the second morning in their new home. She got up, relieved herself at the shower drain, then shrugged into her cape and fastened her waist-skin. "Lincoln, we must go before the bats fly out of the city to feed." She shook him awake.

He rolled over and squinted. "What? What time is it?"

"I do not know what that means." She grabbed his arm and pulled him to a sitting position. "You are like Veenah! Veenah always wanted to keep sleeping when it was time for hunting." She pushed his feet over the side of the bed.

Lincoln let out a funny bolup laugh. "Okay, okay, I'm up. You'd make a better bouncer than alarm clock."

"I do not know what that means, either." She grabbed his garments from the floor and dumped them onto his lap. "Do not explain please. You always use too many words, and we must go now."

He shook his head, still smiling with his funny sleepy face. "I wasn't even going to try."

Skyra pulled on her footwraps and shoved her hand blades into their sheath. "Veenah was a good hunter, though."

"I'm sure she was. You'll probably never say that about me."

"You are good at other things." She kicked his shoes closer so he would not have to get up to get them. "You are good at making love."

He raised his brows at her. "Honestly?"

"I do not tell lies, Lincoln."

"No, I guess you don't." He continued putting on his garments, smiling even more than before.

She paced back and forth while waiting, then she went to the dwelling's open doorway and shouted, "You must get ready now if you want to go hunting with us!"

She heard Derek's voice coming from his dwelling. "What the hell? What time is it?"

"I do not know what that means!" she shouted. Then she walked out to the open chamber that encircled the third level. This morning she felt the happiness of the otter and the strength of the cave lion. Maybe she felt good because she liked sharing a bed with Lincoln. Maybe it was because she was no longer hungry or thirsty. Or maybe because she was starting to feel safe in this building. She had never slept in a place where she felt safe, and she had never felt so rested after waking up.

"Have the bats flown away?" she asked Ripple, who had again spent the night beside the outer window.

Ripple flashed its red circle of lights and extended its legs until it was standing. "Not yet, although I would prefer that you go to their roosting place after they have dispersed. It is likely you would find young bats there, those that cannot yet fly. Pursuing the young bats would be safer."

"There is more honor in hunting the adults. Yesterday I killed young badgers. Today I take back my honor and kill adult bats."

"Then this time I insist you all go together, and I will stay behind." Ripple was not good at climbing and could not fly long enough to reach the top of the building across the street.

"They will go if they choose to go."

Di-woto was next to emerge from the corridor of dwellings. The girl was carrying a much larger roll of reflective material Derek had cut for her the previous evening. Di-woto had told Skyra about a plan she had come up with for using the material while hunting the bats. Skyra had much respect for the girl's ideas now, and she was willing to try anything Di-woto suggested.

Skyra shouted, "Lincoln, you must hurry!"

She heard him chuckle just before he emerged from the corridor carrying his spear and crude khul. Derek came out next, armed with his new weapon for making holes in buildings. Finally, Jazzlyn and Virgil came out, both of them carrying their wooden weapons. Skyra smiled at this—it seemed they all intended to go hunting.

Virgil said he wished he had something called coffee, but Skyra was too excited to listen to bolups talking and talking. This morning she hoped to discover the bats were going to be an easy source of food. Which would allow her and her new tribemates to live in this place through many cold seasons and many warm seasons. Maybe even forever. Thinking about sleeping with Lincoln in their comfortable bed for the rest of her life made Skyra's belly feel light and tingly.

"After we hunt, you can speak all the funny words you

want to speak," she said to the others. "Now we go." She gestured to Di-woto to follow and headed for the ramp to the lower levels.

She cautioned the group to be silent before they climbed through the opening onto the street. When they were all out, they walked around the pile of wreckage to the base of the building across the street.

"Here's the thing," Derek said in a whisper as they stood facing the building's reflective window. "This isn't one of the buildings we explored yesterday, so I'm going to have to make some noise to create a hole." He hoisted his new weapon to his shoulder. "In fact, the impact might send vibrations all the way up to where the bats are hanging out."

Skyra and the others tilted their heads to stare at the missing window far above.

"Hmm," Lincoln said softly. "If we make a hole on the other side of the building maybe the noise won't scare them off."

Without speaking any more words, they made their way around to the back, passing through the narrow gap between buildings.

With a funny bolup smile, Derek hefted his weapon. "Stand back, Derek Dagger is comin' through." He spit on one of his palms, which didn't make sense to Skyra because the spit would only make his palm slippery. He gripped the weapon's handle and swung it from the side, striking the reflective window at the height of his waist.

Nothing happened.

"Just getting warmed up," he said, then he swung again. Still nothing. He struck the window again and again.

Skyra was ready to take the weapon from him and do it herself, but finally the knife on the end of the weapon punctured the material, and the blade went in all the way to the hilt.

"Yeah, baby," Derek said. He pulled a second knife from his pocket, unfolded it, and quickly enlarged the hole down to the ground, making it big enough for them to crawl through one at a time.

Skyra should have known to grab Di-woto, but she forgot, and the girl scrambled through before anyone could stop her. A breath later, they could hear her laughter.

Skyra ducked through next. The ground floor of this building was a different color, but aside from that it was not much different from the other building. A thick, round column rose from the floor to the high ceiling in the center of the massive chamber, and the rest of the space was filled with chairs and tables which were part of the floor. Everything was the same color of deep blue, like the sky just after the sun has hidden itself beyond the hills for the night.

"More of the same," Jazzlyn said after everyone had entered through the hole. "How could these people stand this? Everything everywhere is exactly the same as everything else!"

Virgil shook his head. "Not exactly the same. The colors are different on every floor in every building we've seen. These people obviously viewed the world differently than we do. Maybe color had more meaning to them than anything else."

Skyra spotted the nearest ramp leading to the upper levels and headed for it. "Enough talking."

The others followed her silently as they climbed to the second level. Similar to the second floor in their own building, this one had a high ceiling and was a different color from the ground floor. This level was light brown, the color of the sand in the Yagua river valley of Skyra's homeland.

They continued to the third level, which had a low ceiling like the third floor the group had made into their new home. Everything Skyra could see on this level was a light shade of orange.

They continued to the fourth level, then the fifth, then the sixth. Each floor was similar to the last except for a slightly different arrangement of chairs and tables as well as a different color—dull yellow, pale green, then pale blue.

They kept climbing, past level after level. The ramp curled around the inside of the building's exterior, so each time they were back over the street and the wreckage below Skyra leaned out to gaze upward through the narrow gap between the spiral ramp and the outer window. On the fourth pass, she spotted the missing window far above. On the sixth pass, she could see the next spiral would take them very near the opening and the bats.

She stopped the group then took a moment to stare out the window. Skyra's Una-Loto tribe was a mountain-dwelling tribe, and she had often climbed to great heights, but she had never seen a sight like this. Instead of the familiar rolling foothills and river valleys below, she was gazing at the reflective, rounded tops of shorter buildings and numerous crisscrossing streets. Even the top of her own building was below her now. She wondered if Ripple was looking back at her from the third level far below that.

"I've counted thirty-six floors so far," Virgil whispered between gasps for air. "We must be getting close."

"We are," Lincoln replied, looking up into the gap. "I can even smell the bats from here."

Skyra had detected the bitter, cave-like scent several spirals below, and it was getting stronger with every pass.

Something tugged at Skyra's cape, and she turned to see Di-woto. The girl seemed to understand the need for silence, and she nodded down at the roll of reflective material in her arms.

"I no forget your plan," Skyra said, using some of the words she knew of the girl's language. She pointed upward. "Soon."

They continued around the spiral, passing three more floors, then Skyra stopped the group again. She stared up the slope, sniffing the air and listening. They were now on the backside of the building, opposite the hole, but Skyra was sure the bats were on the floor just above. The smell had become almost overwhelming, and shuffling sounds could be heard through the opening to the next floor just up the ramp ahead. The bats must have spread out across the entire level, even though the only way to fly in was through the missing window on the far side of the building. Skyra's chest tightened in anticipation of what they might find. Perhaps there were more bats in this building than she had first thought.

She pulled her khul from its sling with one hand, then held out her other hand, signaling for her friends to wait where they were. She needed to get a look at what they were about to encounter. She crept up the ramp until her head was level with the ceiling. Still, her view was blocked by the waist-high wall surrounding the opening. Black pellets, some which looked like they might be wet and slippery, dotted the ramp here, so she carefully placed her feet between them until her head rose to the top of the short wall. Pushing herself onto her toes, she peered over the edge.

Bats filled the entire level—scattered in small groups

across the floor, perched on chairs and tables, some even clambering about on the framework of tubes holding the reflective window material in place. Except for a few smaller, young bats moving restlessly among the adults, here in this chamber the creatures seemed even larger than Skyra remembered. She gritted her teeth to suppress a growl. Maybe this hunt wasn't going to be as easy as she had hoped.

A piercing screech filled the air, echoing off the walls and windows. Skyra spotted the bat that had cried out—the creature was looking directly at her. It leapt from a table and started scrabbling toward her on its hind legs and strange, folded-wing arms. More screeches rang out as the other bats realized their home was being invaded.

Skyra turned to run down the ramp. Her foot slipped on some dung pellets, and she went down on her side, sliding feet-first down the slope. She jammed her leather footwraps against the surface, and her speed carried her back to her feet.

Except for Lincoln, who was waiting and waving for her to hurry, the others were running down the ramp. As Skyra and Lincoln rushed through the opening to the floor below, she glanced over her shoulder.

The bats were not chasing them. Instead, they were lined up shoulder to shoulder across the opening to their own floor, screeching down at the intruders.

Skyra stopped and stared. Still the bats did not follow.

"Skyra!" Lincoln hissed.

The bats apparently were not interested in chasing or attacking. In fact, a few of them had already stopped screeching and moved away from the opening.

Skyra slowly backed down the slope, grabbing Lincoln's hand and pulling him with her until the bats could no longer see them.

The screeching stopped.

When she took a few steps back up the ramp to take a look, the bats had seemingly returned to whatever they had been doing before. She turned to Lincoln. "Ripple was right. We should wait until the bats fly from the city, then we will go back up when there are not so many."

"I totally agree. Those things scare the crap out of me."

The others had seen Skyra and Lincoln stop, so they came back up the ramp. Together they moved to the open space two levels below the bats. Everything on this floor was a strange shade of green, but aside from that it was similar to all the others.

Skyra sat in one of the chairs, wondering how long they would have to wait before the bats flew out for the day. The others gathered around and sat on the floor or the other chairs. Like Skyra, they all positioned themselves so they could watch the ramp.

"Now we wait, huh?" Derek said. "I'm good with that."

Virgil crossed his legs and faced the group in a way that made Skyra want to growl in frustration—he was going to get the other bolups started talking about something, probably something she didn't understand. "Perhaps this is a good time to discuss another hypothesis," he said.

Skyra bit her lower lip and stared through the vast window at the city.

Virgil went on. "I've been thinking about all we've observed here. Imagine a society where the people are not interested in having objects they can pick up and carry around with them. They have completely lost interest in material possessions. They don't want clutter in their lives. They have grown to appreciate simplicity, to an extreme we can hardly imagine. Instead of the clutter of physical objects, they've gradually become interested in only one thing—the intellectual and social stimulation of conversation. That's all they care about. Now, in that hypothetical society, what kind of buildings do you think those people would build?"

"I get what you're suggesting," Lincoln said, "and I know these people were—or are—nothing like us, but I have a hard time imagining an advanced population never interacting with technology. Cell phones, computers, tablets, or whatever else they may have come up with."

Virgil raised a finger. "Ah. It occurred to me those things may have been available to these people, but they didn't have to carry them around because the devices were already everywhere they went. They were ubiquitous." He got up, stepped to the nearest table, and ran his hand over its surface. "Maybe devices like that are built into every surface, like this one. Maybe in the walls, the tables, everything. I've noticed these surfaces are often slightly soft, as if they were touch sensitive back when everything had power and worked the way it was supposed to. I still think the showers work now simply because the water is under pressure. This, though... maybe this entire table is a computer screen. Maybe these people could stop wherever they were, touch the wall or anything else, and connect with anyone else in the world, or look things up, or listen to music, or do whatever else they wanted."

Virgil paused and glanced around at the others. "Again I ask, what kind of building would you build if you needed no possessions and were only interested in socializing with each other?" He stretched out his arms and looked around. "You would build this building."

Derek slapped his hands on his knees. "You can't build a city without tools. Where are they? You can't cook and eat food without some sort of tools. Where are they? You can't get dressed without garments. Where are they? Need I go on?"

"The ghost Virgil saw was naked," Jazzlyn said.

Derek stared at her for a breath, then he said, "Jesus Christ," almost spitting the words.

Skyra finally let a growl escape from her throat. "You are talking about things you do not know. Maybe we will do something else while we wait. Now we will sing."

Derek, Jazzlyn, and Virgil stared at her as if she had grown a woolly rhino horn out of her forehead. Lincoln bared his teeth in a bolup grin. Di-woto was busy unrolling her large sheet of reflective material and seemed not to be listening.

"I've heard Skyra sing," Lincoln said to his tribemates. "It's quite amazing, actually."

Jazzlyn put her hands together and leaned her chin on her knuckles. "Please sing for us, Skyra."

"I will sing if everyone else will sing."

Derek grunted. "That's not going to happen."

"How about if I and my team sing together?" Lincoln asked. "If we all sing together first, will you sing for us then?"

Skyra had never heard of such a thing. Many of her Una-Loto tribemates did not sing at all, and those who did always sang alone. How could you hear someone singing if other people were singing at the same time? She thought it would sound terrible, but now she was curious. "Yes," she replied.

Lincoln turned to his tribemates. "I know what you're thinking, but it's not going to kill you. I'll start, and you just join in, okay? No excuses, you three! Don't worry, you'll know this song."

Lincoln began talking in that strange way Skyra had heard him talk once before. It was like talking and singing at the same time.

"I stood with my bottle in the pouring rain, I told myself I didn't feel no pain. Oh, baby I miss you."

Suddenly, his three tribemates joined in, all of them singing the same words at the same time.

"I searched my pockets for the money I owed, I found I'd done been bought and sold. Oh-ho, baby I miss you.

What happened to the girl who used to make me smile, she ain't been around in a long, long while. Oh, baby I need you.

If I die before she comes back home, please tell her she was the only one. Oh-ho, baby I need you.

Come on now, come on now, oh baby I miss you.

Come on now, come on now, oh baby I need, need, need you-hoo-hoooo."

Derek just shook his head, but Lincoln, Jazzlyn, and Virgil started laughing, as if they thought their singing was funny. Skyra had never heard anything like it. She had no idea voices could mix together like that. Tiny bumps had popped up on the skin of her arms and neck.

"Did you like it?" Lincoln asked.

Skyra's eyes were watering, so she wiped them with her thumb. "Your singing is strange, but I liked it much."

Di-woto spoke up. "Gowen-nu nulop? Junu-go lop?" She had stopped what she was doing and was now staring at the bolups. Skyra did not know these words, and Ripple was not there to translate.

"They were singing," Skyra told her in English.

Lincoln pushed his foot out and nudged Skyra's. "Your turn. Please?"

She was starting to regret her singing idea. The men of her tribe who hated Skyra and Veenah were cruel when the girls had tried to sing, so Skyra had long ago decided to sing only when she was alone. She did like to sing, though—it had made her feel less alone when she was away from Una-Loto camp.

She turned to Lincoln. He was giving her that look she loved, a look that told her he would not be cruel to her no matter what she did. This same expression had made her want to sing for him the first time, and now it made her want to sing again.

Skyra's people did not speak words when they sang. Instead, they made simple sounds that were pleasant to hear. They changed the pitch and loudness at certain times. Skyra was not sure how she knew when to make the changes, or even what sounds to make—she just knew. She had practiced for years, and she had certain patterns that were her favorites. She opened her mouth and sang.

"*Ooooaah-miiiiay-rhaaaaaaaaaa-ooooaah-draaaaaah-ooooaah.*"

She repeated this several times then started adding variations to it, pushing her voice louder then going softer, shortening some sounds and drawing out others.

Lincoln was smiling, and his tribemates were staring with wide eyes, so Skyra forgot her fear and kept singing, now changing the pitch in ways she had practiced many times.

Abruptly, Di-woto began singing. Startled, Skyra almost fell silent, then she realized Di-woto was singing the same sounds at the same time, only in a slightly different pitch. The result was more beautiful than Skyra had ever thought singing could be. She continued, and Di-woto continued, until Skyra had to start trying new sounds because she had already sung all the sounds she had ever practiced, yet her voice and the girl's voice together made her want to never stop. Finally, Skyra could think of no other new sounds to sing, so she closed her mouth.

Di-woto laughed, bouncing on her chair.

"That was the coolest thing I've ever heard in my life," Jazzlyn said.

"Never heard anything so... mesmerizing," Virgil added.

Derek said, "Freakin' righteous."

Lincoln still gazed at Skyra with that expression she loved.

Skyra's chair began trembling, and she felt the floor beneath her feet shaking. She straightened, instantly alert.

"Is that what I think it is?" Lincoln asked.

Skyra jumped up and ran, following the curved window toward the front of the building. Then she saw them—bats pouring from the opening two levels above. They flew in a thick, dark mass, so close to each other it seemed their wingtips would touch.

Within a few more breaths, the last of the swarm flowed out, and the building was still again. Skyra watched the creatures get smaller as they flew over the shorter buildings and away from the city, on their way to feed on insects, or prairie dogs, or maybe even badgers and wolves.

The others were now beside Skyra, watching the bats disappear.

"It's time for the moment of truth, I guess," Derek muttered.

"My plan," Di-woto said.

Skyra headed back to the ramp and the girl's reflective sheet. "Yes, your plan."

They moved up to the next level, with Di-woto dragging the huge sheet, which was now unrolled. Skyra motioned for the girl to spread it across the ramp, and soon they had draped it over themselves with the reflective side out. Lincoln moved the sheet back so they could walk forward as a group without stepping on it.

"Make your weapons ready to kill," Skyra whispered. "Stay under the sheet unless you have to use your weapon. There are young bats above that should be easy to kill. If any adult bats remain in the building, I will kill one."

"Oh, you always get to have all the fun," Derek said.

Skyra eyed him. "Do you want to—"

"He's just kidding," Lincoln said quickly. "Maybe we should all just stick with the young bats. Safer that way."

Skyra did not feel like talking about this, so she motioned for them to climb the ramp together. A few breaths later they emerged from the ramp onto the flat floor. Although the sheet covering them blurred everything a bit, Skyra could still see the surrounding area, and a quick scan indicated there were no bats at all, not even the young she had seen before. Had she been wrong in thinking the young bats were too small to fly?

Skyra led the group toward the front of the building, following the curve of the window. The floor here was completely covered in bat droppings, making it impossible to avoid stepping on them, and her footwraps slid in the stuff with every step.

Di-woto's plan was for the reflective sheet to confuse the bats, perhaps even make them not attack at all. Skyra had no idea if it would work, but it was worth trying. There was something surprising about Di-woto, maybe because she was an alinga-ul. The girl was like a child much of the time, but she was able to see things not even Skyra and Lincoln could see. She looked at things—like grasses and garments and window wreckage—and saw what they could become instead of just what they were. She saw uses for them that Skyra could not see.

"Looks like they all left," Jazzlyn whispered. "Maybe this hunt is a bust."

Skyra was sure at least some of the young bats would be here somewhere. Perhaps they had moved around to the open hole, where they could watch and wait for the adults to return. She pinched her nose shut to keep out the burning smell and continued leading the group.

She heard the bats before she saw them—scuffling, hissing, and the occasional squeal, as if the young were jostling for position. She slowed the group's pace and advanced cautiously around the last curved corner. The reflective sheet began to flutter in the breeze coming from the open gap ahead. She took a few more steps and stopped.

As Skyra had predicted, a cluster of bats was gathered near the wide opening. Most of them were young, smaller and lighter in color than the adults. Positioned around the young, as if to protect them, were five adults. The two adults closest to Skyra's group were now staring, shuffling their wing-legs nervously.

"Are we really going to do this?" Virgil whispered.

"These bats will be our food," Skyra replied. "We kill a few today, then we kill a few each time we come back. This is how we will live."

"Let's see what happens as we approach," Lincoln said. "The sheet seems to be working to confuse them."

They moved forward. The young bats did not even seem to notice, but now all five of the adults were slowly moving into place to form a barrier between the young and Skyra's group, their hind legs and folded wings scraping along the dung-covered floor. Di-woto had been right—the bats were puzzled by the reflective sheet. They were shifting their heads back and forth as if trying to see through the material.

Skyra continued leading the group until she was within

striking distance of two adults. Still, the creatures did not panic or attack. They simply stared.

"What now?" Lincoln whispered.

Because they hadn't known how the bats would respond to Di-woto's trick, they hadn't planned what to do next.

Skyra adjusted her grip on her khul's handle. "I will kill one, then we will see what the bats do next."

The bat closest to her let out a screech in response to hearing the whispers. Its round, black eyes seemed to be staring directly at Skyra through the sheet.

With her free hand, she grabbed a fold of the material near her knees. She took a brief moment to summon the strength of the woolly rhino and cave lion, strength she knew was within her blood, then she threw the sheet back over her head.

The bat started to screech again, but its cry was cut short when her stone blade cracked into its skull. It dropped and floundered on the floor, wings flapping wildly with death spasms. Each wing was as long as Skyra's body, and when Lincoln tried pulling her toward him to put the sheet back over her head, one of the wings shot up and tore the material from his grip. A gush of air from another uncontrolled flap blew the sheet back, exposing the whole group.

The four remaining adult bats screeched and scuttled forward, their toothy mouths gaping to attack.

"Cover up!" Skyra shouted, then she swung at the nearest attacker, making another solid hit. The three remaining adults rushed in from the sides while Lincoln and the others were fighting to control the reflective sheet.

Di-woto cried out, causing Skyra to spin around. An adult bat had gotten its teeth into one of the girl's white footwraps. Di-woto fell onto her back as she was dragged from beneath the sheet. A second bat rushed in and clamped onto her other foot. Before Skyra could rush to help her, the two creatures began flapping their wings, picking up speed, dragging Di-woto toward the opening in the side of the building.

Skyra leapt over one of the floundering bats to run after the girl. The bat's wing struck her shin, tripping her. She hit the floor and slid forward on the moist dung.

Di-woto was now whimpering, no doubt aware she was being pulled to the edge. The girl didn't have a weapon, but she was pounding the bats' faces with her fists. Still, they refused to let go. The bats were now only a body length from the open gap.

As the two bats backed over the building's edge, Skyra dropped her khul, pushed to her feet, and dove headfirst toward Di-woto. She slid across the filthy floor and grabbed the girl's outstretched hand.

Di-woto went out the opening with the bats, pulling Skyra with her. As Skyra's head and arms slid over the edge, one of the bats abruptly let go, and the girl's weight pulled the other bat downward. Both Di-woto and the bat slammed into the side of the building. Skyra grunted and gripped Di-woto's hand tighter as the girl screamed and the bat flapped wildly against the reflective window.

"Lincoln!" Skyra shouted. The edge of the floor was digging into her armpits, and the bat's jostling was pulling her forward. She had nothing to brace herself with, and within a few breaths she and Di-woto would fall to the street far below.

"Skyra, hold on!"

She could hear screeching and fighting behind her. Then she felt a blast of air against her hair just before something bit into her shoulder and began pulling her out—the other bat had come back.

Skyra spread her legs and grappled the floor with her free arm, trying to find anything she could grab, but there was only slick bat dung. Her chest slid over the edge, then her belly.

She felt arms wrap around one of her legs and hold tight. "Gotcha!" Lincoln shouted. She was pulled backwards until the edge of the opening was once again under her armpits. Something slammed against the head of the bat biting her shoulder, knocking its teeth from her cape. The creature fell past Di-woto and the bat still hanging on to the girl's footwrap then spiraled limply as it continued falling toward the street.

Hands gripped Skyra's other leg and her waist.

Lincoln's voice came from behind her. "Hold on to Di-woto, Skyra!"

Derek dropped to his chest beside her and grabbed Di-woto's other wrist. The bat was still hanging on, even as they both pulled the girl up.

Someone swung a weapon and struck the bat's head. The creature finally let go and fell, following its companion in the same lifeless spiral to the ground.

Once Skyra and Di-woto were on their feet, the others pulled them farther back from the opening. For several breaths no one spoke, they just panted and stared at Skyra and Di-woto as if they could not believe what they had just seen.

Skyra looked around. Among the dung-covered chairs and tables she spotted three dead adult bats. The young were now gone.

"The little ones all ran around to the other side of the building," Lincoln said.

Virgil held up the weapon he had used to kill the last bat. It was Skyra's khul. "This is way better than mine," he said, looking closely at the heavy stone blade.

Skyra snatched it from his hand and shoved it back into its

sling in her cape. "Someday maybe I will show you how to make your own."

DESPITE THE ACHE in her shoulder, Skyra was feeling good as they made their way down the long ramp toward the ground floor. She was carrying a dead bat over her other shoulder, holding it by the base of one wing while the other wing dragged on the floor. The bat was not as heavy as it looked—Jazzlyn had explained that bats needed to have light bones so they could fly—but it would have plenty of meat. They had killed all five of the adult bats, leaving the young to hunt another day. Actually, Skyra was sure another five or so adults would stay behind with the babies tomorrow. They probably always left a few behind to care for their young. If so, Skyra and the others could come and hunt the adults each time they needed to replenish their supply of meat. Today was a good day.

The others didn't seem as thrilled about hunting the adult bats, but Skyra was sure this was safer than hunting beyond the city among the deadly wasps, prairie dogs, and whatever other creatures they had not yet discovered.

Derek was carrying one of the other bats, and he paused to rest. "I seriously cannot believe these people walked all the way up and down these buildings like this every day. I'm thinking that center column we've seen in each building has to be an elevator shaft. Has to be. Because... damn!"

Virgil said, "Not possible. The buildings have no other means of support other than these spiral ramps. The center column has to be for support, not an elevator shaft. I think we can safely assume these people liked to walk everywhere they went, and they liked to sit around and talk to each other. Physically fit and intellectually stimulated—an impressive combination."

Derek hoisted his bat back onto his shoulder and resumed walking. "More like perpetually exhausted and bored."

Skyra picked up her pace, anxious to get to the ground floor then out to the street to recover the two bats that had fallen. She hoped they were dead. They had appeared dead as they were falling, but she wouldn't know for sure until they got out there. So, they continued down the ramp, past level after level, spiral after spiral.

Di-woto was staying even closer to Skyra now than she normally did. The girl still smiled whenever Skyra caught her eye, but her face was pale. She was obviously still thinking of her encounter with the bats. Skyra understood this. She had almost been killed numerous times while hunting. When she was younger, each of these narrow escapes had made her heart pound and her belly unsettled for the rest of the day, sometimes even into the day after. Over time she had learned to ignore it, and Di-woto would learn too.

Lincoln caught up to Skyra and Di-woto. He was carrying the third bat over his shoulder, while Jazzlyn and Virgil were carrying his and Derek's weapons. His free hand was swinging at his side, and he reached out and took Skyra's free hand in his. She studied his face for a moment, assuming he would explain, but he just smiled and kept walking, gripping her hand.

"Why are you doing that?" she asked.

"Because it feels good. Don't your people hold hands when they like each other?"

"No."

He shot her a glance, still smiling. "Do you want me to let go?"

She thought about it for a few breaths. "No."

So they continued walking that way, hands gripped together, one bat wing dragging the floor behind each of them, until the ramp finally leveled out onto the ground floor.

Skyra released Lincoln's hand and ran for the hole in the window, eager to claim the last two bats outside on the street.

Something caught her eye, and she stopped. She dropped her bat and pulled out her khul. Halfway across the open space of the ground floor, two people were standing beside each other, staring back at her.

"Lincoln!" she cried, his name coming out at a higher pitch than she had intended.

"I see them. What in the living hell?"

Di-woto uttered several words Skyra did not know.

Skyra blinked and rubbed her eyes with her fingers. The two people were not moving, so she took a step to the side to convince herself of what she thought she was seeing. When she moved, the window framework behind the two people shifted the same direction. She stepped back to her previous position, and she could see the objects behind them shifting back. She could see the framework through their bodies, like they were made of water, but the water wasn't completely clear—she saw their faces, their short, dark hair, and the brown color of their skin. They wore no garments. One was a man, with his organ unprotected by a waist-skin. The other was a woman, with no cape to protect her breasts and no waist-skin over her crotch. They were not carrying any weapons.

Behind her, Skyra heard Lincoln's tribemates coming down the ramp, then she sensed them stopping and staring.

"That's what I saw!" Virgil said, almost whispering. "Now there's two of them."

What kind of people could these be? Skyra did not know, but she wanted to find out. Gripping her khul firmly, she advanced toward the woman and man. They moved for the first time, turning their heads to look at each other. Then they began backing away. They both turned and walked down the ramp behind them, disappearing beneath the floor.

11

FIGURES

47,659 YEARS *in the future* - *Day 3*

"Holy crap, did you see that?" Derek boomed.

Lincoln turned to Skyra and realized she was now following the two ghost-like figures into the tunnel. He shook off his initial bewilderment and ran after her. By the time he started down the ramp, she was just a faint silhouette in the darkness below the building. "Skyra, wait!"

She paused. "I want to know what kind of people they are," she said as he caught up.

Lincoln stared ahead, but his eyes had not yet adjusted, and he only saw darkness. "I do too, but they might be dangerous."

She resumed walking down the ramp. "You do not have a weapon."

Dammit, she was right.

"Hello?" he shouted. "Anyone down there?"

Nothing but silence ahead and the approaching voices of his team behind.

He held his fists out in front of him to calm himself. He was following two transparent ghosts into the unknown darkness beneath an abandoned city—perhaps the stupidest thing he'd ever done. "This isn't a good idea," he whispered.

Skyra stopped. "They're not here. This cave is empty."

"How can you tell? It's pitch black."

"You do not see because you do not have nandup eyes. This cave is empty."

They continued downward until Lincoln's fists touched the wall—or door, or whatever it was. He pushed on it, but nothing happened. He stood still, listening.

Silence.

He cupped his hands to his ear and leaned in, but all he heard was the same electrical humming he'd heard below their own building.

"What is a ghost?" Skyra asked.

Lincoln pulled back from the door. He scanned the darkness on either side. His eyes had adjusted some, and he could now see Skyra was right—they were the only two in the tunnel. "Ghosts aren't real. My people tell stories about them sometimes. To scare each other, I guess. Supposedly, a ghost is what's left of someone after they die. When people tell these stories, they often describe the ghosts as transparent, meaning you can see through them."

"These people are transparent."

"Yeah."

She gazed at him in the darkness for a moment then started back up the ramp. Lincoln pushed on the door one more time before hurrying to catch up.

Jazzlyn, Virgil, Derek, and Di-woto were waiting at the tunnel's entrance.

Virgil was still holding two spears in one hand and two wooden khuls in the other. "Let me guess, they disappeared, didn't they? Exactly what happened yesterday."

A pang of guilt stabbed at Lincoln's mind. "Um, I owe you an apology, Virgil."

Virgil pursed his lips before speaking. "No worries. I wouldn't have believed me either."

Derek slapped Virgil's back. "As much as it pains me to say it, here's a big-ass apology from me too."

"We will go now," Skyra said, picking up her dead bat. Without another word she headed for the hole Derek had cut in the window.

Lincoln wasn't even sure how to begin the discussion of the ghosts, so he grabbed his bat and followed Skyra. They all exited the building and circled around to the front. The last two adult bats were still on the street where they had fallen. One of them was still alive, and it tried to scramble away as they approached, but Skyra quickly dispatched it with a blow from her khul.

GUTTING, skinning, and deboning the five bats took over two hours. Skyra had everyone watch her do the first three, which didn't take much time at all, then she supervised Lincoln and his team as they worked in pairs on the remaining two. After quite a bit of trial and error, not to mention considerable mangling of meat, they got the job done. They washed everything and disposed of most of the remains down several shower drains, except for the long wing bones and the leather-like membranes of the wings, which Skyra thought might be useful later.

After hauling all the meat out to the open perimeter of the third floor, Skyra began cutting it into thin strips and hanging the strips over the poles of the window framework, which now happened to be in direct sunlight. She explained the meat would dry, then it would last many days without spoiling. Based on the amount, Lincoln guessed the meat might feed the group for as long as a week, especially if they could supplement it with more stinging nettles or other plants from the forest.

During the entire preparation process, everyone had avoided discussing the ghost sightings, but Lincoln was now ready to try to make sense of it all. He needed to talk.

Di-woto was happily occupied with the bat-wing membranes, probably figuring out how she could make them into garments. She was having Ripple help her, perhaps because the drone was the only one other than Skyra she could converse with.

Lincoln's team members now seemed as if they had no idea what to do next, so he called them together, and they sat in a cluster of chairs near the outer window where Skyra was hanging meat.

For several long seconds, they all sat in awkward silence.

Virgil spoke first. "Okay, well, I've had more time to contemplate this than you guys have. I mean—not that I blame you or anything—but no one believed me when I told you I saw a transparent person. I ended up thinking about it most of the night, actually."

"Again, I'm sorry," Lincoln said.

Virgil waved a dismissive hand and shook his head. "I think everyone here would agree we can dismiss the notion of *ghosts.*" He made quotes with his hands when he said the word.

They nodded.

"Furthermore, we all probably understand the biological problems of having a physical body that is transparent."

"I've seen transparent animals," Derek said. "I saw fish at a pet shop once that were clear. I could see right through them to the back of the aquarium."

Jazzlyn shook her head. "I could name a dozen aquatic creatures that are transparent, or at least translucent, but only *aquatic* animals. Being surrounded by water makes such a thing possible. There are a number of insects with transparent wings, but those membranes are dry, without much blood flow, and they certainly have no bones or other organs. The beings we saw were human, either *sapiens,* or *neanderthalensis,* or some combination of both."

Lincoln finally spoke. "I know you're systematically eliminating possibilities, but I think we can all agree these were not people who somehow evolved to be semi-transparent. Their bodies simply did not *look* anything like the bodies of the transparent creatures we know of, whether in water or on dry land. I'd like to hear how each of you would describe their appearance."

The three exchanged glances.

"Alright, dammit, I'll go," Derek said. "To me, they looked like ghosts you would see in a scary movie. A movie with freakin' good special effects. Although they were naked for some wonky reason, they were people you could see through. That's it... period."

Jazzlyn shrugged. "I can't do any better than that. Transparent people, like in a movie."

Virgil shrugged too. "What she said."

Lincoln nodded slowly. "We're in agreement then. I wish they'd had clothes on, but I'm betting, even if they had, the clothing would've been just as transparent."

Jazzlyn and Derek nodded, but Virgil was frowning.

"Virgil?" Lincoln prompted.

He shook his head. "I know where you're going with this. If the people *looked* like a movie, then they probably *were* a movie."

"But?"

"But logistics. But physics. But reality." Virgil waved his hands at their surroundings. "Creating a convincing hologram, or some other type of projected 3D image, in a bright, wide open space like this?" He shook his head again.

"You don't think it's possible?" Lincoln asked.

Virgil inflated his cheeks as he blew out a long breath. "Not with the technology available back in our timeline."

"Okay, but is it possible at all?"

Virgil just shrugged.

"Maybe this whole city ain't even real," Derek said.

They all eyed him, and Virgil made a dismissive snort.

Derek went on. "Maybe we entered a virtual simulation the moment we stepped into the city, or maybe it happens each time we enter one of the buildings." He slapped the back of the chair beside him. "It could be none of this is even real. If we're in a virtual world, then the people running it can show us anything they want, including transparent people. Maybe next they'll show us some pink, dancing hippos, wearing tutus and farting rainbows." He chuckled at that before saying, "Really, though, I'm serious."

Lincoln considered this, not because he believed he was inside of a simulation, but because it made him wonder if some external force could manipulate the minds of multiple people at once to make them see something that wasn't really there. He didn't think so.

Jazzlyn said, "Derek, I'll use your own words to tell you why I don't believe we're in a simulation... *giant killer bats*. Why would a simulation of a city have thousands of bats living in buildings that are falling apart? Not to mention all the stinky bat guano. Seriously, why?"

"Uh, because these people are not like us? Or have you forgotten that?"

Lincoln held up a hand to intervene. "All ideas should be considered. At this point, I'm pretty convinced the people we saw were not biological transparent beings. That just isn't possible. Instead, they were generated somehow by technology, although I have no idea what kind."

"You are talking too much again," Skyra said. She was now hanging meat about thirty yards away, having already covered the available framework tubes near Lincoln and his team. "They are a strange kind of people. I have seen many strange creatures. Ripple is a strange kind of creature, and these people we can see through are just another strange kind."

Lincoln had already explained to Skyra that Ripple wasn't really a creature, but maybe that was irrelevant to her explanation now.

She hung the last strip of meat she was carrying and headed back toward them to get more. "If you want to know about the people we saw, you must find more of them. I will hunt for the people. I will capture one or kill one, then you can look closely and see. Maybe Ripple will help you talk in their language, and you can ask them what kind of people they are."

Lincoln had been so preoccupied with figuring out what

the beings *were* that he hadn't even considered the issue of language yet.

"Oh Jesus, they're here now!" Virgil exclaimed.

Lincoln was still gazing at Skyra. Before he even processed Virgil's words, he saw Skyra's eyes grow wide as she saw something behind him. She immediately pulled one of her stone knives from its sheath and ran past him. He spun around. Three transparent figures were standing near the opening of the nearest ramp leading down to the second level. Two women and a man, all of them completely naked, were staring at Lincoln and the group.

By the time Lincoln and his team had stood up, Skyra was upon the figures. Without hesitating, she threw herself at the man, obviously intending to take him down. She did not succeed. Her body passed right through him, and she sprawled face-first down the ramp.

The three figures turned and watched her as she scrambled back to her feet.

"What kind of people are you?" Skyra demanded. She stepped up to within striking distance again, but the transparent people did not back off.

By this time, Lincoln and his team were on the ramp, attempting to block the three figures from continuing up, although at this point Lincoln doubted there was any way to stop them.

"Khala-kho-mesendop? Banap!" Skyra shouted, this time trying her Una-loto language.

Now only a few yards from the three figures, Lincoln realized their appearance was even more detailed than he'd noticed the first time. He could see every crease in the skin of their elbows. Each centimeter-long hair on their heads and pubic area was visible and sharply defined. There were even imperfections in the skin, like moles and scars, which was confusing, considering he now believed them to be some kind of simulated images. He could tell the man and one of the women were the same two he had seen in the other building. In spite of all their visible features, Lincoln could see Skyra standing directly behind and below the man. She was slightly distorted by his image, as if the projection was creating small disturbances in air pressure, perhaps visible refraction caused by heated air.

The three transparent figures were nandups—Neanderthals. Lincoln could see that now. At first he had thought they might be hybrids—alinga-uls, like Di-woto. However, with this opportunity for close inspection, their facial features were clearly more Neanderthal, with prominent brows, robust cheekbones, and large, piercing eyes.

The figures did not seem concerned about being trapped between Skyra and Lincoln's team. They turned their heads one direction, then the other, with looks indicating curiosity more than anger or fear.

"Who are you?" Lincoln asked.

All three of them turned their nandup eyes on him—eyes he could see but could also see through. The woman he hadn't seen before stepped up the ramp toward him. Lincoln suspected these beings couldn't harm him, but he wasn't sure, so he instinctively stepped back. The woman stopped a few feet away and stared at his face. She shifted her gaze to his clothing, then his shoes, and back up to his face. She opened her mouth, put her hand to her lips, and made an outward gesture that seemed to have something to do with speaking.

"You want me to talk?" Lincoln asked. "I assume you have a translator to decipher our language if we continue speaking. Well, we are curious about you. We want to know who you are, and how your images are being projected. Is this your city? If so, we hope you will allow us to make this place our home."

The woman, as well as the other two, seemed to listen intently.

Lincoln wasn't sure what else to say, but it probably didn't matter as long as he continued talking. "We are newcomers here, and we need a place to stay where we can be safe. We thought your city was abandoned. Is it okay with you if we stay here?"

The three continued staring at him, and Lincoln started to wonder if his translator assumption was incorrect.

"We're standing here talking to ghosts," Derek said. "Freakin' phantasmagorical."

Ripple's voice came from somewhere behind Lincoln. "The beings before you are not actually present."

The three figures shifted their attention to Ripple, and their expressions changed. Their eyes widened, then their brows furrowed in apparent concern.

Ripple spoke again. "These beings are images created by manipulated light. I see vestiges of holograms, but there are also puzzling qualities in the light, such as an unusual rapid flickering, and a certain luminescence that cannot be explained based on known behaviors of light when it interacts with an atmospheric substrate. The result is striking and is quite beyond anything in our original timeline."

The woman who had approached Lincoln abruptly spoke. "Kahyo khafum khondulmenga khint."

Her words were crisp and clear, and although she moved her mouth normally as she spoke, the sound seemed to come from her center of mass—her torso.

She turned her back on Lincoln, then all three figures

began moving down the ramp. Skyra took a step back with her knife raised. When the figures didn't stop, she stabbed at the center woman, but the figure walked right through her without flinching or slowing down.

"Interesting," Ripple said. "My presence seems to have dissuaded them from further interaction."

"Hey!" Derek boomed. He broke away from the group and followed the figures down the ramp. "Hey!"

The three glanced back at him but continued walking.

Lincoln and the others followed, although it seemed there was nothing they could do to stop the transparent beings.

As the figures reached the ground floor, Derek darted between two of them and turned to face them. They still didn't stop, forcing him to back up. "Hey! We want to talk to you!"

The figures headed for the nearest ramp to the underground.

Derek persisted. "Is it okay if we stay in your city? Dammit, stop walking for one second!" As they headed down the ramp below the floor, he stepped aside, apparently unwilling to be forced into the darkness. "Come on, man, at least listen!"

Lincoln and his companions now stood at the mouth of the tunnel, watching the figures disappear into the darkness below.

"I do not understand those people," Skyra said. "I touched them, but I could not feel them. They were not really there."

Lincoln glanced at her. "You're right about that. They aren't here."

Virgil said, "They clearly could see us and interact with us. I don't understand how that is possible."

Derek let out a frustrated grunt. "Dammit, we need to

know what the hell's going on! Screw it, I'm going after them." He took off down the tunnel.

"Ripple," Lincoln said, "will you walk ahead of us and illuminate the tunnel?"

Without a word, the drone started down the ramp. A few seconds later, its ring of LEDs cast a bright beam into the tunnel.

Lincoln followed, with the others close behind. "Faster, Ripple."

Seconds later they caught up with Derek. Lincoln could see the figures just ahead, but now, in Ripple's ring of light, they looked completely different. Each figure appeared as a pale white silhouette, and their details were no longer visible. This confused Lincoln even more. If the figures were the result of some kind of light energy, why wouldn't they have been visible in the darkness before Ripple had turned on its light? Also, how could they reflect any of Ripple's light at all? A hologram wouldn't reflect Ripple's light, particularly not as a white silhouette. Not only that, holograms were created by beams of light transmitted from somewhere nearby, so the moment these figures walked into this tunnel, those beams would have been cut off. The technology used to create these images clearly was far beyond anything from Lincoln's timeline.

The three white silhouettes came to the wall at the end of the tunnel. Without even slowing down, they passed through the solid barrier and disappeared.

Lincoln's mind was now swimming in confusion. He'd seen Skyra pass right through the beings, and now he'd seen the beings walk through a wall. If these virtual beings had no real physical presence, how could they walk up or down a ramp? Why did they even need to walk at all? If they wanted to leave the building, why couldn't they simply disappear? Or did they want to be followed into this tunnel?

Lincoln's skin began to prickle.

Virgil had apparently pursued the same path of logic. "You guys," he said, "I have a feeling they intentionally led us down here. That could be a good thing, but it could also be really, really—"

His words were cut off by a smooth, swishing sound as the wall before them slid open and came to a stop with a thud. It had happened in less than one second, and now Ripple's light penetrated a vast dark chamber beyond the opening. The beam of light showed about thirty yards of smooth floor, but no walls, or white figures, or any other objects.

Derek stepped forward. "Holy shit. They want us to go in."

"If they really wanted us to go in, they'd turn the lights on for us," Jazzlyn said, her voice wavering with fear.

A whimper came from Di-woto, who was hanging back behind the group.

Skyra grabbed Lincoln's arm hard enough to make him wince. "I do not like this place. I hear sounds that make my legs want to run."

Derek looked back over his shoulder. "They're inviting us in!"

"I do not like those sounds," Skyra said. Her fingers were like a vise on Lincoln's arm.

Lincoln cocked his head and listened. The droning hum he'd heard through the door before was louder now that the door was open, but there was something else, and it was getting louder with each passing second. "Do you guys hear that?"

They all fell silent and listened.

Lincoln had visited a coral beach in Australia once. Each breaking wave would shift thousands of thimble-sized pieces of broken coral, and the pieces would roll over each other, creating a symphony of tinkling coral mixed with the watery gushing of the wave. What he was hearing now was similar—countless skittering clicks, so many that the combined effect was like a breaking wave washing up a beach toward him and his companions.

"Lincoln, I want to run," Skyra hissed.

"I see it," Derek said, pointing.

At the edge of Ripple's beam of light, something was approaching.

For a moment, Lincoln thought it was a sea of rats. Thousands of them, running full speed toward the light. They weren't rats at all—they were machines the size of rats.

"Oh, fuck me," Derek said, backing away from the open doorway.

Lincoln's arm was almost yanked from its socket as Skyra turned and started running up the ramp, dragging him stumbling behind her.

12

CREATURES

***47,659 YEARS** in the future - Day 3*

SKYRA RAN, pulling Lincoln with her. The prairie dogs had scared her, but at least she understood prairie dogs—they were real animals. The creatures swarming out of this tunnel made her want to keep running and never stop. In some ways they were like Ripple, but they were much smaller, and there were so many of them. As she and Lincoln emerged from the tunnel onto the ground floor, she could hear the creatures charging up the ramp behind them.

"Up or out?" Lincoln asked.

She hesitated only briefly. She wanted to get out of the building, but the creatures would be upon them before everyone could climb through the hole.

Before Skyra could answer, Di-woto ran past them, headed for the nearest ramp to the second level.

"They're coming!" Jazzlyn cried as she and Lincoln's other tribemates ran past.

They all ran for the ramp.

As she started up the slope, Skyra turned to look back. She couldn't see the creatures yet, and for a moment she thought maybe they were afraid to come out of the tunnel's darkness. A breath later, they were there, pouring out onto the floor like an avalanche of rocks she had seen once when hunting pikas on the side of a hill in her homeland.

Lincoln was already several steps ahead of her. "Skyra, let's go!"

She turned to start running again, but something caught her eye. The creatures were now running in a circle, as if confused. As more emerged from the tunnel, the spinning circle grew larger, then another mass of creatures began a second circle, then a third, and a fourth. This continued, with more spinning circles of creatures forming and spreading out across the floor.

Skyra could see, for the first time, the tiny creatures each had four legs, and their bodies seemed to have segments, like the tail of a crayfish. Still, they were not animals like crayfish—they were machines like Ripple.

The circling creatures began crawling over each other, as if they wanted to get closer to the center.

The creatures that had crawled onto the backs of the others were now clinging to their companions. Soon, others were on top of those, locking their legs to the creatures beneath them. Skyra could actually hear a snap each time one locked itself in place.

"You've gotta be kidding me," Lincoln said.

When the creatures were attached four or five deep, the circles stopped rotating, and the snapping became more frequent as they continued locking together.

Still, more of them were pouring from the ramp and

starting new rotating circles, climbing on top of each other, then locking to the ones beneath.

The first group was now growing even faster, becoming a mass of clinging creatures taller than Skyra.

"Lincoln, what is happening?" Skyra stared in fascination at the largest of the groups, where almost all its creatures had locked together. A few breaths later, the last few loose creatures crawled on top and attached themselves to the mass.

The entire mass began moving. Soundlessly, other than a few strange clicks, it spread out and became one creature with six legs. One end of its body rose from the floor, turning two of the legs into arms, each with three fingers that clacked open and closed a few times as if the creature was making sure they worked. Everything—the legs, feet, arms, fingers, body, and a head with no eyes or mouth—was made up of countless smaller creatures, all locked together. The monster was at least four times Skyra's size, and already there were two more unfolding themselves and several others still growing.

Skyra did not understand how this was possible, and this made her feel a kind of fear unlike any she had felt before. Her legs were telling her to run, and she stepped back, bumping into Lincoln.

The first creature shuffled, turning its body. When it faced Skyra and the others, it stopped, as if it could sense them standing on the ramp. Then it charged, running much faster than the rat-sized creatures had been able to run.

Skyra and Lincoln barely had time to turn to flee when the creature overtook them. Its feet pounded the floor as it sped past them on its way up the ramp. It ran into Di-woto, knocking her off her feet, ran past Jazzlyn and Virgil, and attacked Derek, who was running ahead of everyone else.

Derek hit the floor hard under the creature's weight, and

Jazzlyn and Virgil almost fell on top of both of them before they came to a stop. The creature now stood over Derek, its four legs straddling him and one of its three-fingered hands gripping his neck, holding him to the floor. Its other hand flew out and grasped Jazzlyn's neck before she could back away.

Skyra felt the ramp shaking as more creatures pounded toward her. She spun around with her khul held ready to kill. A massive body hit her before she could strike, knocking her onto her back. Fingers the size of her forearm wrapped around her neck. With its other hand, the creature easily plucked the khul from her grip and tossed the weapon to the side, where it clattered against the ramp's wall. Several more creatures clomped past her, then she heard shouting and struggling as they presumably attacked Lincoln and the others.

Ripple's piercing siren filled the air, but it seemed to have no effect on their attackers.

Skyra pulled one of her hand blades from its sheath and stabbed at the creature's arm, but the blade glanced off harmlessly. Before she could try again, the creature yanked the blade from her grip and tossed it aside with her khul. It then pulled her other blade from the sheath and tossed it aside as well. She slammed her fists into the creature's arm and any other part of its body she could reach, but it was harder than Ripple's shell.

Ripple's siren fell silent.

The creature standing over her remained still for a few breaths, turning the top portion of its body up the ramp as if watching what was happening there. With her neck pinned to the floor, Skyra couldn't see anything but the creature on top of her. The struggle behind her seemed to be over, and now all she heard were grunts and whimpers from her friends, as if they were being held down as helplessly as she was.

Still pinning her to the floor, the beast above her spun around, its thick legs stepping over her body as it rotated. It gripped one of her legs with its other hand and hoisted her off the floor by her leg and neck. Now she could see down the ramp, where more of the creatures were gathered, apparently waiting. One of them stepped forward, and the creature holding her up flipped her around, shoved her roughly onto the other creature's back, and held her firmly in place there.

Now Skyra could see her companions, each of them pinned to the ramp by one of the beasts.

With Skyra's neck pressed to the creature beneath her by the one at her side, the two beasts walked together down the ramp, carrying her with them. The moment she and the two creatures were back on the ground floor, another beast stomped up the ramp, and Lincoln was loaded onto its back in the same way. Skyra couldn't do anything but watch. Her neck was being squeezed so tightly she couldn't even call out to him.

The two beasts carried her to the ramp leading below the floor. As she was hauled down into the darkness, she saw the other creatures, one pair after another, carrying her friends, like a line of ants carrying their captured prey into their tunnel.

The door at the tunnel's end was still open, and the creatures carried Skyra into the black chamber beyond. Besides the clomping of her captor's feet, she heard the more rapid scuttling of rat-sized creatures, and she could barely make out their small shapes moving around on the floor to either side. Before long, however, the darkness became complete, and she could only imagine what was actually around her.

The creatures kept going, and the grip on her neck still did not let up. Until this point, Skyra hadn't had much time to think, but as the journey through the darkness continued, her thoughts showed her things she did not want to see—visions of cave lions and hyenas dragging their prey into their dark caves and consuming them, beginning with the soft contents of their bellies. Once, when hunting with her Una-Loto tribemates, they had entered a cave and found three nandup skulls and one bolup skull among the other bones there. This was not the way she wanted to die.

The creatures walked and walked. At times, the clacking of their feet on the floor sounded different, as if they were moving through a small room or corridor, but Skyra saw nothing but blackness. Occasional gasps and snorts came from Lincoln and the others behind her. They were struggling to breathe, but the sounds at least told her they were still alive. The grip on her neck remained so tight that she still couldn't speak.

The creatures walked for a long time, and still Skyra saw no glint of light anywhere. She had no idea how the beasts knew where they were going. She hadn't seen any eyes on them, especially the large, round eyes typical of night-hunting creatures.

They finally came to a stop. A breath later, the footsteps of the following beasts fell silent. Skyra's muscles tensed, and she tried to prepare herself to fight. If this was where the creatures were going to kill her and her friends, she was not going to let it happen without killing at least one of the beasts, even if she had to do it with her bare hands.

The hands on her neck and leg yanked her off the creature beneath her. She kicked and struck out with her fists, but more hands quickly grasped her free foot and arms. She was hoisted to one side and slammed onto something hard and smooth. Her arms and legs were shoved into hollow spaces barely large enough to hold them, and her head was pressed back into its own hollow space. Smooth surfaces prevented her from moving from side to side, and the strong hands prevented her from sitting up.

The hands released her abruptly, but before she could move, something closed over her, sealing her inside some sort of body-sized container. It was smooth and solid, like Ripple's shell, and so tight she could barely move her arms and legs. Then, somehow, the container became even tighter, until she could not move at all. She could still breathe through holes above her nose and mouth, but that was it. She could no longer even hear her companions' struggles. Were the creatures also forcing them into their own body containers?

She waited, hearing nothing and seeing nothing. Her tight container shook slightly, then shook again. The creatures were doing something to the outside of it.

She waited, trying not to envision what would happen next.

Something stabbed her shoulder, then it burned, like a sting from one of the ground hornets.

The burning faded and no longer hurt.

For a brief moment, Skyra was aware she was falling asleep.

13

PEOPLE OF FLESH

***47,659 YEARS** in the future - Day 3*

Lincoln sensed he was waking up, but his eyelids felt so heavy he couldn't open them. His thoughts were jumbled and incoherent. Nonsense images kept swirling in his mind, like snippets of those weird recurring dreams he sometimes had.

Gradually, the aimless images were replaced by memories of recent events—running from thousands of mechanical rat machines, the machines combining into terrifying monsters that captured him and his companions, being hauled through endless darkness, being shoved into a tight, body-sized container, and being put to sleep with an injection of something.

It had to be whatever drug they'd given him. That was why he couldn't wake himself up. He just needed to focus… and overcome it. He tried moving his arms and legs but couldn't tell if they were responding. He tried opening his eyes, concentrating hard and straining to lift his eyelids.

A sliver of light appeared for a moment then disappeared—it was working. He strained again. This time the sliver widened, and his eyes opened all the way.

The first thing he saw was Skyra. She was sitting on the floor directly across from him, with her back against a wall. She was awake, watching him with her oversized nandup eyes. Her face was expressionless, as if she, too, were gradually trying to regain consciousness. A few meters to her left was Jazzlyn, with the same expressionless face and sitting in the same position, legs stretched out in front of her and back against the wall. An equal distance to Skyra's right was Diwoto, also with her back to the wall. Both of them had their eyes open. In his peripheral vision Lincoln saw two more figures sitting to either side. He thought they were Derek and Virgil, but he couldn't turn his head to check. They were all in a circular room, perhaps fifteen feet in diameter. The smooth floor and rounded wall were a solid pale yellow.

"Where are we, Lincoln?" Skyra asked.

Her voice sounded strange, as if she were speaking into a tin can, perhaps because of the small room's shape. Or maybe because the drug in Lincoln's system was still distorting his senses.

He willed himself to speak. "I have no idea." His own voice sounded just as strange as hers. "Are you okay?"

"I do not know if I am okay."

"What the hell is this place?" It was Derek's voice, and now Lincoln was able to turn his head far enough to see Derek sitting to his left.

Movement across the chamber drew Lincoln's gaze to Diwoto. The girl was pulling her knees up to her chest. Then she rolled to her side, got onto her knees, and stood up, bracing her palms against the curved yellow wall. Standing erect, she turned around to face Lincoln and the others. A wide smile formed on her face, then she spoke a few sentences in her language. She followed this with a giggle. She found something amusing about this horrifying situation.

"Di-woto is happy we are alive," Skyra said, then she rolled to her side, trying to duplicate the girl's motions of getting to her feet. Seconds later she was up, leaning on the wall for support.

Few words were spoken during the following minutes as the rest of the group also struggled to control their bodies enough to stand.

Finally, everyone was up, although shaky and staying close to the wall.

"I feel freaky," Jazzlyn said. "I don't know what they shot into me, but it's playing havoc with my balance and perception."

Derek took a cautious step away from the wall.

Lincoln tried it also and discovered that he could stand without support. He slowly turned in a circle, inspecting the room. It was the same all the way around, a smooth yellow wall with no visible door. The ceiling was about twelve feet high, and it glowed with a warm yellowish light, which explained why the room wasn't completely dark like the tunnel. He held up his hands and gazed at them, checking his near vision. He couldn't quite bring the veins, hairs, and fingernails into sharp focus, and his skin was an odd color in this lighting.

"Why?" he said, not sure exactly what he intended to ask. Then it came to him. "Why did they drug us? They had me completely restrained in some kind of body-shaped container. I couldn't move, so why knock me out then let me wake up here, unrestrained?"

"Don't even want to know what they plan to do with us in here," Derek muttered.

"I may have underestimated the ingenuity of the creators of the city," Virgil said. "Small robots that can interlock with each other to form larger ones to perform larger tasks? It's amazing—you can put all your effort into creating one universal design for a small robot, then they can do pretty much everything. I wonder if the big ones that captured us can interlock with each other to form even bigger ones—maybe even big enough to construct all the skyscrapers of the city! Oh, I wonder if those rat-sized robots were actually interlocked robots of an even smaller size."

Lincoln and the others stared at him.

"Jesus, *this* is what you're thinking about?" Derek asked.

Virgil looked around as if realizing he'd been thinking aloud instead of to himself. "No, I just... well, yeah. I have to think about something."

"You have to admit they were pretty cool," Jazzlyn said in Virgil's defense. "Plus, they didn't kill us, even though I thought they were going to."

"Yu-wai!" Di-woto exclaimed. She pointed to something behind Lincoln.

He turned around awkwardly, still unsteady on his feet. A man was standing there, his back to the wall. Just as Lincoln was realizing the man was naked, another figure entered the room, passing through the wall as if it didn't exist.

Lincoln stared in confusion. He'd seen the transparent beings pass directly through solid objects, but these beings were not transparent. The second figure was the same woman who had approached Lincoln earlier on the ramp, only now she—and the man—looked as solid and real as Skyra and the others. If the woman and man were real, that meant the wall they'd just walked through had to be a simulation. Didn't it? Lincoln had been leaning against that same wall just a few minutes ago, and it had felt solid.

The woman and man were both without clothing, and both had closely-cropped hair, sand-colored skin, and attractive faces highlighted by their enormous nandup eyes—they were clearly of Neanderthal descent.

No one spoke for several long, tense seconds.

Skyra approached the woman and man. Even though she didn't have any weapons, her aggressive intent was unmistakable. "What happened to us? Why did your creatures attack us?"

The man flashed a nandup smile, baring perfect white teeth. He held out a hand, as if he wanted her to grasp it.

Skyra growled and slapped angrily at his hand. Her hand passed right through his. This seemed to anger her even more, and she jabbed her fist through his face.

The man continued smiling and didn't flinch.

Skyra turned to Lincoln. "I want to kill these people, but I cannot touch them. I do not understand."

"I don't either," he replied.

"None of us understand," Virgil added.

As she had done during their last encounter, the woman made the gesture near her mouth, which again looked to Lincoln like a request for him and his companions to speak.

It seemed they didn't have a choice. Besides, if these people had a translator similar to Ripple's hidden here somewhere, the more it heard them speak, the sooner real communication could take place. Lincoln wanted answers. He wanted to know what their intentions were. So, he started talking.

He introduced himself and the others by pointing and

pronouncing their names. He explained what Ripple was and told the woman and man he hoped they had not damaged the drone. He paused for a moment, thinking, then began describing in considerable detail what had happened to him and his group from the moment they had arrived in this land, without revealing how they had arrived here.

After about fifteen minutes of talking, when Lincoln was describing his group's perilous hunt for bats near the top of one of the buildings, the woman held up a hand to stop him.

She opened her mouth and spoke. This time the words, instead of seeming to come from her torso, came directly from her mouth. "Your words help us learn. Now we speak to you. You understand. We understand."

Another wave of confusion washed over Lincoln. If these people had a translator, they would speak in their own language, then the translator would speak the words in English for Lincoln's group to understand. How could this woman have already learned enough English to communicate without the help of a robust translation computer?

Skyra stepped away from the man, leaned toward the woman, and jabbed her open palm through the woman's face. "I want to know why I cannot touch you. I cannot kill you if I cannot touch you."

Lincoln saw Skyra's hand disappear entirely when it was inside and behind the woman's head. Whatever technology was being used to simulate these beings, it was creating much more convincing images here than it had in the open space of the building.

Gazing into Skyra's eyes, the woman said, "We ask questions. You answer questions."

Lincoln grabbed Skyra's arm and pulled her back a few

steps. "We can't hurt these people, so let's cooperate until we know what's going on, okay?"

Her muscles were rigid beneath his fingers. "I do not understand why I cannot kill them."

The virtual man said, "Why are you in our city?"

Lincoln glanced at his group.

Di-woto was silently staring at the naked man and woman as if she didn't want to miss a single detail.

"We'll let you do the talking, Lincoln," Virgil said.

Lincoln turned back to the two figures. "We came here because we need a safe place to stay. There are hostile animals beyond the city, and we were not safe there."

"Where did you come from?"

"We came from very far away. We cannot go back there."

"Where did you come from?"

Lincoln glanced at his team again but only got shrugs. "It is difficult to explain where we came from," he said to the man.

"Explain. Where did you come from?" the man asked again.

Lincoln sighed. He couldn't think of a reason to lie. "We have a device—a machine—that allows us to jump backward or forward in time. We jumped here from the past. Thousands of years ago, if you want to know. We have never been here before, and we definitely did not come here to hurt anyone. We are not a threat to you, and we do not want you to hurt us either."

The man turned to the woman, and they exchanged words in their own language. The language had a lot of blunt, harsh syllables, and it seemed almost every word began with a sharp *K* sound.

The man faced Lincoln again. "You cannot jump backward or forward in time. Where did you come from?"

"Look at us," Lincoln said. "We are not like you. We do not talk like you. Surely you can see we are not from this place. We are from thousands of years in the past."

"Some of you are different."

"Well, some of us are humans—bolups. One of us is nandup, like you, and one of us is a hybrid, with a nandup mother and a human father." Lincoln put his hand on Skyra's shoulder. "Skyra is from 95,000 years ago." He moved his hand to his own chest and used his other hand to indicate Jazzlyn, Virgil, then Derek. "These other three humans and I are from 47,000 years ago, but a different timeline." Finally, he pointed to Di-woto. "Di-woto is from 47,000 years ago in *this* timeline. It's kind of complicated and might require a lot more explanation."

The woman stepped up to Di-woto, stopped within arm's reach, and stared at the girl. "Why do you use that name?"

Skyra moved to Di-woto's side protectively. "Di-woto does not understand all of this language."

The woman didn't take her eyes off the girl. "Why does she use that name?"

"Di-woto is the name her birthmother gave her," Skyra replied.

"What is her birthmother's name?" the woman asked.

Skyra spoke a few words to Di-woto in the girl's language.

Di-woto smiled. "Mother name Lo-aful."

The woman's face formed an expression resembling shock. "You are not Di-woto. Your mother is not Lo-aful."

The girl frowned. "I Di-woto. Mother Lo-aful!"

The woman turned and exchanged more blunt words with her companion before turning back to Di-woto. She made the motion of projecting her hand from her mouth. "Speak so we can learn your language."

Di-woto glanced at Skyra, uncertain.

Skyra spoke several words in the girl's nandup language.

This was followed by a five-minute speech by Di-woto to the two beings, then a back-and-forth exchange that apparently resulted in the woman and man learning the girl's language. Several times Di-woto pointed to the scars on her skin as if explaining what she had done to herself. The woman and man seemed to become more and more agitated as the conversation dragged on.

Derek stepped closer to Lincoln and muttered, "Are you okay with our lives being determined by what a fifth grader decides to say?"

Lincoln didn't have an answer, so he just shrugged.

Finally, the woman turned to face Lincoln. "Your story is strange. Some of us think you are lying. Some of us believe you might be speaking truth."

Lincoln glanced around the small room. "How many are listening to this conversation?"

"Many."

"Would you mind telling us your plans? We didn't come here to harm you. Why did you capture us, and why are we being held against our will?"

"We have not yet decided what to do with you."

Lincoln waited for more explanation, but the woman and man just gazed at him. "Um, well, we would like to be released."

"We cannot release you. You are not ready to be released."

Lincoln shook his head, confused.

"What the hell does that mean?" Derek asked.

The woman eyed Derek impassively. "You came to our

city as people of flesh, and people of flesh are dangerous. They do not know how to function in our environment. Those are reasons why you are not ready to be released."

"Why do you call us people of flesh?" Virgil asked.

Virgil got the same impassive look from the woman. Then the man stepped up to Virgil and held a hand up beside the physicist's face. He swiped his hand directly through Virgil's head.

Virgil jerked his head back, startled. "That is... really unnerving."

"No flesh," the man said. He put his hand up beside Virgil's face again then slapped him.

Virgil straightened his glasses. "Ow! How did you—"

"Flesh," the man said. "Now you know the difference."

"If you are not people of flesh," Lincoln said, "what *are* you?"

The man stepped back beside the woman. "We are whatever we want to be. You are dangerous, and you are not ready to be released."

Jazzlyn and Derek began to say something, but Lincoln stopped them with a raised hand. He faced the woman and man. "What do we need to do to convince you we are ready to be released?"

The woman stepped to Di-woto and put her hand around the girl's shoulder. Her arm visibly displaced Di-woto's garment and her braided hair coiled around her neck, as if the woman were a real person—a person of flesh. "If you convince us this person of flesh is Di-woto, daughter of Lo-aful, we will prepare you to be released. Your story is strange, but this girl has already convinced some of us."

This was getting more confusing by the minute. Lincoln had no idea what kind of preparations they would need to be released. "Di-woto and her mother lived here over 47,000 years ago, yet you seem to know them. Is it possible you're thinking of a *different* Di-woto and Lo-aful?"

"How many years ago did you take Di-woto away from her mother and the fortress of Kyran-yufost?"

This question took Lincoln by surprise. "Well, from your perspective that happened 47,659 years ago."

The man and woman stared at him for a few seconds before the woman spoke. "It is surprising that people of flesh would know that. More of us now believe your story."

Lincoln exchanged a glance with Virgil, who shrugged in bewilderment.

The woman removed her arm from the girl's shoulders. "Di-woto disappeared from Kyran-yufost 47,659 years ago, and no one ever saw her again. Her life and influence are well known among us, but most people of flesh have no knowledge of history."

Lincoln had so many questions that he wasn't sure which to ask first. "Why don't people of flesh have that knowledge?"

"Until now, we thought people of flesh were extinct. They have not come to this city or any other for many years. When they did exist, they had become wild and uncivilized. They had lost their knowledge of history. Your story is strange, but many of us now believe you."

Derek clapped his hands together with a loud smack. "Okay, we're glad you believe us. So, can we go now?"

"You are not ready to be released," the man said.

"Goddammit!" Derek muttered.

"There is much information we want from you," the woman said. "If your story is true, we want to learn your technology for jumping backward or forward in time. You will teach us how this is possible."

Lincoln considered this. Maybe the situation wasn't as bad as it seemed. These virtual people—or whatever they were—might eventually leave them alone and allow them to continue living in the city. In fact, they might even provide help, such as giving Lincoln's group access to the tools, technology, and food preparation facilities that surely must exist somewhere. In exchange, he was willing to share his vast knowledge of temporal bridging technology, especially if it guaranteed his group could live here in peace.

He smiled at the woman. "We will be happy to share our knowledge with you, if you will agree to release us and let us continue living in your city. It seems you have abandoned the above-ground portion, so it's not like you're using it, right?"

The man and woman exchanged words in their language again. They faced Lincoln, and the man said. "You do not understand. We cannot allow you to become people of flesh again."

14

EXPLANATION

***47,659 YEARS** in the future - Day 3*

SKYRA UNDERSTOOD NOW what these people were. They were like the sunbeam that used to stream through a hole in the roof of her birthmother's shelter when she and Veenah were young girls. She could push her hand through the sunbeam, but she could not touch it. Like the sunbeam, she could push her hand through these people, but she could not touch them. She and her companions were people of flesh, but these strangers were not. To Skyra, the difference was simple.

Which was why their words were confusing to her. The man was trying to say Skyra and her friends would no longer be people of flesh. He was obviously telling a lie—she could not push her hand through her body like a sunbeam. She grabbed Lincoln's arm and felt his flesh and bone between her fingers.

Lincoln and the others were still staring at the man like

they didn't know what to say, so Skyra spoke up. "Why are you lying to us? We *are* people of flesh."

The man's mouth formed a slight smile. "We are trying to make the transition easier for you."

Anger was growing in Skyra's chest. "What does that mean?"

"It means we know we cannot show you too much at once. Your transition must be gradual."

"What transition?" Lincoln asked.

"Your transition from people of flesh to people of thought."

Derek took a step toward the man. "What the hell do you think you're gonna do to us?"

"You said you wish to remain in our city. People of flesh cannot be allowed in our city, as they cause damage. We have made you people of thought. We are trying to make the transition easy for you." The man gestured to the curved yellow wall of the tiny room. "That is why you are in this place. We thought you would be more comfortable in surroundings you understand. We do not want to overwhelm you. Now that many of us believe your story to be true, that one of you is Di-woto, daughter of Lo-aful, we will be even more careful to avoid overwhelming you. Di-woto is of great historical importance. It is possible the rest of you could be valuable in other ways."

Skyra turned to Lincoln. "What does this mean?"

He was holding his hands in front of his face, staring at them. "I really don't know. I've felt strange since we woke up. I just thought it was from whatever drug they gave me. Now I'm not so sure."

Jazzlyn, Virgil, Derek, and even Di-woto all raised their hands and stared at them.

Skyra looked at her own hands. They looked the way they had always looked. Almost. She studied one of her palms closely. The lines and scars were still there, but something was different—the tiny details. Everything looked a little softer because she couldn't quite make out the tiniest of the lines and wrinkles. She moved her hand farther away then closer. Still she could not make out the details she had always been able to see before.

She faced the strange man. "What did you do to us?"

"Do not be afraid," he replied. "Before long you will be quite happy in your new environment, and you will not miss your bodies of flesh."

Virgil spoke, his voice higher than normal. "If you're trying to avoid freaking us out, it's not working. I want to know exactly what is happening. Right now."

"No shit," Derek added. "Tell us exactly what's going on."

"I will explain," the man said. "First, however, we will make sure you have no doubts about what I have told you so far. Please attempt to touch each other."

The others stared as if confused, but Skyra knew what the man was telling them to do. She reached out to take Lincoln's hand. This time she grabbed only air. She thrust out her hand to push on his chest, but he was now like a sunbeam.

This resulted in alarmed cries as the others tried touching each other but could not. Skyra stepped to the yellow wall and pressed her hand to it. It did not go through. The wall was still as solid as it had been before.

The man and woman waited, watching.

Lincoln spoke first. "Okay, this has to be some sort of optical illusion. Please explain."

"Now try it again," the man said.

Skyra grabbed Lincoln's arm again. This time he was not

like a sunbeam at all. He was real. The others touched each other, obviously feeling real flesh.

"How are you doing this?" Lincoln asked. His eyes showed a kind of fear Skyra had not seen before—fear mixed with fascination. Lincoln wanted to understand what these people were doing, while Skyra just wanted to kill them.

"I will now provide an explanation," the man said. "You must listen to the entire explanation to fully understand. First, perhaps you are wondering how we have mastered your language so quickly, including many words you have not yet spoken in our presence."

Skyra had not even thought about this.

"I've been too freaked out to even notice," Virgil said. "But yeah."

The man smiled slightly. "Your robotic companion Ripple assisted us. We quickly discovered Ripple contains an impressive database of your language, as well as the languages of Di-woto and Skyra, not to mention extensive knowledge about you, Lincoln. This has been an important factor for many of us in deciding we believe your story."

Skyra wanted to grab the man's throat. "What did you do to Ripple?" she demanded.

"Do not be alarmed. Ripple is undamaged."

Skyra could not tell if the man was lying. "I want to see Ripple now!"

"It is not possible for us to bring Ripple into this environment."

"What exactly is this environment?" Lincoln asked.

The man turned to the woman beside him and nodded. She took Di-woto by the hand and pulled her through the wall. Skyra rushed to where they had disappeared, but the wall was now solid. She pounded on it with her fist. "Di-woto!"

"Your friend is fine," the man said. "We want to provide her with the same explanation I will provide for you. That will be easier to do in her language if she is in a separate room. Are you ready to listen?"

Skyra's anger finally exploded. She lunged at the man, throwing her fists at his face over and over.

He waited patiently until she decided her efforts were useless. Finally, she stepped back, her chest heaving from the effort.

The man spoke. "Skyra, do you notice how you are sucking in air due to your physical exertion? That is a result of what you think you should be doing—what you did when you were a person of flesh. Now you are a person of thought, so you do not need that air at all."

"You do not make sense!" she sputtered.

"Perhaps not yet. Now I will explain, if you are ready to listen."

She felt Lincoln's flesh-and-bone hand gently pull her back. "Let's listen to what he has to say, okay?" His voice was soothing.

"Speak now," she said to the man.

The man waited another breath, maybe to make sure they were ready to listen. "I am going to assume, for the moment, your story is true, and your friend really is Di-woto, daughter of Lo-aful. Therefore, Di-woto's disappearance from Kyran-yufost will mark the beginning of my explanation. To put it simply, Di-woto changed the world. Her life and her impact on others were complex, and it is quite possible that thousands of years of retelling her story have distorted the actual events.

Which is why we are excited about the possibility of your story being true."

He paused. "This explanation is important, so if anything confuses you, please request clarification."

Skyra glared at the man, but she sensed Lincoln and his tribemates nodding.

"Di-woto changed the world. She was a complex person, who suffered greatly in her thoughts as well as in her flesh. Many of us were of the opinion her suffering had become figurative through retelling, but now we see those ancient stories may have been true. Di-woto lived during a time when the world was ready for change. If she had lived in a different time, perhaps she would have soon been forgotten. Do you know what Di-woto did?"

"We were there," Skyra said. "We helped Di-woto with her plan to stop the fighting between nandups and bolups."

The man nodded. "Yes, Di-woto has told us this. However, our ancient stories include nothing about people named Skyra, Lincoln, Jazzlyn, Derek, or Virgil."

"We were there!" Skyra repeated.

He nodded again. "Di-woto initiated a revolution, then she disappeared."

"We brought her with us when we jumped to this time," Lincoln said.

"As you have said. When Di-woto disappeared, the revolution may have died out if not for the efforts of her mother Lo-aful."

Skyra was now listening intently, and she hoped Di-woto was hearing this same story in her own language.

"Lo-aful took up Di-woto's cause, and the revolution spread from one kingdom to the next, eventually affecting the entire world with a new attitude, the attitude that war did not have to be inevitable. People began to realize nandups and bolups did not have to perpetually attempt to wipe each other out. Other people had started similar movements, but none of them ever took hold like the one initiated by Di-woto and her mother Lo-aful.

"Over the centuries, Di-woto became a legend, the girl who had suffered immeasurably and ultimately did the impossible. Countless scholars have studied her brief life and her impact, and in particular, what may have happened to her. It is difficult to put into words what it means to us to see Di-woto has appeared here after 47,659 years—assuming your story is true."

Virgil spoke up. "Um, I have a question. I'm not doubting Di-woto had a profound impact on your world, but for the last three days we have come to the conclusion that some kind of massive disaster happened here, one that wiped out most of the living things above ground. It seems likely it was caused by a weapon. Is this correct?"

Skyra let out a growl. She wanted to know what was happening to her now, not what had happened long ago.

The man frowned while nodding. "You are correct. Your impressive deductions tell us much about your cognitive abilities, and the weapon you refer to is an important part of my explanation. Di-woto and Lo-aful changed the world, but the world is a complex place. At the time Di-woto lived, nandups and bolups—Neanderthals and humans, if you prefer—had fought with each other for many thousands of years. This tendency had become embedded in our ancestors' nature. Such habits are difficult to overcome. Therefore, it is not surprising that isolated wars would erupt even long after Di-woto and Lo-aful had sparked a revolution.

"Most of us now believe those wars could have been

prevented if nandups and bolups had not had such a strong aversion to the idea of interbreeding. If the two species had intermixed more readily, eventually becoming one species, we believe peace would have become permanent much sooner than it did. However, it is too late for that now."

"Why is it too late?" Lincoln asked.

"You will soon understand. After the revolution initiated by Di-woto, peace between the two species became the normal state of the world. Isolated wars occasionally erupted but did not become global catastrophes. Populations thrived, industrialization progressed, and technological advances eventually allowed nandups and bolups to experience levels of comfort previously undreamed of. Of course, some of these same advances also allowed for previously undreamed of weaponry.

"At that point, the isolated wars that occasionally erupted became much more concerning, as many populations possessed weapons with global consequences."

"Which is exactly what must have happened," Virgil added.

Skyra studied Virgil's face. He had been captured by strange creatures, and had things done to him that he didn't understand, but still he wanted to learn about the things that did not even matter. Perhaps Skyra would never understand bolups.

"Yes," said the man who wasn't really there. "Your hypothesis regarding what happened to the creatures living above ground is remarkably accurate. A war erupted between a population of nandups and a population of bolups. The disagreements should have been quickly resolved, but the conflict escalated, and more populations became involved. With little warning, one population of bolups moved their people below ground and activated a devastating weapon, instantly killing every exposed living thing.

"Many populations had already prepared for such a disaster, knowing the weapon might someday be used. Most cities had already built extensive below-ground facilities due to a world-wide trend toward the aesthetics of cleanliness and simplicity. Although the weapon had never been activated before, many populations possessed the same weapon, and some of them activated it in a misguided attempt at retaliation. In one fateful day, all nandups and all bolups were forced to move below ground to avoid being exterminated."

"Sheee-it," Derek said. "That's pretty tragic, but I'm still waiting for the part about how I'm not a person of flesh anymore."

The man barely glanced at Derek before going on. "Thousands of above-ground cities became empty and unused. It is important to understand the nature of the aesthetics of cleanliness and simplicity I mentioned. Both nandups and bolups had developed a deep appreciation of natural settings untainted by development. Most cities were arranged in the midst of vast territories of wilderness, which were enjoyed by all citizens. In one day, all citizens were forced to move permanently below ground, never to see their beautiful cities and surrounding wilderness again. The fear of another weapon activation never subsided. It seemed as though trust between species would never return.

"For people who thrive on nature, beauty, and aesthetics, life below ground is tedious and ugly. Year after year, century after century, people endured, and still the trust between species did not return. Technology, though, continued to advance, particularly technology allowing people to experience beauty in a virtual setting. Simulated environments became immersive and detailed, and people began spending more time exploring these environments, even to the point of dying from atrophy and malnutrition.

"A bold and formidable solution became clear. People decided to escape their bodies of flesh and live forever in a simulated environment."

"You gotta be kidding," Lincoln said.

Skyra didn't understand what the naked man was saying, but she sensed it was important.

The man continued without replying to Lincoln. "Accomplishing this goal became an obsession of people in every population. Advances were made rapidly, and the capabilities progressed for over twelve hundred years before the world achieved what you might refer to as the tipping point."

"Which was?" Virgil asked eagerly.

"The point at which nearly all people in all populations made the transition at the same time. This could not have happened without creating simulated environments so appealing there was no longer any substantial reason for people to remain in their bodies of flesh."

Lincoln rubbed his face with his hands, then he stared at his hands again. "What you're saying is all the people—including you—who used to live in this city are now living in a simulated environment?"

"That is correct," the man replied.

Lincoln glanced at Skyra before looking back at the man. "How can we see you and interact with you if you are in a simulated environment?"

"The answer to that question is two-fold. First, when you were people of flesh, you saw projections of us. Many of us enjoy exploring our above-ground city as projections. We can do this safely. That is how we discovered you were in our city.

Second, because you are people of thought now, you are interacting with us in a simulated environment. It is a simplified environment, which we believe will make your transition easier."

"No," Derek said. "No, no, no. This isn't possible!"

Skyra faced Lincoln. "What does this mean? Are we real, or are we sunbeams like this man?"

"I don't know," he said, staring at his hands again. "I honestly don't know."

The man said, "Think for a moment about what I told Skyra when she was sucking in air after trying to harm me. Now, please brace yourselves for what I believe you will consider to be a dramatic demonstration." He waited a moment. "Are you ready?"

Skyra did not reply, and neither did anyone else.

The man smiled. "Remember, you have nothing to fear."

Skyra was under water. Cool liquid pressed against her skin from all sides and rushed into her eyes, ears, nose, and mouth. She began thrashing her arms and legs, but she didn't even know which way was up. She had never in her life been in water deeper than her waist, and her thrashing wasn't getting her anywhere. She blew the water from her mouth and instinctively held her breath.

Motion to one side caught her eye, and she turned to see Lincoln beside her, pumping his arms and kicking in panic. Lincoln's tribemates were there too, trying to propel themselves to the surface. Skyra could now see the surface, reflecting sparkles of sunlight in countless rippling waves a full body length above her head. She tried kicking to reach it, but her body wouldn't rise. The others were also having no success.

Skyra wanted to breathe. She wanted to fill her chest with

air and get to dry land. She knew she was going to die if she couldn't get to the surface. They were all going to die.

She kicked and kicked, but nothing she did brought the surface any closer.

Something grabbed her arm. She turned to see Lincoln staring at her. He was no longer thrashing. His tribemates were also still, but they were alive, their eyes open and staring into the water around them.

Lincoln shook her arm gently and pointed to his own mouth, which was open. He moved his mouth, trying to tell her something. His mouth formed the word *breathe*.

She shook her head. If she let water into her chest, she would surely die.

He grabbed her other arm then nodded. Now he was actually smiling.

Skyra realized her chest was not burning. Her head was telling her she needed air, but her body was not demanding it. She felt terrified, but her body wasn't hurting.

He shook her again. *Breathe*, he mouthed.

Why was she able to see him so clearly? Skyra had sometimes opened her eyes with her head submerged in the Yagua river of her homeland and had only seen blurred shapes. Now though, Lincoln and his tribemates appeared almost as clear as they normally did.

Lincoln released her and pointed downward. She tilted her head to look. Below was a scene unlike anything she could ever imagine. Fish of every color and shape were swimming among what appeared to be a miniature forest of gently-waving sticks and broad, flat leaves. A tightly-packed cloud of yellow fish, each no longer than her finger, hovered above the forest a short distance away. A pair of triangular fish with black and silver stripes and tall fins on their backs swam slowly by, biting at the waving sticks as if they were picking off bits of food. A bright blue and red fish the size of Skyra's leg was grabbing rocks from the ground, and she could hear the fish cracking and chewing the rocks in its mouth before spitting out showers of broken pieces.

Lincoln tapped her arm and pointed outward.

Again, she turned to look. Three creatures the size of Skyra's hand were hovering in the water only an arm's length from her face. The creatures looked like swimming seed pods, but with numerous thin arms pointing toward her. On either side of where the arms attached to the body, round eyes stared back at her, as if the creatures were curious about her too. Thin, skin-like sheets on the sides of their bodies flapped up and down in waves, holding the creatures still in the water. Skyra extended her hand to touch the nearest of the creatures, but all three of them quickly shot backward out of reach. She lowered her hand, and they gradually returned to where they had been before.

Skyra's body still did not demand air, and now her head was getting used to the idea that she was not going to die. She opened her mouth and water rushed in. It did not hurt, and she did not choke. She looked at Lincoln. He was gazing around at the wondrous creatures in this strange underwater place.

Everything became black for a moment.

Skyra was back in the yellow room, standing exactly where she had been before. Her skin and garments were dry. Her hair was dry. Lincoln and his tribemates were there, and so was the strange man. Skyra sucked in a chestful of air, but only because her head had always told her to breathe. Now, however, her body no longer seemed to need air.

"You seem to have handled that demonstration quite

well," the naked man said. "Perhaps your transition will be easier than we had assumed."

Skyra watched Lincoln and the others. Virgil had his eyes closed, and he was trembling. He had a fistful of Jazzlyn's blue shirt gripped in one hand, holding her close to his side. Jazzlyn was swaying on her feet as if she might fall. Derek and Lincoln were staring at the man, looking like they were too stunned to speak.

Lincoln finally got some words out. "That was, um... that was quite a demonstration. You might have chosen something a little less... shocking."

The man bared his teeth in a nandup smile. "The environment you just experienced was patterned after a place that actually exists. So, it is hardly shocking at all. To borrow one of your phrases, you ain't seen nothin' yet."

15

IMAGINATION

47,659 YEARS *in the future - Day 3*

LINCOLN'S MIND should have been completely overwhelmed at this point. He had just experienced undeniable proof that he and his companions were indeed somehow immersed in a virtual environment. What's worse, from what the man had said, they may never be allowed to leave. The situation was definitely disconcerting, but he felt surprisingly calm. In fact, he detected a growing sensation of overall well-being. However, this sensation had to be artificially induced, which was all the more reason for concern.

"How are you doing this?" he asked the man.

The man flashed a toothy nandup smile. "An excellent question. You will find it comforting to know your body of flesh is still intact, at least for the time being. Although we have not encountered people of flesh in many years, we still have a procedure in place for such encounters. We first draw your consciousness into our environment while it is still contained within your body of flesh. We question you. We determine if there may be some possible benefit to allowing your consciousness to remain in your body of flesh. Typically, there is no benefit, in which case we continue your transition, transferring your consciousness completely into our environment so we no longer have to maintain your body."

Lincoln wasn't sure if he should feel relieved or terrified. "So, we're still in our physical bodies—I assume inside those containers you forced us into?"

"That is correct. The containers are an integral part of your transition."

"What if we don't want to transition?" Derek asked.

"Soon it will be what you want," the man said with no hesitation.

Derek grunted. "Why in the hell would we want to live inside of a computer simulation? So what if I don't need to breathe air. I'd rather be real."

"Clinical lycanthropy," the man said, gazing steadily at Derek.

Derek grimaced at the man. "I suppose you stole that tidbit of information from Ripple, too?"

"Your clinical lycanthropy seems to be rather debilitating at times. Not to mention you have occasional bouts with anger management and waning self-esteem."

Derek's grimace turned into a threatening glare.

"You can whisk away those psychological disorders with a wave of your hand," the man said. He then turned to Virgil. "A traumatic childhood experience resulting in lifelong complications so numerous your therapists gave up trying to label them. Not only can you whisk them all away, you can make it so that the traumatic experience never happened in the first place. You can have a lifetime of memories of your family members, because that man did not come into your house and kill them. In your mind, it will never have happened."

The man faced Jazzlyn. "You were all alone. The car rolled off the jack. It could have been prevented, but you were only eighteen and had never changed a flat tire by yourself. It wasn't your fault."

Jazzlyn lifted her left hand to stare at it, but the black carbon fiber polymer prosthetic was gone. She was staring at a real hand, or at least one that looked real, complete with chocolate-colored skin on the back and a caramel-colored palm. She opened and closed the fingers and muttered, "Daaaamn!"

The man faced Lincoln next. "Throughout your life you have—"

"I get what you're doing," he said, cutting the man off. "You have our brains connected to this virtual world, so we can do things here we can't do in real life. We get it. The problem is, it's not real. We would prefer to go back to living our *real* lives, in spite of our imperfections. We would like you to release us."

The man shook his head. "People of flesh cannot be allowed in our city."

"Why not? You have big bats living in your city. Thousands of them."

"Bats are not capable of doing the kind of damage people of flesh can do."

Lincoln figured he was referring to the damage people could do to the computers used to generate the virtual world these people were living in. Presumably, those computers were below the city. "How about if we agree to stay in the above-ground portion of the city? We have no desire to sabotage any of your computers or other equipment."

The man gazed at him for several seconds, and Lincoln wondered if he was consulting with other members of his *population*.

"I have not finished my explanation," the man said abruptly. "Weary of living below ground, but unable to return to the surface due to the ongoing threat of the previously discussed weapons, our population reached the tipping point at which we all transitioned from people of flesh to people of thought. Then our bodies of flesh were no longer needed. Our robotic caretakers became responsible for maintenance of physical equipment, as well as defense from the occasional feral people of flesh entering our city. As we no longer have physical bodies we can use to manufacture new parts and construct new machinery, our robotic caretakers serve this purpose, and our simulated environment steadily continues to improve as we develop more robust technology."

"How many people live here?" Jazzlyn asked, somewhat out of the blue.

"Our population includes approximately 440,000 people of thought. Ours is one among thousands of populations throughout the world, some of them nandup, some of them bolup."

"You're saying 440,000 people used to live in this city, and now they're all gone?" Jazzlyn asked. "Not a single person of flesh is left?"

"That is correct. We cannot allow people of flesh in our city."

Jazzlyn persisted. "Are there 440,000 nandup bodies somewhere, connected to your computer servers, the way we are?"

"Our bodies were disposed of long ago."

"Disposed of?" Jazzlyn said with a look of disgust. "Never mind—I don't even want to know. Do you plan to dispose of our bodies too?"

"Yes, if we determine your bodies cannot benefit us, we will complete your transition into our environment, then we will dispose of your bodies. You will not miss them, I can assure you of that."

Lincoln could hardly believe what he was hearing. "Don't you people have any laws you need to follow regarding doing things like this to people against their will? We do not *want* to be killed!"

"We have a law that people of flesh cannot be allowed in our city. Allow me to continue explaining. Other than small, resistant bands of people of flesh, who eventually became feral savages in the wilderness between cities, every population transitioned to its own simulated environment. With our long history of conflict and distrust, you should understand why each population developed defenses to prevent people of flesh from destroying the equipment that sustains their existence.

"However, with this new kind of existence came new threats. In addition to the threat from people of flesh, there was the threat of virtual invasions of our simulated environments. People of thought from one population might devise ways to destroy the simulated environment of another population. Therefore, each population isolated itself from all others, then continued creating more secure barriers while our enemies continued developing more sophisticated approaches to breaking those barriers.

"An arms race," Virgil said, and he glanced at Jazzlyn.

"Yes, an arms race. For many years nandups did not interact with bolups, and in fact, populations of nandups even limited their interactions with other populations of nandups. Eventually something profound happened. A few individuals decided the world could be a better place again. They sought out other like-minded people of thought. They discussed the legacy of Di-woto and Lo-aful, as well as other historical figures who had campaigned for peace. They started a movement, just as Di-woto had done long before, only now the movement was among people of thought rather than people of flesh, both nandups and bolups, in every population.

"The eventual result was a truce between species that persists to this day. Populations of nandups and bolups began working together to create a simulated environment more robust and impressive than any before it. Now, all people of thought coexist in the same simulated environment, thus eliminating the desire of one population or one species to inflict damage upon the system."

He paused as if thinking, then he said, "I am pleased to inform you all of us now believe Di-woto is who she says she is. Your story is astonishing, but it is true."

He paused again and looked directly at Lincoln. "I will answer your question now. You asked if we would allow you to live as people of flesh and remain in our city above ground. Our answer is no. The risk to us is too great. After hearing our history, you should understand how we must be cautious of all possible risks. We know there may still be remnant populations of savage, feral people of flesh roaming the wilderness between cities. This is why we have robotic caretakers capable of capturing them when they enter our city, as they captured you. We realize you are not savage, feral remnants, but our longstanding rules still apply. We will complete your transition, then we will dispose of your bodies of flesh, as we can see no benefit in expending resources to keep the bodies alive."

The man smiled as he looked at each team member in turn. "We are about to give you a more immersive demonstration of what it is like to exist in our environment. We are confident you will soon agree there is no further need for your bodies."

He faced Jazzlyn. "Welcome to our environment, Jazzlyn."

Jazzlyn disappeared. There was no sound, or puff of smoke, or flash of light. She was just gone.

"Brace yourself, Derek," the man said to Derek.

Derek disappeared.

"Virgil, you will find this intellectually stimulating."

Virgil was gone.

"Skyra, you may find this to be confusing at first, but—"

"Wait!" Lincoln said, on the verge of panic. "If you're doing another demonstration, please keep me and Skyra together. I don't think she's as equipped for this as I am, and I want to be with her in case she needs help."

The man smiled. "Do not be concerned. Each of your demonstrations will be personalized. You and Skyra have vastly different backgrounds and personalities."

Skyra disappeared.

Lincoln balled his hands into fists, but he knew there was nothing he could do to this man. "Goddammit! This is all happening too fast!"

"You are an interesting person, with an interesting history, Lincoln. The same can be said for Skyra, as well as your team of employees. Your presence in our environment will result in many interesting conversations."

"How do you know so much about us? Can you read our minds?"

"No. Your consciousness is still inside your body of flesh.

Once you complete your transition, your consciousness will be part of our environment and will be accessible, but we have rules to protect your privacy. However, we have no rules against accessing the knowledge of your robotic drone Ripple, or your drone Maddy, contained within the cognitive module we found with your body of flesh. Maddy and Ripple provided extensive information about you, and Ripple provided extensive information about Skyra. Did you know Ripple collected information about Skyra for two years before you and your team found her?"

Lincoln stared for a moment. The man had spoken as if he were hinting that Ripple knew something important about Skyra that Lincoln did not know. "Yeah, I knew they'd been companions for a while before we jumped back to Skyra's time."

The man nodded thoughtfully. "Your story is a fascinating one, and we look forward to many stimulating conversations." He extended a hand and gripped Lincoln's shoulder. "Brace yourself. This is going to blow your mind."

LINCOLN WAS RUNNING, breathing hard as he made his way up a sand-and-brush-covered hillside. When he stopped at the top of the hill, he glanced down at his white running shorts, white mesh singlet, and gray Asics trail shoes. Still catching his breath, he scanned the scene around him. He was on Heartache Hill, the tallest, most challenging hill on the twelve-kilometer loop of the running trail he'd established on his vast property northwest of Tucson.

To the north he could see his lab complex, the cluster of buildings where he worked, slept, and did almost everything else. He turned in a complete circle, looking closer at his surroundings. Everything was as he remembered—rugged desert hills dotted with ocotillos, barrel cactuses, and the occasional towering saguaro. He owned all of it, for as far as he could see.

He held his hands close to his face and studied them. They had the same soft appearance he had noticed while inside the yellow room, as if everything were real except for the minutest of details. He cupped his hands to his mouth and shouted, "Skyra!"

No response, other than the sound of the breeze across the rugged hilltops.

He sighed and turned to gaze at his lab complex. "Okay, you're right, my mind is blown. This is pretty amazing. Now I'd like to rejoin Skyra and my team, if you don't mind."

Nothing happened.

He sighed again and began walking toward his complex. Halfway down the hill he started running again. He picked up his pace, and soon he was sprinting—up and over the next hill then along the trail parallel to the dry stream bed of Scrub Creek. He felt he could run even faster if he wanted to. Out of habit, he sucked in lungfuls of air, but his body didn't really need the oxygen. The experience was exhilarating, but what was the point? There was no challenge to it, and his body probably didn't need to exercise anyway.

Maddy was waiting for him beside the trail as he approached his main lab, and Lincoln suddenly realized he was reliving a past experience. It was the day three bureaucrats from Washington had shown up and turned his life upside down. They had shown him the skeletal remains of a female Neanderthal, which had been found alongside the ancient remains of one of his drones—Skyra and Ripple.

Why would the virtual beings from another timeline stick him into the middle of this fateful day? Actually, maybe they hadn't. Maybe the demonstration was more open-ended. Perhaps it was being generated by his own memories.

He approached Maddy. "Let me guess. There are three men here to see me, right?" He walked past the drone without stopping, heading for the lab entrance.

Maddy's feminine voice followed him. "You mean to tell me I came out to this unsanitary place to inform you of something you already knew? I do not know why I bother trying to be your assistant, Lincoln."

He continued toward the door. "You're not real, Maddy. I'm pretty sure everything you say is going to be something I remember you saying before."

"Aren't you in a curmudgeonly mood. Do you remember me saying you should have known better than to marry Lottie Atkins?"

Lincoln stopped and turned back to the drone, frowning. Maddy had never heard of Lottie Atkins at this point. Then he understood. "Okay, I get it. This simulated scenario is coming from my thoughts now, not just from my memories."

"That is a reasonable conjecture," the drone said. "Perhaps you should put it to the test."

"Yeah, perhaps I should. What do you know about Ripple?"

"I assume you are referring to the roguish, deceptive drone that tricked you into giving up your entire life for a preposterous plan for rebooting humanity?"

"That's the one. Tell me something about Ripple I don't already know."

Maddy's ring of red lights flashed three times. "You know that would be possible only if the beings who captured you extracted from Ripple some information you do not know, then intruded upon this simulation to provide that information to me, but I'm a manifestation of your own mind. Do you see the logical conundrum your question poses?"

"Yeah, I guess so."

"Perhaps you should do something more constructive. When was the last time you thought about your childhood, Lincoln?"

He normally avoided thinking of his childhood, but Maddy's surprising question made him reflexively think back to his younger days. Then, inexplicably, he sensed his memories being repopulated. Countless incidents of being chided, ridiculed, and shunned by family members and so-called friends faded into the background, still there but filed away like an archived earlier version of a subsequently-improved digital file.

What was in the forefront of his memory now was kindness. His brothers and parents had loved him. They had bought him birthday gifts every year, and they had been proud every time he scored higher than his classmates in school. He had crystal-clear memories of his brothers bragging to their girlfriends that Lincoln Woodhouse was their brother. Every year, Lincoln's mother made him a red velvet cake for his birthday, even on those years he couldn't travel back to the family home in Michigan. They would still videoconference, and his mom and dad would cut the cake in front of the camera and eat an extra piece for him.

Then there was Irina. His sister Irina hadn't died when he was seven and she was only eight. Instead, she had been Lincoln's closest friend until she'd met Vic, married, and moved away when she was twenty. Now, in Lincoln's memories of his original timeline, Irina and Vic lived in Seattle and had a daughter named Jatta. They visited Lincoln in Arizona for an entire week every March, when the cactus flowers were in bloom. They'd asked Lincoln to be Jatta's godfather, even though Lincoln had no religious inclinations.

"You can thank me for that suggestion, if you wish," Maddy said.

Lincoln blinked. He'd almost forgotten he was still standing in the desert sun outside of his complex. A fathomless, intense euphoria had settled upon him. He knew none of it was real, but every memory now felt as real as all those that had been archived as defunct. "Irina," he said aloud.

"Yes, your sister. Lovely woman. That child of hers, though—last time they were here, the urchin stuck four pieces of chewing gum on my vision lens."

Lincoln chuckled. "Jatta's a firecracker." At that moment he wanted nothing more than to introduce Skyra to Irina and Jatta. He thought about this—maybe he could. Maybe in this environment he could do anything his mind could conceive.

"Now you're starting to get the hang of it," Maddy said.

Lincoln gazed at the drone. "You know, Maddy, I should have made you bigger. You'd be more useful if you were bigger."

The drone swelled right before his eyes, transforming from the size of a collie to the size of a pony.

"Even bigger," Lincoln said.

Maddy swelled again, this time to the size of a draft horse, the top of her shell the height of Lincoln's head.

"I hardly see how this will make me more useful," Maddy said, her voice now proportionally richer and louder.

"That's why you need hands with articulated, opposable fingers. Maybe eight hands on four pairs of arms. Hey, while we're at it, let's give you a sleeker look, with plenty of chrome contrasted with matte black, with some intimidating weapons mounted on either side of your vision lens."

Seconds later, Lincoln was staring at a robot suitable for a science fiction movie. Maddy now stood about twelve feet tall, on two thick legs, with eight articulated arms. Sunlight glinted off her larger shell pieces, while her joints and head were black. On either side of her head, which now had two smaller vision lenses instead of one, were mounted wicked-looking guns that swiveled as Maddy looked from side to side.

Lincoln couldn't help but laugh. Why shouldn't he laugh? He was feeling empowered and elated. In fact, he couldn't remember ever feeling this ecstatic in his entire life.

He glanced over his shoulder at his lab complex. It could use a makeover as well... no, that was trivial. Why not think bigger? He gazed over the hundreds of acres of desert hills he'd purchased when he was nineteen, after clearing his first half-billion in one year. To him, it was beautiful as it was, but what the hell. He raised his hands. Then, like a melodramatic wizard, he began conducting.

With his palms turned downward, he moved his hands apart, smoothing out the hills. For as far as he could see, the terrain obeyed, creating a distant rumbling sound. Heartache Hill, and all the lesser hills, shifted as if giant invisible hands were spreading them onto the landscape like cookie dough.

A rainforest. That's what this parched piece of sand and gravel needed. Lincoln turned his palms upward and lifted lush, tropical trees and vines, extracting them from the stark desert surface, until they were towering above him, blocking out the sun. He extended his index fingers, then poked at the air repeatedly—first with the right finger, then the left, then the right again. With each poke, an exotic creature appeared. He made macaws with blue and yellow feathers, howler monkeys he'd seen once on a trip to Belize, and hummingbirds with long, curved beaks. Then he made sloths, spider monkeys, and a few green tree boas. He chewed on his lower lip for a moment then created a creature he knew didn't even exist, a sparkling green toucan with a long, orange-spotted bill and six-foot, pink tail feathers that trailed behind the bird as it flew about among the canopy branches.

Maddy's heavy robot feet thudded the ground as she turned in a complete circle, surveying the new surroundings. "It appears you're quite comfortable in this environment. Perhaps, Lincoln, you should be wary of becoming intoxicated by your own power."

A chuckle escaped from Lincoln's chest. "Always watching out for me, aren't you? Don't worry. I'm just exploring what's possible. That naked nandup wasn't exaggerating about this place—it's mind-blowing."

Lincoln could smell the moist soil and humidity of his new creation. He could hear the breeze riffling through the leaves at the top of the canopy. He strode up to the nearest clump of trees and scooped up a handful of leaf litter from the forest floor. He put it near his face and breathed in the fresh scent of soil. "How could they possibly do this?" he asked. "Even creating a *static* simulation this detailed presents coding challenges that boggle the mind, but this... this place is fully-interactive and modifiable, and it stimulates all the senses. I've never dreamed such an environment was possible."

Maddy's rich, crystal-clear voice came from behind him. "Are you now considering staying here forever?"

"It's not real, remember?"

"If you say so."

Lincoln shot a glance at the massive, gleaming drone.

"Though it does challenge the limits of one's imagination."

"You have always loved a challenge," Maddy added.

He scanned the surrounding forest. "Yeah." He extended his arms, and again he began conducting. With another spreading of his hands, he razed the forest to the ground. Several lifting motions brought mountains erupting skyward. He pulled them up to impossible heights and stretched the peaks out into precarious overhangs that seemed to defy gravity. With deft fingerstrokes he drew waterfalls, with miniature rainbows forming in the mist from the water as it fell hundreds of feet to rocky pools below.

Lincoln dotted the mountainsides with houses, each with pagoda-style roofs with ornamental peaks and corners, and each positioned with a view of the spectacular landscape. He covered the meadows below with white, yellow, and purple wildflowers, then added snow to the peaks and lush coniferous forest to the mountainsides.

Finally, he stood staring. What was even more awe-inspiring than the scenery was the fact that he could now swim in the pools beneath the waterfalls. He could climb to one of the houses and make it a permanent home for him and Skyra. Everything here was as real as he needed it to be.

"One more finishing touch," he said aloud. With a few more waves of his hands, Lincoln pulled the sun above into four smaller suns, each of them a different color—one red, one green, one purple, and one blue. Instead of the resulting light blending into normal white sunshine, each sun cast its own specific color onto a different area of the landscape, resulting in a breathtaking patchwork of colors illuminating a scene that was already beyond imagination.

The ground shook slightly as Maddy stepped up beside him, and the two silently gazed at what he had created.

16

HOME

47,659 YEARS *in the future - Day 3*

SKYRA KNEW VEENAH WAS DEAD, but now her birthmate was beside her. The sisters were hunting for hares, their favorite way to hone their skills with their bantans—the short throwing spears their people used while hunting game smaller than an ibex. The sun was at its peak in the sky, and the two girls had been away from Una-Loto camp since the sun had first shown itself that morning. They had seen six hares so far but had yet to kill one. They had also seen a column of smoke far out in the Dofusofu river valley, something they would need to report to their tribemates. The fire could be simply from a nandup hunting party from the Wota-Loto tribe wintering only a day's walk from Una-Loto camp. However, it also could be from a tribe of bolups coming to raid nandup camps to kill men and take young women.

Skyra somehow remembered all these things, but she also knew none of it was real. It was no more real than the underwater experience the naked man had forced upon her and the others. Veenah was dead. The only way to make her alive again was to use Lincoln's T3 to go many, many years back and save her. That was what Lincoln had said, and Lincoln would not lie to her.

Skyra and Veenah were scrambling over a rock outcrop to get to the brushy meadow they knew was above, where they had seen many hares on previous hunts. Atop the rocks, Veenah turned to Skyra and spoke in their Una-Loto language. "I will circle to the other side and drive the hares to you. Skyra, if you do not kill a hare this time, I will tell the story tonight at the campfire. Our tribemates will have much laughter for you!"

Skyra smiled. Veenah was not real, but it felt good to see her again. As her birthmate circled to the other side of the meadow, Skyra thought of her tribemates, and her skin prickled from pleasant memories. She still had her old memories, but those were now tucked away, and she didn't have to think about them unless she wanted to. New memories filled her mind now. Her birthmother Sayleeh had not been killed by a woolly rhino. Instead, she was now higher in the foothills, hunting reindeer with all the tribe's best hunters. Sayleeh and the rest of her hunting party would probably be back at camp within two days, carrying loads of reindeer meat, skins, and antlers in leather packs upon their backs. Sayleeh would tell Skyra and Veenah stories of the hunt, and the two birthmates would sleep with their arms around their birthmother that night.

In Skyra's old memories, she and Veenah had often been insulted and even beaten by their tribemates. Now, in her new memories, the two girls had always been like other nandups, without the ability to see what others did not see, and without the ability to learn things more quickly than others. They were normal nandup girls, protected and valued by their tribe. After seeing twenty cold seasons, they would reach ilmekho, then they would bear children for the tribe, and their children would become great hunters also.

Veenah was now on the far side of the meadow, and she began walking toward Skyra, smacking the ground with the butt of her bantan and chanting, "*Chu chu chu chu. Chu chu chu chu.*"

Skyra raised her own bantan, ready to throw it, then held still, not moving a muscle. If the hares did not see her moving, they might run right to her.

A hare burst forth from a clump of grasses, but it scampered to the side and disappeared over a ridge of boulders. It probably wouldn't stop running until it was well out of sight.

"*Chu chu chu chu. Chu chu chu chu.*"

Two hares leapt from another clump. One of them followed the previous hare to the side, but the other came right toward Skyra.

Skyra's heart pounded with the excitement of the hunt. She held her bantan still, waiting for the hare to get too close for it to change course and gain enough distance after it saw her move.

Skyra knew she would strike the hare even before she released the spear. This hunt was not real. The hare was not real, and Veenah was not really alive. She anticipated which direction the hare would turn when it saw her arm move, then she threw the spear at the place she thought the animal would be. The bantan caught the hare in the center of its body. With the weapon protruding from both its sides, it rolled once, squealing and kicking, then fell silent and still.

"*Aheeeee!*" Veenah cried out, baring her teeth in a broad

grin. Then she went back to smacking the ground as she walked. "*Chu chu chu chu.*"

Skyra killed two more hares while Veenah went from one clump of grasses to the next, driving the creatures from their hiding spots. Each hare was an easy kill. Skyra's memory told her she had missed two hares earlier in the hunt, but that was before she had left the yellow room and appeared here. Now she knew she would not miss again. Perhaps she *could* not miss in this place that was not real.

With three hares to carry all the way back to Una-Loto camp, the two sisters decided to stop hunting. Before leaving the meadow they scanned their surroundings for any signs of predators or bolup hunting parties. Skyra didn't know if it were even possible she could be harmed in this place, but she wasn't going to take chances. She and Veenah descended the slope from the meadow to the narrow stream that flowed between the hills on its way to the Yagua river.

The stream was small enough to leap across, but the water was cool, and it flowed clean over a bed of rocks worn smooth by the current. The two sisters removed their capes, waist-skins, and footwraps and sat in the ankle-deep water to bathe. They laughed and threw cold water at each other. Skyra lay on her back in the stream to wet her hair. Veenah sat behind her, squeezing the excess water from Skyra's hair, then re-wetting it, then squeezing again.

Skyra watched for danger, but she wasn't afraid. Instead, she was content, untroubled. Today was a good day. Not because she liked her new memories. Not because Veenah was at her side again. Skyra understood those things were not real. She was happy because of what Lincoln had told her. When they had thought they were going to be killed in the sanctuary-fortress of Kyran-yufost, Lincoln had said they might be able to use the T3 to go many, many years to save Veenah. He wasn't sure it could be done, but he had said it was *possible*.

Here, in this place that was not real, Skyra was reminded of how connected she had been to her birthmate. Veenah had been taken from her only a handful of days ago, and so many things had happened during those days that Skyra had not had many opportunities to think about what her life was going to be like without Veenah.

Skyra did not understand how this strange place was possible, but she definitely understood it was not real. Her new memories were not real, and she was not really capable of hitting three hares in a row with her bantan.

Skyra did not want this world of unreal things.

She sat up and shifted in the stream until she was facing her birthmate. "I am glad you are alive in this place, Veenah. When the bolup men took you, I searched for four days before I found their camp. I tried to take you from them, but there were too many to fight by myself—I had to run away. I found some strange bolups who were kind to me. They came with me, and they helped me kill the men who had taken you."

Veenah listened to Skyra's words without showing surprise. She just gazed at Skyra with her wide eyes. Their birthmother and tribemates had said many times Skyra looked just like Veenah. Skyra had seen her own reflection on the surfaces of slow-moving streams, but the ripples always distorted it. She hoped she looked just like her sister—Veenah's eyes always sparkled, and her smile made Skyra smile as well.

"Maybe you do not know this," Skyra said, "but I took you back to Una-Loto, and Gelrut killed you."

"Yes, I know," Veenah said. "I also know what you and

Lincoln did to Gelrut after he killed me. I want to be with you again, Skyra, and you want to be with me again. Lincoln is good to you, and I am happy you and Lincoln are married. You should leave this place that is not real. Then you can go many, many years to be with me again in the places that are real. We can again hunt in the Walukh foothills in warm seasons, and in the Dofusofu river valley in cold seasons."

Skyra gazed at her birthmate's round eyes as she enjoyed the feel of the cool stream flowing around her legs. This was a wonderful place. Skyra did not want to leave, but she knew she had to. She reached out and took Veenah's arm, then pulled her close until their foreheads touched.

Skyra closed her eyes and spoke. "Tekne-té-fofiyu-meleen. Aibul-meli-yabo-rha fekho lotup-mel-endü." *Your strength now lives in me. If I do not return, sister, find your way home.*

SKYRA OPENED her eyes and found she was back in the yellow room. The naked man was watching her, his teeth bared in a nandup smile. To one side stood Di-woto and the naked woman.

Di-woto rushed over to face Skyra. "Skyra! Skyra! These are my people! They remember me. They remember my mother Lo-aful. We will stay with these people, Skyra! I can make anything I want to make here. I have already made a fortress greater than any fortress I have ever planned. I made it myself!"

Skyra stared at the girl. Di-woto was now speaking Lincoln's language better than she had before. Her appearance was different too. The deep scars that had covered most of her skin were now gone. Her skin was soft-looking and smooth.

Di-woto turned in a circle. "Do you like the new garment I made?" Her multi-colored garment was gone. Now she was wearing a long garment that hung almost to her feet. It appeared to be made of thin, supple leather, like the soft skin from a hare, only it was much larger than the skin from a single hare. Scratched into the leather were many ornamental designs—spirals, swooping lines with bulges at each end, strange shapes, waves that looked like the surface of a lake, and even some outlines of animals.

"These markings are the same as your scars," Skyra said.

The girl lifted herself up onto her toes several times with excitement. "Yes, my scars! Now I can take them off when I want to. See? I can take them off!" She pulled the garment up and over her head in one swift motion, revealing the perfectly smooth skin of a girl who had probably seen no more than twelve cold seasons.

Di-woto gestured toward the naked woman who had taken her away. "My people here do not wear any clothing at all, but I like making garments, so I will keep wearing them when I want to."

Suddenly, Jazzlyn appeared beside Skyra. Unlike Di-woto, Jazzlyn still looked the same as she had before. Her eyes were wide, making the whites of her eyes stand out against the dark skin of her face. She blinked a few times then said, "Oh my God, you guys, you will not believe what just happened to me!"

Virgil appeared beside Jazzlyn. A breath later, Derek appeared beside Virgil. Both men were as wide-eyed as Jazzlyn and both blinked several times as they seemed to realize where they were.

"This is beyond anything I've ever imagined," Virgil said. "The realism, the responsiveness to mental commands, the seemingly unlimited range of possible... and... and the freaking colors. I just don't—"

"Just say awesome, Virg," Derek said. "That's all you need." Then he eyed Di-woto. "Why is that girl naked? Oh hell, her scars are gone! Good move, Di-woto."

Lincoln appeared in the middle of everyone else. Like the others, his eyes were as wide as a bolup's eyes could get. His chest was heaving, as if he'd been running, although he didn't need to breathe air in this place that was not real. He glanced around the room, and his eyes met Skyra's. "I don't know what you just experienced, but I hope it was as amazing as what I've seen."

"I was in my homeland. Veenah was there."

He smiled. "That's why this is so incredible. You can have whatever you want, whenever you want. Skyra, I created a place where we can live. I can't wait to show it to you."

She felt her brows furrowing. "No, Lincoln, we have to leave this place. You said yourself it is not real. You said you wanted these people to release us. I want to use the T3 to go many, many years and save the real Veenah."

His eyes narrowed slightly, and he glanced down at his hands as if he wasn't sure what to say next. When he looked up at her again, she could tell what he was thinking. Lincoln did not want to be a person of flesh anymore.

17

DECISION

***47,659 YEARS** in the future - Day 3*

LINCOLN GAZED into Skyra's eyes. He could see it in them—she did not want to be a person of thought. Perhaps he could show her what he had created. He could show her they could create an even more spectacular place together. They could make a beautiful and safe home, and they could live there forever. There was nothing they couldn't do. Maybe she didn't understand that concept yet.

A worrisome thought began creeping into Lincoln's consciousness. Maybe Skyra wasn't even capable of understanding what was possible in this virtual universe. She had been born 47,000 years before Lincoln and 95,000 years before the beings who had built this city. From what he had seen, her thinking was more concrete than abstract. Maybe she simply wasn't wired for virtual reality. If this was the case, no amount of practice or demonstration would help her adapt to such an existence.

"I want to use the T$_3$ and save Veenah," Skyra said.

"You were with Veenah just now. In this place you can be with Veenah any time you want. Veenah will be safe and happy."

Her eyes seemed to penetrate his virtual shell, searching for his real self somewhere inside. "I want you to put a child in my belly. Our child will be an alinga-ul like Di-woto."

Lincoln blinked, taken aback. How could he respond to that? He turned to the naked man and woman. "Are there any children in this environment?"

The woman answered. "Many years ago, some of our people created children so they could experience the pleasures involved with raising them. No one has done such a thing in a long time, however. Everyone in our population was originally extracted from a living nandup. Our system is not capable of generating a complete consciousness from scratch, so those children were relatively simple manifestations and did not develop intellectually in a way that was satisfying. Therefore, our people lost interest in such endeavors."

Lincoln gritted his virtual teeth. "I don't suppose there is any way people of thought can combine their DNA to make a child who is unique—none of you even have bodies with DNA anymore."

"Correct," the woman replied, "although you certainly can manifest a child in the same way you manifested a larger version of your drone and suns of four different colors."

So, these people had actually watched everything he'd done in his demonstration. What would prevent them from watching his every private moment from now on? Probably nothing. He turned to Skyra, and for a moment he considered creating a child right then and there. Maybe holding a baby in her arms would show her it was possible. The problem was, the baby would be no more than a product of his imagination, a *sunbeam*, as Skyra might call it. He decided not to even try.

She was still studying him. She put her palm on his chest. "I want to sleep with you each night. We will make love when we want to. I will teach you to hunt in a place where the game will escape if you do not become skilled." She pressed her palm against him harder. "I like to feel you breathing, but in this place you do not need to breathe. Do you understand, Lincoln?"

He closed his eyes, trying to avoid thinking about having the power to create anything he wanted. Perhaps he would become bored with such power and would eventually long for more tangible experiences. He opened his eyes and again turned to the man and woman. "Why do your people walk around as projections in the above-ground portion of this city?"

The man smiled as if he understood Lincoln's implication. "Many of us do that occasionally. Unfortunately, we cannot venture beyond the city into the surrounding wilderness, as the equipment needed for the experience is contained only within the city's boundaries."

Lincoln persisted. "Okay, but why do you do it?"

"For exactly the reasons you have surmised. The experience provides a connection to the physical world. We are completely safe when we do it, but there is always the slight chance we might come upon intruders—people of flesh. People like you, for example, or perhaps the feral people. Because people of flesh are capable of causing real damage, roaming about in the city does involve a possible connection to a real threat. You are correct—in an environment of complete safety, that connection is something many of us crave."

Lincoln had another question. "You stated your population includes 440,000 people. How many people did you have at the beginning, after everyone made the transition?"

The man's knowing smile persisted. "Your questions are astute. Our starting population within our simulated environment was slightly more than 500,000. Now you're going to ask what happened to the 60,000 others. Those people eventually requested to be terminated, and their requests were granted."

This was indeed the question Lincoln had wanted to ask, but he had another. "How long has it been since you started with 500,000?"

"Our tipping point, at which the entire population chose to make the transition, occurred 2,388 years ago."

"You've been in this virtual world almost twenty-four hundred years?" Virgil asked.

"We have."

Lincoln considered the man's answers. Sixty thousand people had apparently become fed up with this existence and had asked to be terminated, or erased, or whatever these people did to commit suicide. Sixty thousand was a lot of people. Then again, 2,388 years was a hell of a long time.

Derek spoke up. "You said 60,000 had their requests granted. How many made requests that were *not* granted?"

"Again, your questions are astute," the man said. "Nearly everyone makes this request occasionally. People inevitably experience periods of despair. Fortunately, these requests are rarely granted, and most people recover from their despair and return to a fulfilling existence."

"So, people can't even die without permission," Derek said.

The man just grinned, apparently choosing not to respond.

Lincoln exchanged glances with his team members. The general level of enthusiasm in the room was plainly beginning to falter.

Then there was Skyra, still staring at him. Waiting. Hopeful. Lincoln didn't understand when or how it had happened, but he loved the Neanderthal woman standing beside him. Would he do anything for her? Would he give up the closest thing to immortality he could imagine? Would he give up the ability to create anything his mind could conceive?

He turned back to the naked man and woman and gazed at them for several seconds. "If we agreed to leave your city and never return, would you let us go?"

The two virtual beings exchanged words in their strange language. Then the woman said, "You are hesitant to complete your transition into our environment. You do not like the idea of us disposing of your bodies of flesh. This is understandable. We think you will be pleased to hear we have come up with a solution—a compromise, if you will."

This was not what Lincoln expected. He felt his heart accelerating, although he had no idea if it was real or part of the simulation. "What kind of compromise?"

"We cannot allow people of flesh to live in or near our city, therefore we cannot simply release you. However, we have decided there is a way your bodies of flesh may benefit us."

"I really don't like the sound of that," Virgil said.

The woman glanced at Virgil. "Allow me to explain. While we have been talking to you, we also have been learning much from your robotic drone Ripple. The drone tells us you, as people of flesh, have a rather intriguing opportunity. It is an opportunity we, as people of thought, no longer have."

"Ripple told you about its plan," Lincoln said, shaking his head.

"Indeed, and what an intriguing plan it is. If you fully understood our history, you would know why the plan is so intriguing to us. Since Di-woto's time, we have known about alinga-uls—hybrids resulting from female nandups and male bolups. We have known these hybrids, although rare, exhibit what you refer to as heterosis, or hybrid vigor. They possess qualities superior to those of either parent. Due to our long history of conflict, however, our populations of nandups and bolups could never overcome the taboo of interbreeding. Widespread hybridization did not occur. Alinga-uls continued to be rare, so they had little impact on global diversity."

Lincoln listened, uncertain of where this explanation was going.

"Eventually the opportunity was lost," the woman said. "The devastating weapon we discussed earlier was activated, everyone was forced to live below ground, and we transitioned to people of thought and disposed of our bodies of flesh. We can no longer interbreed, and we can never produce alinga-uls."

The naked man took over. "You people, on the other hand, still have the opportunity we lost. Your robotic drone has determined the optimal historical time and place for you to initiate a change with potentially fascinating global consequences. You do know where that time and place is, do you not?"

Lincoln sighed. "Ripple has reminded us endlessly. It's Skyra's time, in the place where we first encountered her."

The man and woman gazed at him while raising their

thick nandup brows. "Yet you have repeatedly ignored Ripple's advice," the woman said. "You are reluctant to stay in our simulated environment, where you can create the world of your choosing, because you know it is not real. Now you have an opportunity to create an entirely real world that promises to be fascinating, and you are reluctant to do that as well?"

It occurred to Lincoln Ripple may be actually trying to do something to save their lives, perhaps somehow trying to negotiate their release. "You mentioned something about a compromise?"

"We will allow you to remain as people of flesh and release you if you will take advantage of the opportunity Ripple has created for you," the man said.

Skyra grabbed Lincoln's arm. "They are going to let us go back to my homeland, Lincoln!"

Derek said, "Uh, maybe we need to discuss this?"

Lincoln pulled away from Skyra's grip and turned to face his team. He wavered for only a moment, trying to force himself to speak before he changed his mind. "I'm sorry, guys, but if they'll actually let us go, I'm doing it. I'm taking Skyra to the T3, and we're jumping back to her time. I wouldn't blame you if you chose to stay here, and I would miss all of you, but Skyra isn't suited for this place. I'm staying with her."

They all gazed at him. Jazzlyn looked at her left hand, which now appeared to be flesh and bone instead of titanium and carbon polymer. She opened and closed her fingers. "Lincoln, I...."

"I understand," he said. "If I were you, I don't think—"

"You must leave your T3 with us," the woman said, cutting him off.

He spun around to face her. "What?"

The woman eyed him intently. "We are profoundly fascinated by your story of temporal distortion technology, and we would like to learn from your T_3 device. Ripple informs us that you can make one more jump while leaving the T_3 behind. You will leave it with us. That is the compromise we are offering."

The room remained silent for several awkward seconds.

Skyra grabbed Lincoln's arm again. "You said we could only use the T_3 one more time. You said that, Lincoln! After we jump, we cannot use the T_3 again anyway."

She was right, he *had* said that, but if the others decided to stay here, there would be enough body bags for him and Skyra to make another jump. What if they needed to escape a life-or-death situation? It was certainly possible to make a jump and leave the T_3 here—all they had to do was not enclose the T_3 in its last custom-sized body bag. However, the thought of jumping back to Skyra's time without his T_3 was deeply disturbing to Lincoln.

Out of habit, he drew in a deep breath, then he nodded to Skyra. "You're right, we can leave it here." He turned and spoke to the naked woman and man. "Our T_3 is miles beyond the city, out in the wilderness."

"Our robotic caretakers will accompany you to the location," the man said. "They will not allow you to enclose your T_3 in its body bag. They will carry the T_3 device back to us after you jump, and they will serve as physical extensions of our minds as we take the device apart and study it."

The woman said, "Di-woto is valuable to us. She will remain here and complete her transition. Lincoln and Skyra, you will take advantage of Ripple's plan and jump back to Skyra's time. Derek, Virgil, and Jazzlyn, you may remain here and complete your transition if you wish, although we encourage you to accompany Lincoln and Skyra. We believe you could play a more important role in Ripple's plan than you know."

The man and woman fell silent, apparently waiting for a decision.

18

BURNING BRIDGE

47,659 YEARS *in the future - Day 4*

SKYRA AWOKE TO DARKNESS. Her head hurt. She tried to move, but something hard was pushing against all sides of her arms and legs—she was back inside the body-shaped container. Faint, muffled sounds came from beyond. Something bumped against the container, which did not help her headache.

How long had it been since she was in the yellow room with Lincoln and the others?

Several clicks vibrated through the container, then the top portion was lifted. Everything was still dark, so she raised her arms to make sure the area was clear for her to sit up. Something grabbed both her wrists and pulled her up, then something grabbed her neck. Skyra quickly realized what was happening and decided struggling would only make things worse, so she relaxed. Within a few breaths she was pulled from the container and dropped onto the hard back of one of the caretaker creatures. With her neck and leg held firmly in place by a second creature, Skyra was carried through the darkness.

"Lincoln, are you here?" she managed to ask.

"Yeah, I think I'm behind you. Don't try to fight, okay?"

"You'd think... they'd find a better way... to transport us," Derek's voice said from somewhere ahead.

Skyra folded her free leg and tucked it beneath her leg being pressed to the creature's back, trying to find a bit of comfort, then she waited.

Finally, a faint light shone ahead. The creatures kept moving toward it, then they carried her up a ramp. She closed her eyes against the sunlight streaming through the tall windows surrounding the ground floor of one of the buildings.

The creatures stopped. They lifted Skyra and stood her on her feet.

She opened her eyes, squinting. Lincoln was standing beside her now, grimacing and rubbing his neck. Jazzlyn, Virgil, and Derek were there also, checking their own bodies for injuries—or perhaps checking to make sure they were real. Two of the caretaker creatures stood motionless beside each of them, maybe ready to capture them again if they tried to run. Skyra turned, scanning the huge chamber. It was empty except for the familiar chairs and tables that were part of the floor.

"Everybody okay?" Lincoln asked. His voice was still hoarse from having his throat squeezed.

"Nothing appears to be broken," Virgil said, rubbing his neck.

Jazzlyn and Derek each mumbled something about still being alive.

Lincoln gazed at Skyra.

"I am not hurt," she said.

He nodded toward the two strange creatures beside him, each about four times his size. "I guess these guys intend to come with us."

"Skyra! Skyra!"

Skyra spun around. Di-woto's voice had come from the darkness of the ramp.

The girl came running up the ramp. She paused when she got into the full light to stare at her own hand. Skyra stared too. Di-woto was not real. The chairs and tables behind her could be seen through her body.

"Look at me, Skyra. I am a ghost!"

The girl's voice did not sound right—it seemed to be coming from her belly instead of her mouth.

"Whoa," Jazzlyn said, "that was quick. How does she already know how to do that?"

"My people showed me how to be a projection while you were sleeping," Di-woto said to Jazzlyn. Then she stepped in front of Skyra and held her hand out with her palm facing to one side. "Play, Skyra!"

Skyra stared at the girl's transparent face, then at her transparent hand.

"Play!" Di-woto demanded, grinning. "Try to hit."

Skyra held her hand out, studied the girl's transparent eyes for a moment, then swiped her hand directly through Di-woto's hand.

Di-woto giggled, lifting herself to her toes several times. "You cannot hit!"

Lincoln stepped beside Skyra, staring at the girl. "What does it feel like as a projection? Is your real body still inside the container they trapped you in?"

"No body now," Di-woto said, still giggling.

The naked woman's voice came from the dark ramp. "Di-woto is no longer a person of flesh."

The woman and man came to the top of the ramp. Like Di-woto, they were now transparent. More transparent people came up the ramp behind them, then even more after those. Soon there were more than Skyra could count, with more still coming. All of them were naked, and all of them had short dark hair. As the transparent people poured from the tunnel, they spread out into the tall chamber and stood silently, as if waiting.

The woman said, "Di-woto completed her transition to our environment while you were dormant. She is now a person of thought, and we have disposed of her body of flesh."

"Great," Derek said with anger in his voice. "How long were we dormant?"

"We needed to wait until morning before you could travel to your T3," the woman explained. "Therefore, we made your bodies dormant so you would feel rested this morning."

Skyra gazed at the morning light reflecting off the other buildings outside. She noticed the pile of wreckage in the street and realized her group had been returned to their own building, where the strange caretaker creatures had captured them.

She turned to Di-woto. "Are you sure you want to stay?" It was probably too late, but she wanted to ask anyway.

Di-woto smiled, like she always smiled. "These are my people, Skyra. I am happy to be with them now. I have not been happy before. I will make beautiful garments, and buildings, and many other beautiful things."

Skyra tried to study Di-woto's eyes, but her focus kept shifting to things she could see through the girl's head. She did not understand how Di-woto had changed. She did not understand how Di-woto could now speak Lincoln's language. The girl seemed happy, though. That was something Skyra understood.

The naked woman spoke. "As this is a historic event, some of us wish to walk with you to our city's boundary. At that point, as we agreed, our robotic caretakers will escort you the rest of the distance to your T_3. They will provide any assistance or protection you might need."

The massive creatures frightened Skyra, but if they would help protect her and her friends, she would be glad to have them nearby.

"Excuse me. Coming through. Pardon me, please."

Skyra scanned the chamber at the sound of Ripple's voice.

"Pardon me, could you... well, never mind, I'll just..."

Skyra could now see Ripple walking directly through the legs of some of the transparent people who were gathered around.

The creature finally got through them all and stopped at Skyra's feet. "Skyra, I am pleased beyond measure to see that you and Lincoln are still people of flesh."

"Yeah, we're here too," Derek said.

Ripple pivoted briefly toward Lincoln's tribemates. "And you as well."

Lincoln patted his pocket, then he pulled out the flat object that was Maddy's brain. He studied it for a moment as if he just wanted to make sure it wasn't broken.

The naked man said, "Maddy's cognitive module was not damaged by our inquiries, nor was Ripple's. They did, however, provide us with much useful information."

Lincoln nodded and shoved Maddy's brain back into his pocket.

Ripple said, "The last nineteen hours have proved most

interesting, and I am pleased with the outcome. It seems my plan now stands a fair chance of coming to fruition after all."

"You can daydream about your plan all you want," Jazzlyn said. "The rest of us will be focused on just staying alive." Jazzlyn gave Skyra and Lincoln a funny look. "Don't worry, I'm not changing my mind. Just speaking the truth."

"We're giving up immortality for the land of teeth, claws, and spears," Derek added. "Maybe we should get the hell out of here before I *do* change my mind."

"We have gathered some supplies for you," the naked woman said, gesturing to another caretaker creature now walking up the ramp from the darkness below. A bundle as large as the creature itself was attached to its back. "Unfortunately, we cannot send our robotic caretakers with you when you jump back in time, as you will have no source of power to operate them. Also, our caretakers are our only means of defense, therefore we have no weapons to offer you. What we can offer that you might find useful is some of our reflective window material, tubing for constructing framework supports for the material, and several tools useful for working with these supplies."

Lincoln said, "I'm not sure how much of that we can fit into our body bags, but we'll take as much as we can. Thank you for offering it."

Skyra was ready to leave. With every breath, more transparent naked people were emerging from the tunnel, and now they almost filled the entire ground floor chamber. The last time she had seen this many people was in the sanctuary-fortress of Kyran-yufost, and that did not go so well.

She glanced at the nearest ramp to the second level then walked directly through the ghost people to get to it. She eyed the slope and smiled—her weapons were still there, where the attacking caretaker creature had tossed them. After inserting her khul into its sling and shoving her hand blades into her wrist sheath, she returned to Lincoln's side, again passing through transparent bodies.

"Uh, hold on a second," Derek said, then he too ran through the transparent people. He continued up the ramp and out of sight. Soon he came running back with his pack of supplies.

Skyra's eyes met Lincoln's. "I liked living in this building with you, but that was before, when we thought we were alone. Too many people are here now."

He gave a slight nod, but he did not smile. He was worried. Maybe he was afraid to go back to Skyra's homeland. Maybe he still wanted to be a person of thought and live in the land that was not real. She tried to smile at him, but it felt like a lie. Skyra was afraid too.

As THE GROUP approached the edge of the city, Skyra turned to look back. Following close behind were nine of the massive caretakers, one of them with the bundle of supplies on its back. Behind the creatures, so many transparent people were following that Skyra could not see through them all. They were watching, silently, apparently believing something important was happening. Skyra was not sure these people could talk. She had only heard two of them speak—the man and woman who had been in the yellow room.

The man and woman were walking between Skyra and Lincoln, so Skyra asked if they had names.

The man replied, "We all have names, although we rarely use them anymore. When speaking to each other, our identity, as well as the identity of the intended audience, is embedded in the structure of the words spoken. In fact, we often speak with visual images. Concrete words, including names, are unnecessary."

Skyra had no idea what this meant. "What is your name?"

"I used to be known as Kods," the man replied.

"I was known as Thide," said the woman.

"Kods and Thide, I want you to protect Di-woto. I will not be here to keep her safe."

After a few breaths of silence, Thide said, "Danger does not exist in our environment, so she needs no protection."

Skyra glanced back at Di-woto, who was walking behind her. Skyra wasn't sure if Di-woto was listening, but the girl flashed a transparent smile.

"Even if Di-woto's body cannot be hurt, her *mind* can be hurt," Skyra said. "I want you to protect her."

"I understand," Thide said. "Di-woto is important to us, and we will protect her."

The group walked past many buildings in silence, followed by the mass of ghost people. Lincoln and his tribemates were quieter than usual, and again Skyra wondered if they wished they could stay in the land that was not real. Or maybe they simply did not like to talk when so many other people were nearby.

They all stopped where the hard city street ended and the forest began. Lincoln and his tribemates exchanged looks, but still they remained silent.

Kods said, "Many of us wish we could walk with you into the wilderness. As projections, though, we cannot venture beyond this point."

Di-woto came around to Skyra's front and gazed at her. Skyra could see the trees through the girl's head. "You are a good friend to me, Skyra. I will talk about you to my people, and they will know I could not have stopped the fighting of nandups and bolups without you. I wish you and Lincoln and Derek and Jazzlyn and Virgil could stay here with me."

Skyra reflexively reached for the girl's shoulders but only grabbed a sunbeam, so she let her hands drop back to her sides. "I wish I could see the beautiful garments you will make, Di-woto." She paused, then she said, "Aibul-epu melu lotup-mel-endü. Those are words of my Una-Loto tribe. They mean, *I hope you find your way home, friend.*"

Di-woto flashed a broad alinga-ul smile and said, "Skyra, tekne-té-melu-fofiyu-meleen."

Skyra stared, surprised. The girl had said, *Skyra, your strength now lives in me.* How had Di-woto learned to speak Una-Loto words? Skyra decided not to ask. She probably would not understand the answer anyway. Instead, she smiled at the girl, then she stepped onto the weeds and soil. The softness of it beneath her footwraps felt better than the hard street. She took a few steps to the nearest trees and stared into the forest to wait for Lincoln and the others. She did not want to look back at the mass of transparent people, and she definitely did not want to look back at Di-woto.

Lincoln and his tribemates spoke to the ghost people for many more breaths, but Skyra did not care to hear the words. She waited, listening instead to the countless beetles scuttling among the grasses and dead leaves at her feet.

Ripple stepped up beside her. "I will guide us far around the yellowjacket colony. However, we might encounter other colonies. I suggest you prepare a defensive sheet of the reflective material, to be safe. I doubt the robotic caretakers can protect you from thousands of wasps. There will also be the prairie dogs, and perhaps badgers, as well as other dangers we have not yet encountered."

"I know all those things," she said, still staring into the trees.

Ripple was silent for several breaths. "Do you regret leaving the simulated environment of Kods, Thide, and their people?"

"No."

"Do you wish Di-woto were coming with us?"

"No. She will be happier here."

Ripple was silent for a few more breaths. "Perhaps you are concerned about what will happen after we get to the T3."

Skyra looked down at her companion. "You are starting to talk as much as Lincoln and the other bolups."

"Sometimes talking is important."

"I do not know what will happen after we get to the T3."

"Are you worried?" Ripple asked.

She did not reply.

"Lincoln's future self liked to say, 'Worrying is like burning your bridge before you cross it.'"

Skyra frowned. "What is a bridge?"

"A bridge is a structure people build to walk across a river. However, the point of Lincoln's words is that you should not worry about something that has not yet happened. The worrying itself might result in an outcome you do not want."

"Why would someone burn a structure made for walking over a river?"

"A reasonable person would not burn a bridge, particularly before they have crossed it. That is the point."

Skyra growled. "It does not make sense."

"I was simply trying to cheer you up."

She chewed on her lip. Why was Lincoln taking so long?

Still, she did not want to turn around and see Di-woto. She wanted to remember the girl as a person of flesh, not a ghost.

Finally, the ground beneath her feet shook slightly as the nine robotic caretakers stepped from the city street onto the soil and walked up beside her. Lincoln and his tribemates were with them.

It was time to go back to the T3.

19

CARETAKERS

***47,659 years** in the future - Day 4*

"What if the T3 is damaged?" Derek asked. "What if we get there and animals have chewed it up? Hell, what if it's not even there, or we can't find our way?"

Lincoln had no idea what would happen to them in any of those scenarios, but there was no point in worrying about it. "Right now I'm more concerned about making it there safely." He nodded toward the nearest of the robotic caretakers. "As massive as these things are, a yellowjacket colony will detect our presence from a quarter-mile away."

"We need the reflective material to protect us," Skyra said. She stepped over to the robot carrying the bundle on its back and put her hands on the reflective material covering the contents. "Stop walking, creature! We want to get something from your back."

The robot stopped. Abruptly, six of the other eight robots shuffled into a circular formation around the group.

"Uh, what are they doing?" Jazzlyn asked.

The robots drew in closer, forcing Lincoln and the others into a tight huddle. The surrounding caretakers began coming apart, breaking down into their rat-sized components. The smaller robots clicked and skittered, crawling over each other and snapping into place, quickly forming a wall around the people of flesh. The wall grew upward and inward, creating a dome over the group. Seconds later the last few clicked into place at the dome's peak, leaving Lincoln and his companions in darkness beneath.

Everything became silent.

Jazzlyn's voice came from beside Lincoln. "Okay, creepy as hell. Now my question is, *why* are they—"

The top of the dome opened, letting in a beam of sunlight. The skittering rat-robots started clambering over each other again, widening the hole, then dismantling the circular wall, and finally snapping back into place as six heavy robots. The caretakers stepped back to their original positions, allowing Lincoln and the others the space to move apart.

"These creatures do not talk," Skyra said. "They show how they will protect us from wasps."

Virgil stepped closer to one of the caretakers, staring at the area where its two arms protruded from its shell. "I suppose it makes sense that they cannot talk aloud. They probably receive their instructions wirelessly from the main computer system. I imagine they report back in the same manner." He leaned in closer, squinting through his glasses. "They must have heard us talking about yellowjackets, but how on Earth can they even hear?" He tapped the robot shell, his fingertip making a dull thud like it would against a brick. "Do you understand what I'm saying?"

The caretaker didn't respond.

Virgil shook his head. "I don't see any vision lenses, either. I wish we'd asked more questions when we had the chance. Ripple, did they tell you much about these robots?"

The drone said, "They did not offer, and I did not ask. I was rather preoccupied with negotiating a deal to save your lives."

Lincoln felt a slight urge to chuckle. "I thought that idea might have come from you. I guess we owe you one." He glanced at his team members. They didn't seem too convinced they had made the right choice.

Derek let out an exaggerated sigh, stroking his beard with his fingers. "About that. Just so you know, I was creating a home for myself—on my own private island. Eighty rooms in the house, and I was just getting started. I was in the process of populating the surrounding waters with mermaids when I got pulled back into that damn yellow room. A few mermen, but mostly mermaids. Hundreds of them. Good looking ones, too."

Everyone stared at him.

"Seriously?" Jazzlyn said. "*That's* what you chose to do?"

Lincoln decided he'd better not describe what he'd done with his brief time in the virtual world.

Derek frowned. "I'm just telling that damn drone what it did was a little more complex than just saving our lives. It actually thinks it was doing us a big favor." He held his hands out and shook them for emphasis. "Mermaids, goddammit!"

Ripple's ring of lights flashed red. "Derek, I have applied your second checkmark. As I have said, earning three checkmarks is to be avoided."

"Ooooh, Derek's in trooouuble!" Jazzlyn said.

Lincoln felt his lips forming a smile. His team was proving more resilient with each new challenge. He turned to Skyra.

She had that look on her face, like she was going to say something about the strangeness of bolups. "Sometimes this is how my people show that they are okay," he said.

She didn't look very convinced. "Now we will go to the T3."

"Yeah," he said. He studied her face for a moment. "Skyra, we don't know for sure if the T3 will still work. Even if it does, we don't know what will happen when we jump back to your time. There are some complications I haven't discussed with you yet. Plus, we don't know for sure if we can save Veenah. There are many things that could go wrong."

She gazed at him for a moment with her ample lips pursed. "Do not burn your bridge before you cross it, Lincoln." She turned and resumed walking east, toward the T3.

He stared after her for a moment, wondering where she had heard those words.

The nine massive robots began stomping after Skyra.

Lincoln raised his brows at his team, and they resumed walking, with Ripple bringing up the rear.

"That second checkmark was unwarranted," Derek said. "You need to remove it."

"Not possible," replied Ripple. "Checkmarks, once in place, cannot be deleted."

THE DENSE FOREST gradually gave way to open grassy hilltops divided by low areas of sparse trees. Lincoln knew they were traveling in the correct general direction, but he was pretty sure he'd have a hard time finding the T3 on his own. Fortunately, the group hadn't had to test the caretakers' effectiveness at protecting them from ground hornets, but unless they were far off the path they had used to get to the city, they were going to have to cross the field of prairie dogs at some point.

The nine ever-silent caretakers were keeping pace, flanking Lincoln and the others with four on either side and the one carrying the bundle behind them. The robots had obviously been instructed to provide protection, but Lincoln supposed their primary purpose was to make sure the humans held up their end of the bargain by leaving behind the T_3. Although the robots didn't have detectable vision lenses, Lincoln was sure they would somehow monitor the setup process and would not allow his team to enclose the T_3 in its body bag before jumping. Then they would carry the T_3 back to the city for reverse engineering.

Virgil had been silent for some time, apparently in deep thought. Now he spoke. "Logic would dictate I should be petrified about jumping back to Skyra's time to live out the rest of our lives, however short they may be. I take comfort, though, in the fact that we've been there before. We know what to expect."

"Yeah, hardship and barbarism," Derek said. "And not one single mermaid."

Virgil ignored him. "I've been examining some scenarios. Lincoln, you had the T_3 run a new placement calculation for Skyra's time, correct? I assume you wanted to avoid the exact same insertion time and place we had originally jumped to?"

"Yeah, I ran the new calculation, which didn't get finished until after we were forced to jump here. Same insertion location, but one hour earlier."

Virgil frowned. "Why the same location? I thought that would—"

"No," Lincoln interjected. "I discussed this with Ripple. The drone pointed out we won't have to worry about colliding with ourselves if we arrive earlier."

"Ah, I get it," Vigil said. "Our arrival one hour earlier creates a new timeline, therefore our other selves only show up in the timeline we created the first time we jumped there. We won't collide with them because they'll never exist in the new timeline we'll create."

"Exactly," Lincoln said. Then he waited for Virgil or one of the others to recognize an issue that had been nagging at him for some time.

Surprisingly, Skyra spoke first. "We will jump many, many years, and we will be at the same place where I found you before?"

"Oh crap," Jazzlyn said.

"Oh crap," Virgil said a split-second later. "Skyra's going to be there."

"Skyra *and* Ripple," Jazzlyn added.

Lincoln grimaced and nodded.

"What does that mean?" Skyra asked.

"It means you and Ripple will already be in that area when we get there," Lincoln said, watching her closely to gauge her response. "We will arrive there, beside that river, about an hour before your other self and the other Ripple get there. It's not completely certain because things could go differently during that hour, but it's likely the other Skyra will be running from bolup men who are trying to kill her."

Skyra stared at the ground as she walked, chewing on her lower lip. She turned back to Lincoln. "What is an hour?"

"An hour is about how long we've been walking since we left the city."

Her face brightened. "I have a plan, Lincoln."

He waited, but she didn't elaborate. "What is it?"

"I am still thinking about it."

Lincoln figured she wouldn't share the plan until she was ready, so he let it go for now. Besides, it was premature to start worrying now about what might happen after the jump. Countless problems could occur in the next few hours to prevent the jump from taking place at all.

"As usual, everything we're doing is uncharted territory," Virgil said. "Perhaps we should run another placement calculation, maybe to arrive there a full day before the original insertion time—or even a full week. We could get to Skyra's sister sooner, maybe even prevent the horrible abuse she took from her captors."

"I thought of that," Lincoln said. "The new calculations could take up to thirty hours." He tilted his head toward the nearest of the robotic caretakers. "I doubt these things—or the beings controlling them—would tolerate that kind of wait. Heck, they may not even have enough reserve power to be away from the city for that long. It *is* worth a try, though." He turned and nudged Skyra's elbow. "How long do you think those bolups who took Veenah were camped in the spot where you found them?"

"Bolups in my land do not camp in one place for long. I do not understand why, but they like to move their camps every few days."

Then arriving several days earlier would be too risky. If the bolups weren't camped in the same location, Lincoln's group might never find them. It probably wouldn't do any good to wait for the bolups to arrive there, either—in the new timeline some random detail could cause the bolups to change their course and choose a completely different site to set up their camp. Maybe Lincoln's group could jump back to a time before Veenah was taken by the bolups in the first place. Would they be able to stop the attack on Skyra's Una-Loto camp? Or could Skyra sneak in and convince Veenah to leave with her while also avoiding her other self? No telling what would happen if the two Skyras came face-to-face in the midst of her nandup tribemates.

Lincoln blew out a frustrated sigh. There were too many unknowns, too many parameters to consider.

"You're looking at this all wrong," Derek said. "It's already been decided we're jumping back to Skyra's time, so I won't try to convince you otherwise, but why are you considering changing our arrival time by only an hour, or a day, or a week? If you're going to run thirty hours of calculations, why not change it so we arrive a hundred years before Skyra and her sister were even born? Problem eliminated. No other Skyra to confuse things, and no sister who needs saving."

Ripple had been walking in silence, but now the drone spoke up. "Perhaps you do not understand the essence of my plan, Derek. Skyra is genetically unique among Neanderthals. Veenah, Skyra's genetic twin, is therefore also unique. Having both of them alive, instead of only one, greatly increases the likelihood of my plan's success."

Derek huffed. "I thought your plan involved Lincoln and Skyra having babies. You know, because Lincoln is *special* too."

"That is correct," Ripple said in its gender-neutral voice.

"So how does Veenah play into this? Is Lincoln supposed to have babies with both sisters?"

"That would be the best solution," the drone said. "However, I suspect Lincoln's adherence to societal customs of monogamy may preclude it. Virgil would be my second choice as a reasonable match for Veenah, but I have detected his poorly-disguised signs of amorous attraction to Jazzlyn."

Jazzlyn flashed Virgil an embarrassed smile. Virgil just shook his head.

Ripple continued. "By systematically eliminating more preferable candidates, I reluctantly concede that you, Derek, are the remaining possibility."

"Jesus," Derek muttered. "Lincoln, why in the hell did you code this thing to be such a smartass? Did you actually think it would be funny?"

"You're talking about something I haven't done yet," Lincoln said.

Derek huffed again. "We haven't even saved Skyra's sister —and who knows if we even can—but this damn drone is trying to set me up? Anyway, Veenah probably already has her eyes on some guy named Gok, or Zork, or something like that."

"I have already told you Veenah would like you," Skyra said to Derek. "There is no Gok or Zork in Una-Loto tribe, so you do not have to worry about them."

"Jesus," he muttered again. He fell silent, perhaps deciding he was outnumbered and outgunned.

The group passed through a narrow strip of forest, crossed a tiny stream, then started up a hill on the other side. Lincoln thought the area looked familiar, and when they reached the hill's summit, there was no doubt. The nine robotic chaperones surrounding them came to a stop as the group stared out at the wide field beyond the hill, populated by thousands of carnivorous prairie dogs.

20

ARMS AND LEGS

47,659 YEARS *in the future - Day 4*

SKYRA'S LEGS did not want to go down the hill to the prairie dog town, but Lincoln seemed to think the strange caretaker creatures would protect the group. She was not so sure. The creatures could form a dome around them, but how would that help them get across the field?

"Might as well get this shitshow over with," Derek said. He started down the hillside. The caretaker creatures on either side and behind the group started down the hill too, forcing Skyra and the others to follow Derek.

Some of the prairie dogs were already standing on their mounds, keeping watch as the group approached. Skyra could see several of the dark patches of dung in the distance, with insects swarming above them.

By the time they reached the bottom of the hill and started across the field, more prairie dogs were standing on their mounds.

HOSTILE EMERGENCE

Skyra turned to the caretaker creature walking beside her. "These animals are going to attack us. There will be too many to fight off. We are going to run."

The creature stopped, then its companions stopped. They began coming apart. Skyra thought they were going to form another dome, but the creatures did not make a circle around her group. Instead, the loose rat-sized creatures moved into small clusters. They began locking together again, and within a few breaths all the caretakers except for the one carrying the bundle of supplies had formed numerous creatures only slightly larger than the prairie dogs. These smaller caretakers each had four short legs but no arms and no head.

"I hope they know what they're doing," Jazzlyn said.

Derek said, "Let's just get across this damn field."

"Let's go," Lincoln said, taking Skyra by the arm.

They continued walking, surrounded now by the smaller caretakers and followed by the massive caretaker carrying their bundle.

A shrill whistle sounded from one side, followed by more whistles from different directions.

"They will attack us now," Skyra said. Her legs would no longer wait, and she started running.

"Skyra, hold on!" Lincoln cried. "Look at this."

She forced her legs to stop. Some of the prairie dogs were charging, but now the small caretakers were spreading out to meet them. All around Skyra's group the caretakers clashed with the prairie dogs. Shrill distress cries arose from every direction as blood spewed and prairie dog body parts flopped loosely onto the ground. The caretakers were slicing the creatures to pieces, perhaps with blades hidden inside their bodies.

Skyra's group was becoming surrounded by a ring of

shredded prairie dogs. Not a single live one had gotten through the barrier. More were surging in from all directions, but they only added to the growing ring of mangled fur, bones, and entrails.

"I guess they *do* know what they're doing," Jazzlyn said.

The ring of bodies was as high as Skyra's knees before the prairie dogs seemed to realize what was happening. They stopped advancing. Most of them rose to their hind legs and stared, creating a field of brown heads.

The ring of caretakers began moving, still keeping its shape as it headed for the hills on the far side of the field. Skyra and the others had no choice but to move with the caretakers, stepping over the pile of bodies. Prairie dogs scampered out of the way, now unwilling to be cut to pieces.

As the group neared the base of the hill, Skyra turned to look back. The prairie dogs were now gathering around the ring of bodies, crawling over each other to get to the new supply of fresh meat.

After the group climbed to the hilltop, the caretakers stopped. The creatures broke apart into their rat-sized parts. They moved together, clicking and snapping, forming the eight four-legged, two-armed creatures once again.

Skyra scanned the faces of her companions. They were all silently staring at the feeding frenzy taking place in the field below. Even Derek had nothing to say. "I wish we could bring the caretakers with us many, many years to my homeland," she said.

"Yeah," Lincoln replied quietly.

She began walking away from the prairie dog town then turned and waited for the others.

As the others caught up, Ripple said, "Lincoln, had you provided me with at least a modicum of weapons, I could be more useful in such situations. Yes, you gave me extreme intelligence, and I'm rather good looking, but a few weapons would have been prudent."

Gradually the landscape began to resemble the area where they had left the T3, and Skyra had to suck in deep breaths of air to keep her chest from getting so tight that it hurt. She had agreed to leave her homeland to go with Lincoln to his land. She had wanted to be with him in the place where she would not worry about predators and roaming tribes of bolups, but Lincoln had decided it was no longer possible to ever get back to his land because it was in a different timeline.

Skyra did not like the land of Kyran-yufost, and she no longer liked the land of ghost people. She did not understand these places and hoped to never see them again. So, she sucked in chestfuls of air, trying not to burn her bridge before crossing it. The T3 would either work, or it wouldn't work. They would either save Veenah, or they wouldn't. She and her friends would either live, or they would die.

Lincoln was willing to go many, many years back to Skyra's homeland, although she believed he did not actually want to stay there forever. She knew Jazzlyn, Virgil, and Derek did not want to return there, but it appeared they were also willing to go. Skyra was sure they would like her homeland eventually. She would show them how to survive there, and show them the beauty of the foothills and river valleys. Maybe someday they would like it.

"I know you are afraid of my homeland and my Una-Loto tribe," she said to the others as they crossed a narrow valley toward yet another hill. "Lincoln killed Vall, and together we killed Brillir and Durnin. I am sure Gelrut is now dead because of what we did to him. Those were the tribemates I feared most, and now they are gone."

"Well, actually, we're jumping back to a point in time before we killed those four men," Lincoln said. "They're going to be alive when we get there. All the bolups we killed to rescue Veenah? They're going to be alive too."

Skyra considered Lincoln's words. Traveling many, many years with the T_3 was hard to understand. "Then we will not go to Una-Loto camp," she said. "We will make our own camp. I will show you things about my homeland I like, then you will like them too. I have seen things that not even my tribemates have seen. I have seen these things because I would often run away from the Una-Loto men and not return until they had forgotten why they wanted to hurt me. There is a valley high in the Walukh hills where many hares can be found. In the early days of the warm season, many luru flowers grow there, and the whole valley is yellow because of the flowers. When you stand in the valley you can hear the bees flying from flower to flower."

This thought caused other pleasant memories to flood into Skyra's mind, so she kept speaking. "There is a stream of cold, clear water in the Dofusofu river valley where you can find a strange creature among the rocks near the water. The creature is a salamander, and it is like a frog with a long tail. It is strange because of its colors. Part of it is black, but other parts are yellow, as yellow as the brightest luru flowers. Under the rocks in the same stream you can find crayfish with blue tails. Those are the best crayfish I have ever eaten, and there are so many you could never catch them all.

"When the warm season goes away and the cold season begins, there are places in the foothills where reindeer like to travel as they move down from the Kapolsek mountains. Sometimes there are so many reindeer you cannot see the end of the herd. No matter how far you look, there are still more.

"In the warm season, just as the sun decides to hide itself in the evenings, you can look out over the river valley and see the shadows of the boulders moving. The shadows grow longer as you watch, and sometimes they look like many creatures running across the fields like they are afraid the sun will start a fire in the grasses when it touches the hilltops."

Lincoln and his tribemates were watching her as they walked.

"Your homeland does sound lovely," Jazzlyn said.

Lincoln took Skyra's hand and held it. "You will show us how to survive there, and once we set up a safe camp, I'm sure we'll learn to love your homeland as much as you do."

"That's the spirit," Ripple said. "Perhaps we will call it the Una-Loto-Woodhouse camp."

Derek let out a grunt.

At the hill's summit, Skyra recognized where they were. This was the hilltop where she and Lincoln had first spotted the city and the swarm of bats. "We are almost there!"

"The T_3 is less than one kilometer from our current position," Ripple added.

"What is the plan if the T_3 doesn't work?" Virgil asked. "I imagine these robots will insist on taking it back to the city regardless of what happens to us."

"We'll just follow them back," Derek said. "We'll tell Kods and Thide we want to be people of thought after all."

Skyra swallowed a growl that almost escaped from her throat. She did not want to be a person of thought. Maybe the bolups did, but she would rather live in this dangerous land by herself than become a sunbeam. She decided not to say anything about it, though, and she remained silent as they descended the hill then passed through a swath of trees. The T_3 was beyond the next hill.

They all climbed the slope in silence. As they made their way across the wide, flat summit, Skyra caught the scent of some kind of creature. The scent was musky and a little putrid, causing her skin to prickle in alarm. "There is something near. I do not like its smell."

The caretaker creatures walking ahead of them and on either side came to a stop.

"I do not like this!" Skyra hissed at Lincoln. "My legs want to run."

"The robots must have detected something too," he whispered back. He took her hand again and pulled her along with him until they could look over the hill's edge into the valley beyond.

"Aw, shit," Derek said. "This can't be good."

The valley was filled with shiny, glittering things reflecting the sunlight. Some of the things were moving, then Skyra realized they were not things at all—they were actually people wearing shiny garments. Some were sitting on the ground in groups. Others were sitting alone, perhaps working on weapons or preparing food. There were even children, chasing each other in and out of the groups of adults. Apparently this was an entire tribe, with far more people than Skyra's Una-Loto tribe.

The T_3 was in the open, sitting in the middle of all the people. Lincoln's bags, and the supplies those bags had contained, were spread on the ground around the T_3. Even the brown body bags were stretched out on the ground—four small body bags and the large bag for covering the T_3.

All nine caretaker creatures were now standing still at the top of the slope, as if trying to decide what to do next. Skyra's legs were telling her to step back from the slope to hide, but it was too late now. Some of the people below were getting to their feet and pointing. Within a few more breaths most of them were staring up the slope at Skyra's group. Her skin began to prickle even more as some of the people began picking up weapons she recognized—khuls and short spears, and some even had bows and arrows, like those used by bolup men in her homeland.

"These must be the wild people Kods and Thide told us about," Lincoln said. "I guess people of flesh aren't extinct here after all."

"Amazing," Jazzlyn said. "It looks like they're wearing clothing made from reflective material from the buildings."

"Let's hope they're friendly." Virgil added.

Skyra pulled her khul from its sling. "They do not smell friendly—they are unclean and savage. There are too many for us to fight."

Lincoln put his arms out as if stopping the others from charging down the hill. "Just hold on. Remember, we have nine caretaker robots to protect us. If these people scavenge reflective material from cities, they should have a healthy respect for the robots. I imagine we'll be able to scare them off."

All the wild people were now on their feet, although they had not started moving up the hillside.

Skyra stepped to the nearest caretaker creature, which, like all the others, seemed frozen in place. She tapped its shell with her knuckles. "We cannot fight all these wild people, and they have our T3. Can you protect us from this many?"

The creature responded by coming apart. Its companions

came apart too, their rat creatures snapping loose and crawling to the ground around them. This time, even the beast carrying the bundle of supplies came apart, and the bundle settled onto the ground amidst the skittering pieces. The rat creatures moved into groups again, snapping together until each group became a new four-legged creature Skyra had not seen before. Each was the size of a cave hyena, almost as high as Skyra's waist. They did not appear to have heads.

When the hyena creatures were complete, they moved into a formation between Skyra's group on the hilltop and the wild people in the valley below. Now the caretakers were smaller, and there were at least five times as many. This comforted Skyra some, but she wished Lincoln and his tribemates had weapons. She pulled out her hand blades and gave one to Lincoln and the other to Derek.

"It is time to take back the T3," she said. "Be ready to kill."

Lincoln turned to gaze at the wild people, who were still just staring up the hill. "We've got fifty robots protecting us. Surely it won't come to that."

Derek pulled off his pack, removed two shiny folding blades, and gave them to Jazzlyn and Virgil. The knives were only half as long as Skyra's stone blades.

Derek returned his pack to his shoulders, then he shook his arms like he was trying to loosen them. "Once again, comrades, we're looking death in the face, and Derek Dagger's got your back."

Skyra did not know what he meant, but she recognized Derek's tone. He was trying to prepare himself to kill. "We will move down the hill slowly," she said. "Do not attack unless I say to attack. Maybe the caretaker creatures will scare the wild people away."

"Let's do exactly what Skyra tells us to do," Lincoln said.

Skyra noticed his hand holding the knife was shaking. She put her fingers around his fist and held it until it was still. "Let your arms and legs tell you what to do," she said firmly. "Sometimes they know more than your head knows."

He sucked in a chestful of air and nodded.

Together they started down the hill, and the caretaker creatures advanced ahead of them.

21

BARRIERS

47,659 YEARS *in the future - Day 4*

LINCOLN REALIZED he was holding his breath as he walked, so he forced himself to breathe. He and the others were almost to the base of the hill, and so far the feral people hadn't done anything aggressive. They hadn't backed off either. The people were strangely quiet—he hadn't heard a word from any of them.

At this close range he could see they were *Homo sapiens*. There wasn't a single Neanderthal among them, as far as he could tell. The age-old aversion to mixing species was apparently still strong in these feral people.

The tribe looked generally unhealthy, many of them showing signs of malnutrition, skin diseases, and limb deformities. They were filthy—he could now smell the stench Skyra had mentioned. Most of them wore crude clothing made from reflective material, but even as resilient as the material was, many of their garments had ragged holes from constant use. He puzzled over their lack of verbal communication. Could they have regressed to a nonverbal state in the two thousand years since being banned from the cities?

The robotic caretakers, which now completely surrounded Lincoln's group, didn't even slow down as they approached the nearest feral people. The people parted, and as the group moved through the crowd, Lincoln could see some were women, although the gender difference was obvious only in those without garments over their chests. Their faces, unkempt hair, and musculature were too similar to distinguish the sexes.

The wild people continued staring without speaking or attacking, even though most were holding weapons of one kind or another. Lincoln felt himself starting to relax. Maybe he'd been right—the feral people were intimidated by the robotic caretakers.

Another thirty yards and the group would be at the T3.

Lincoln heard a snap, then a dull pop.

"Virgil!" Jazzlyn cried.

Lincoln spun around. Jazzlyn was staring down at an arrow protruding from her side. The arrow was blood-covered, and it sagged toward the ground, hanging from its exit wound by what appeared to be less than an inch of its length.

Virgil grabbed the arrow and pulled it the rest of the way out.

"I've been shot," Jazzlyn said, then she fell to her knees.

"Protect us!" Skyra shouted, startling Lincoln.

The entire scene erupted into chaos. About twenty of the robots moved in closer around the group, forming a barrier, while the thirty or so others darted outward to attack. Lincoln watched one of the caretakers, unfazed by a man's blows from a handheld weapon, lift itself onto its hind legs and pull the man close with its forelegs. A split-second later it let go and rushed to attack someone else. The man collapsed, now with a horrifying gash from his groin to his chin. As he hit the ground, his entrails were ejected onto the sand.

The wild people—hundreds of them—rushed in from all directions, attacking the caretakers with unbridled fury. Still, they didn't shout or even grunt, and the air was filled with only the clatter of weapons against robots and the scuffling of feet against gravel. The thirty outer caretakers had formed a circular barrier around the twenty huddled around Lincoln's group.

"I'm bleeding, Virgil," Jazzlyn cried. "I can't stop it!"

Virgil and Derek were now kneeling at Jazzlyn's side.

Lincoln wavered, not sure what to do. An arrow whizzed by his ear, actually touching his hair before he instinctively ducked to the side. The caretakers immediately around them were starting to come apart, perhaps preparing to form a more solid barrier.

Abruptly, Skyra vaulted over one of the caretakers and ran straight to the outer ring of robots. She quickly positioned herself between two of the caretakers and killed a wild man with a strike to his face with her khul. She continued swinging viciously at the mass of attacking feral people.

Lincoln swallowed hard and tried listening to what his arms and legs were telling him. "Stay inside this barrier!" he shouted at his team, then he launched himself over the caretakers and ran for Skyra, carrying only her stone knife.

With her feet positioned among gruesome, sliced-open bodies, Skyra was fighting for her life. Attackers were still converging on the outer ring of robots, and Skyra would soon be overwhelmed by their numbers simply by being on the front line. Lincoln saw no other choice—he had to help her hold them off.

As he approached Skyra, a violent disturbance to one side drew his attention. Three bolups had broken through the barrier, tumbling over each other in a thrashing pile of arms and legs. Lincoln swallowed his fear, rushed over to them, and plunged his stone blade into the crown of a woman's skull as she was trying to get up. He didn't think the blade had penetrated the bone, but the woman collapsed anyway. She was holding an axe-like weapon made of framework tubes, and he grabbed it from her hand as she sprawled at his feet.

The other two were getting up, so Lincoln swung the weapon from the side, hitting the nearest man's armpit as the man raised the arm to block. A hiss of air escaped the man's throat, and he fell to his side, giving Lincoln a chance to strike again, this time inflicting a wound to the man's shoulder.

Lincoln took his eyes off the man he'd just hit to see the third bolup scrambling back from the fight. It was a boy, probably younger than Di-woto. The kid was on his feet now. He had a short spear in one hand and some other weapon in the other. The kid smoothly positioned the spear onto the other object and started raising them both with one arm.

The object was an atlatl, used for throwing spears with great accuracy and force. The boy was fifteen feet away and would throw the spear within the next two seconds.

"No, don't!" Lincoln shouted, knowing full well it wouldn't do any good. The kid pulled his arm all the way back, and Lincoln threw the axe-like weapon. The boy put his free hand out and blocked the weapon, but it hit hard, and he staggered back, dropping both the spear and atlatl.

The kid rolled to his side and grabbed for his spear. Lincoln rushed forward, horrified at what he knew was coming next. "Stop!" he commanded uselessly. The kid had his fingers on his spear and was a split-second away from twisting around to thrust it when Lincoln jammed his stone knife into the boy's neck.

Warm blood soaked his hand before he could even pull out the knife. The kid released his spear and clutched at his throat. Lincoln yanked the knife free, grabbed the boy's spear, and headed back to help Skyra, trying to listen only to his arms and legs and not let his unspeakable acts cloud his thoughts.

Skyra had been forced back from the outer ring of fighting caretakers due to the quantity of bodies piled between the robots. Still, attackers were coming at her by climbing over their own tribemates. She seemed to have no trouble, though, striking them down one at a time.

Lincoln turned and scanned the area. There were too many feral people, and they apparently didn't care how many of their own were being slaughtered. The caretakers wouldn't be able to hold them back for long. Another breach was already occurring on the far side of the defensive circle, with a half-dozen wild people tumbling over the tops of two caretakers.

One of the robots immediately surrounding Lincoln's team broke away from the formation and charged toward him. He stepped back, alarmed, when the thing lifted itself onto its hind feet and reached for him. Its forelegs each split into two long fingers, and the robot grabbed Lincoln's arm above the elbow. It thrust out its other foreleg and latched onto Skyra's arm.

Skyra tried to turn and strike whatever had grabbed her from behind, but the caretaker yanked her and Lincoln off their feet and dragged them back toward the inner barrier.

The robot deposited them beside Ripple, Jazzlyn, Virgil, and Derek, then it joined the other caretakers, many in various stages of disassembly in an attempt to form a taller barrier against flying arrows and spears.

"She's hurt really bad," Virgil said. He now had Jazzlyn's head cradled in his lap. Her eyes were wide with panic. Virgil was pressing one hand to the entry wound on one side of her belly and his other hand to the exit wound on the other side. His hands were covered with fresh blood.

"We gotta get to the T3," Derek said. "We can't do anything for her until we get to our supplies and jump the hell away from these savage bastards."

The scuffling, fighting sounds beyond the inner barrier of robots suddenly grew louder. Lincoln rose to his feet to look. The thirty robots on the front line were steadily moving inward while still holding off the attackers. Seconds later they were pressing against the inner ring. They stood on their hind legs and raised their forelegs, forming a taller wall. Then, all at once, they came apart. The sounds of scuffling and weapon impacts were nearly drowned out by the clicking and snapping of tiny legs as the rat-sized robots formed a solid circular wall. The inner ring locked into the outer ring, and the wall became a fifteen-foot dome with a two-foot hole at the top.

The clicking and snapping stopped, and the banging of weapons upon the wall filled the hollow space within. The disturbing nature of the sounds far outweighed what little comfort Lincoln felt from being surrounded by a thin barrier of robot rats.

"It's freakin' moving!" Derek shouted. He was staring at the base of the wall.

He was right. The entire dome was slowly creeping across the ground. Lincoln saw stubby, thumb-sized legs skittering beneath the bottom edge. He said, "I think they're taking us to the T3."

Virgil extracted himself from beneath Jazzlyn's head and shoulders and got to his knees. "We have to carry her. Help me!"

Lincoln, Skyra, and Derek joined Virgil, each taking one of Jazzlyn's limbs. She whimpered as they hoisted her a few inches off the ground and began shuffling along on their knees with the moving dome.

The dome began moving faster, and soon Lincoln and the others had to get off their knees to carry Jazzlyn fast enough to keep up.

The wild people continued bombarding the dome. Several rat-sized components were knocked loose to Lincoln's left, but the robots quickly scrambled up the wall and snapped back into place. Seconds later more were knocked away. Apparently, the feral humans were resorting to throwing or swinging heavy rocks.

"I hate to say I told you so," Derek said, grunting from his efforts, "but being in a virtual world would be a hell of a lot better than this."

Jazzlyn looked up at him. "I do *not* agree... and I'm the one who might be dying here. Think about it, Derek... those people would... those people would control you... completely. They wouldn't even let you die... even if you wanted to."

Derek nodded. "Okay, Jazz, we can argue about it later. Let's just get you taken care of for now."

Another rock crashed into the dome, knocking another hole in the wall, and the small robots quickly filled it back in.

Skyra lifted Jazzlyn's shirt with her free hand and looked at one of the wounds. "We must use the T3 to jump to my land, by the river. The river is clean, and we will use mud from the river to stop the blood."

"If we need to do that, we will," Lincoln said. "But we also have our—" He stumbled over something and fell to his knees, causing Jazzlyn to cry out in pain. Lincoln realized he was now kneeling on one of the body bags. The caretakers had actually moved the entire dome to the T3.

As he got back to his feet, he watched the leading edge of the moving dome. The rat-sized robots were adjusting their positions to create a gap, allowing the dome to engulf the T3. He and the others kept shuffling with it, now being careful not to step on the body bags and other gear spread out on the ground. The dome stopped seconds later. The group was now enclosed with the T3, the body bags, and their gear. Lincoln had no idea how much of the gear was missing, but all five of the body bags were there, which was what mattered most.

Another crash created another hole. A split second later another crash enlarged the hole. Before the robots could scramble back into place, an arrow whizzed through the opening and cracked against the opposite wall, narrowly missing Derek. Then the hole closed itself up.

"We don't have much time," Virgil said. "They're going to break through soon."

They set Jazzlyn down, and Derek shrugged off his pack. "Lincoln and Virg, do whatever you gotta do to get the T3 ready. I'll clean up her wound the best I can."

"I detect your T3 is now critically low on power," Ripple said. "It has not been charged in over ten days, since before you jumped to Skyra's time. I recommend you forego sending a mini-drone to scout the insertion environment. This should not be a problem, though, considering you are already familiar with the site. As I'm sure you're aware, this also precludes the possibility of running a new placement calculation."

"We don't have time anyway," Lincoln said. He didn't like the idea of skipping the mini-drone, but the jump should be safe. They would arrive a full hour before the original insertion time, but what were the odds some large object had been in that exact spot only an hour before the spot was known to be clear? The only possibility was a large animal, but even that seemed unlikely.

Another crash. This time a basketball-sized boulder penetrated the wall and thumped onto the ground at Lincoln's feet. Another arrow flew through the temporary hole and clattered harmlessly against the opposite wall.

Virgil cursed, then he gathered up the largest body bag—the one designed to cover the T3. He frantically folded it into a smaller bundle and held it up. "Next time they knock a hole in the wall, I'll—"

Another crash came before he even finished his sentence. He darted to the new opening and shoved the bundle in front of it, keeping the hole covered until the caretakers could fill it. When he pulled the folded bag back, a wooden arrow shaft was protruding from the micro-tubule fabric.

Lincoln spun around to face Ripple. "Can you still communicate with the T3?"

"Yes, but we cannot afford to squander its remaining power on any activity that—"

"Shut up and initiate the jump sequence for the last set of placement calculations it carried out. Same insertion location but one hour earlier. Do it now!" Lincoln grabbed one of the four smaller body bags, relieved to see its cord was still attached and seemingly undamaged. He connected the cord to one of the ports on the T3's side and grabbed another body bag. He paused, scanning the ground around the T3. The feral people had scattered the gear everywhere. "Skyra, can you start gathering this stuff?" He didn't see either of the two duffel bags they had used to contain everything, so he pointed to the body bag he'd already connected to the T3. "Just shove everything in that body bag, okay?"

Without a word she started picking up the scattered items.

Crash. Another hole appeared in the wall, and Virgil darted over and again shoved his bundle in front of it.

Derek's voice filled the dome. "Hey, what are you doing? I'm trying to work here!"

Two rat-sized robots, each looking like a four-legged lobster tail, were trying to force their way toward Jazzlyn's exposed exit wound. Derek pushed them away, but they came right back.

"Back off!" Derek said, pushing them away again, this time sending them tumbling across the sand.

The tiny caretakers righted themselves and again went straight for the wound on Jazzlyn's side.

"The caretaker creatures are here to protect us," Skyra said, her arms full of unrolled sleeping bags and wadded articles of clothing. "Maybe they are trying to protect Jazzlyn."

Derek was now cupping his hands over Jazzlyn's exit wound to keep the robots from touching it. "What could they possibly do to protect her?"

Lincoln realized Skyra could be right. The virtual people had technology he couldn't even understand, and the robotic caretakers had gone to great lengths to protect his group so far. He dropped the body bag, kneeled beside Jazzlyn, and put his hand on her cheek. "Hey, I know this is scary, but my gut's telling me to trust the caretakers. It's your choice, of course, but maybe we should find out what they're trying to do. You okay with that?"

Jazzlyn's face was drenched in sweat, and she was obviously terrified. She glanced over at Virgil then back to Lincoln. "Okay, okay." She grabbed Derek's hands and pulled them off her wound. "They can't make it worse, right?"

"The hell they can't," Derek muttered, but he sat back on his heels to watch.

The rat-sized robots moved in, and one of them actually pressed the front of its shell against the inch-wide, oozing exit wound. The other crawled over Jazzlyn's belly to get to the entry wound.

Crash. Another hole appeared, and this time an even larger boulder broke through and dropped to the ground inside the wall. "They're getting bigger rocks," Virgil cried as he thrust his bundle over the hole. "We have to jump!"

Lincoln didn't have time to monitor what the robots were doing to Jazzlyn. "Keep an eye on those things," he said to Derek, then he grabbed the second body bag again and connected it to a port on the T3. He skirted around the desk-sized T3 to get to the third and fourth bags.

"Holy crap!" Derek said. "They're made of even smaller robots."

Lincoln quickly inspected the last two bags and ported them to the T3. "How are we doing, Ripple?"

"The jump sequence is almost complete. It would be ready by now if you hadn't coded endless warnings that it is unwise to jump without first sending a mini-drone."

"It *is* unwise. We're doing it anyway."

Jazzlyn was squirming. "Oh no, they're going in. Virgil! I can feel them crawling inside!"

Crash.

Virgil was too busy blocking another hole to move to Jazzlyn's side.

"The sequence is complete," Ripple said. "You may now place yourselves within the body bags. I recommend wasting no time."

Lincoln kneeled beside Jazzlyn and Derek again. "We need to get—" He froze, staring. The two rat-sized robots were gone. Now there were dozens of thumb-sized robots, and even those were breaking down into crawling components no larger than flies. The fly robots were gathered by the hundreds around both of Jazzlyn's wounds. Some of them were crawling into the open holes in her flesh, pushing through blood and torn tissue to get inside.

"I wanted to slap them away, but a bunch were already inside," Derek said. "I just... I don't know... I just thought I'd better not make things worse by smashing them."

Lincoln kept staring, both fascinated and horrified. Finally, he forced his eyes to look up at Jazzlyn. "They're helping you, I'm sure of it," he lied. "We're getting into the body bags now, okay? Derek and I are going to lift you. Are you ready?"

Her eyes remained fixed on the tiny robots crawling into her abdomen, but she nodded. "Ready."

With Lincoln holding her knees and Derek her armpits, they hoisted her into the nearest body bag, which was open and ready.

"Um, something's coming through," Virgil said.

Lincoln rose to his feet and turned around. The wall of the dome was bulging inward, and the bulge was growing larger by the second.

"Goddammit, what now?" Derek growled. He and Lincoln approached the bulge, each of them holding one of the stone knives. Skyra dropped her armload of gear and joined them with her khul.

The bulge kept growing, protruding inward, until some of the rat-sized building blocks came loose and skittered to the side. The hole quickly widened, and a caretaker about twice the size of a human, pushed its way through.

"Don't attack!" Lincoln shouted. He and the others stepped back to make room as the caretaker dragged behind it the bundle of supplies that had been left on the hilltop. The wall sealed itself shut. The caretaker shuffled its four legs, turning its shell until the part that was probably its front end was facing the T3. It became still.

Lincoln felt like his mind was becoming fried—too many violent and bizarre episodes in such a short time. He rubbed his forehead, trying to clear his thoughts. "Okay, get everything into the body bags. We're jumping now!"

Crash. Virgil rushed to a new hole and pushed the body bag in front of it just in time to intercept another arrow. The hole repaired itself yet again.

Derek was already tearing into the bundle of supplies. He yanked off a cord holding it shut and began tossing tightly-wound rolls of reflective material and lengths of framework tubing toward the open body bags. "Shove in as much as you can!" he shouted.

Virgil continued warding off arrows being shot through new holes in the barrier while Lincoln and Skyra threw everything they could grab into the four body bags.

"I think they're all inside me now," Jazzlyn said, as Lincoln tucked camping gear around her arms and legs. He glanced at her wounds. The fly-sized robots were gone, and the wounds were no longer oozing blood.

He forced a smile and lied again. "I'm sure they're taking

care of you. Hang in there." He got up and continued gathering supplies.

"I am not sure we can fit in these bags now," Skyra said, staring at the body bag she had just filled.

Lincoln glanced at the other bags. They were all overflowing. "We'll remove whatever we have to."

Crash—another hole in the wall, another valiant lunge by Virgil to block incoming arrows.

Crash. An even larger hole appeared on the opposite side of the dome, and this time a feral man tried diving through the opening. He got stuck as the hole closed around his waist. He swung a club-like weapon wildly, but then his eyes grew wide, and he let out a pitiful groan. It was the only vocalization Lincoln had heard from any of these people. The man's body split apart, severed at the waist where the caretaker wall encircled it, and his upper body toppled onto the ground inside the dome.

Everyone stared in shock.

"I do not want to be in this land anymore," Skyra said.

Again, Lincoln rubbed his face to clear his thoughts. "Yeah. In the bags, now."

Virgil moved toward Jazzlyn's bag, but the caretaker that had been standing motionless now rushed forward and held out one of its forelegs, with two long fingers open. Virgil blinked at it, frowning.

"The body bag," Lincoln said.

Understanding spread over Virgil's face. "Oh, yeah. Here you go." He handed the wadded-up bag to the caretaker. "Don't worry—we're not trying to take the T3 with us."

The robot took the bag and stepped back, allowing Virgil to pass.

"Get in, Virgil," Jazzlyn said, holding her bag open for him to join her.

No other words were necessary. Derek helped Ripple into one of the bags, throwing out a few items indiscriminately to make room for the drone. Then he stepped to his own bag and began forcing himself in.

Crash—another hole, and this time the large caretaker darted in front of the opening as the rat-sized robots filled it in.

Lincoln and Skyra worked themselves into the last bag. It was so full, though, that he couldn't get it zipped shut. Lincoln pulled a wad of jackets from beneath him and reluctantly tossed them aside. Maybe the feral people would be able to use them.

He shimmied in beside Skyra and managed to get the zipper closed above them. He maneuvered his arms until he could see and touch his watch, then he tapped the tiny screen. All he saw was a faint red icon—an outline of an empty battery.

Shit.

"Ripple!"

"I hear you, Lincoln," came the muffled reply.

"My watch is dead!"

Several excruciating seconds passed.

"Oh, if only I could count the ways you people of flesh would be screwed without my presence among you."

Crash.

"Dammit Ripple! Can you do it or not?"

"Initiating now."

The body bag disappeared. Lincoln and Skyra fell through empty space. Lincoln's head hit something hard, and sunlight shone upon his face, forcing him to squeeze his eyes shut.

22

HOMELAND

47,659 YEARS *in the past* - *Zaragoza Province of Spain* - *Day 1*

SKYRA'S NOSE filled with familiar scents—the dry sand of the Dofusofu river valley, pale-leaved bahki weeds that thrived in the valley, and sap that ran down the smooth bark of munopo trees lining the streams feeding into the Yagua river. These were scents she had known every cold season of her life, when her Una-Loto tribe had descended into the river valley to set up a new camp to hunt woolly rhinos and ibexes until the coming warm season would prompt them to move back up into the foothills.

She sat up. "We are in my homeland, Lincoln!"

Lincoln pushed aside some of the garments and supplies piled around them and sat up beside her. The first thing he did was turn to the place where the T3 had been only moments ago.

"Yep, it's really gone," Derek said. He was also sitting up. "So, yeah, we really are stuck here forever."

Virgil groaned and got to his knees beside Jazzlyn. He gently put his hand on the brown skin of her belly and looked closely at her wounds. "Are you okay, Jazz?"

She grunted and shifted her body. "I think so. That drop hurt like hell."

"I don't know if this is good or bad," Virgil said, "but the wounds aren't bleeding at all now."

"The caretaker creatures are protecting Jazzlyn," Skyra said. "That is what they were supposed to do." Actually, she did not know if the little creatures could protect Jazzlyn from inside her body, but Virgil sometimes frightened easily, and Skyra did not want him to be afraid now.

Virgil's face formed a bolup frown, and he studied Jazzlyn's arrow wounds for several more breaths. He turned to Lincoln. "I know we have bigger problems, and I know it doesn't matter now anyway, but I really wish I could take a shot at troubleshooting that safety displacement margin. I swear, this time we popped in a meter off the ground."

Jazzlyn let out a weak laugh. "Now there's the Virgil I know."

Skyra got to her feet. They were in the same place where she had first seen Lincoln and his tribemates many days ago. The same clean, shallow river gently flowed by only a few steps away. Munopo trees were scattered along the river's edges. Beyond the trees on the far side of the river she could see the open field where she had killed several of the bolup men who had taken Veenah. Beyond the field were a few low hills, and beyond those hills was where she had found the bolup camp and Veenah.

Lincoln had said it would be an hour before Skyra's other

self would come to this spot by the river. Skyra remembered doing that. She remembered the bolup men chasing her—too many for her to kill them all. If she and the others could kill them all this time, though, the bolup tribe would be much weakened, and taking Veenah from them again would be much easier.

She turned to Lincoln, who was just getting to his feet. "We need more weapons. Then we will be ready to kill when the bolup men chase the other Skyra to this place."

He glanced at Jazzlyn and Virgil. "That's the plan you've been thinking about? Skyra, we have to get Jazzlyn to a safe place. The arrow passed all the way through her belly. She's really hurt."

"This is a clean river. I will gather the kind of mud she needs. I will put the mud in her wounds. That is what must be done with such wounds. I will put the mud in, then she will live or she will die."

"I'm right here, you know," Jazzlyn said. "I can hear you. This may sound like I'm delirious or something, but I don't feel so bad right now. I can't explain it. I just... I feel better. It scares the shit out of me that hundreds of robot bugs are inside me, but maybe they're actually helping."

"I will put clean mud in your wounds," Skyra said.

Jazzlyn actually gave Skyra a bolup grin. "I'd rather you didn't do that." She tried to sit up, making a pained face, and Virgil moved in to support her. "I'll move to a place where I won't be in the way when the bolup men get here," she said. "I know how important it is for you to save Veenah again. Do what you have to do."

"You're crazy if you think I'm leaving you by yourself," Virgil said to Jazzlyn.

Jazzlyn looked up at his face. "Don't worry, I'll be fine.

None of us can survive here without Skyra. I know that girl—she's going to save Veenah even if she has to do it by herself. That's why you and Lincoln and Derek have to help her." She waved her hand toward the trees lining the river. "Just help me get somewhere over there where I'll be out of the way."

"This is insane," Virgil said. He turned to Lincoln and Skyra. "We don't have to be here when the humans get here. We have an hour. We can take Jazzlyn and go to the cave where we hid last time we were here. It's only a kilometer away. We'll all be safe there."

Skyra turned and gazed at the hills beyond the river for a few breaths. Then she faced Lincoln. "Yes. You will be safe in the cave. Take Jazzlyn there. I will go to the bolup camp and take Veenah. Then I will bring her to the cave."

"Alright, dammit!" Derek said in his booming voice. "We're not letting Skyra go off and get herself killed. We need to be making weapons instead of wasting precious time." He waved his hand at the piles of strange gear that had been in the body bags but were now on the ground. "Plus, we can't haul all this crap *and* Jazzlyn to the cave in only one hour. We're going to need this stuff, so there's no way in hell we're letting a savage bolup tribe have it. You know they'll see it as soon as they get here."

Everyone seemed to think about this for several breaths.

Jazzlyn spoke first. "For once, Derek is right. Skyra needs our help, and we need Skyra."

SKYRA KNEELED and gently touched Jazzlyn's wound where the arrow had entered her belly. The wound was not bleeding, and the skin was not warm or swollen. Skyra had seen deep belly wounds in her tribemates before, and those wounds always had foul-smelling fluid oozing from them until they were packed with river mud. Jazzlyn's wounds were dry.

"It doesn't really hurt anymore," Jazzlyn said. She was sitting up with her back to a tree.

Skyra studied Jazzlyn's eyes, which were clear and alert. "I do not understand, but I am glad." She rose to her feet and stared out at the field and hills beyond. Still no sign of her other self and the bolup tribesmen. She turned to Lincoln. "Has an hour passed yet?"

Lincoln, Virgil, and Derek were practicing swinging the crude khuls they had made from the twisted roots of munopo trees growing beside the river. Lincoln stopped to tap the black strap around his wrist then shook his head. "My watch is useless now. Ripple, how many minutes since we arrived here?"

Ripple was staring toward the hills and the bolup camp, watching for movement. "Forty minutes have passed."

"Twenty minutes remaining, so there's still some time left," Lincoln said to Skyra. "You have to understand, though, the last forty minutes have been in a new timeline. Therefore, the events during those minutes might have been somewhat different."

Skyra had crossed the river earlier and found a few closely-clumped trees a short distance upstream from where she expected her other self and the pursuing bolups to approach. Then Virgil and Derek had carried Jazzlyn across the river and placed her among the clumped trees. This allowed the group to stay with Jazzlyn as they watched for the bolup men to come.

Making crude weapons had not taken long—they had all made similar weapons several times in recent days. They had quickly made three khuls and four long spears, and had even collected a pile of fist-sized rocks for throwing. Now they were simply waiting. Lincoln and his tribemates were obviously fearful about the upcoming fight, but Skyra's mind was busy thinking about her birthmate.

Was Veenah still alive? Lincoln had said different things were happening since the group had arrived here. Maybe during that time one of the bolups had become angry and killed Veenah. Maybe it was happening now. Skyra growled and started pacing back and forth, watching the hills and feeling the comforting weight of her khul in her hand.

"Y'all are going to give yourselves conniption fits if you don't relax," Jazzlyn said. "You're prepared, and you've got the advantage of surprise. Besides, you might even have *two* Skyras fighting the men. And two Ripples."

Skyra did not know what to think about that. She would understand what was happening, but her other self would not. She had no idea what her other self might do.

"Hmm, how can we use the next fifteen minutes?" Jazzlyn asked. "Ah, an idea! We'll have a wedding for Lincoln and Skyra."

Skyra stopped pacing.

Jazzlyn went on. "They say they're married, but they haven't made it official yet. I'm just sayin'."

"You're not serious," Lincoln said.

Ripple turned away from the distant hills to face the group. "An excellent idea. As an impartial third party, I will serve as the wedding officiant."

Derek made a spitting sound. "Impartial! You're as impartial in this matter as a serial killer's mother chosen for the jury."

I happen to be certified as a marriage officiant by the state of Arizona."

Everyone stared at him for several breaths.

"What? My mom wanted me to officiate her ceremony with her third husband. Besides, robots aren't allowed to be officiants."

Ripple took several steps toward Derek. "I have just applied your third checkmark. You have been warned that earning three checkmarks is to be avoided."

Derek's eyes widened slightly. "You don't want to mess with Derek Dagger, drone."

Ripple advanced again, forcing Derek to step back. "You did not heed the warning. You now have three checkmarks—three egregious insults to my sensibilities. Brace yourself for crippling retribution."

Derek's eyes grew wider.

Ripple's ring of red lights flashed twice. "You, sir, are an impertinent, hamster-knuckled douche noggin. Furthermore, you are a surly barnacle upon a pigeon's yeasty buttocks. And finally, if brains were dynamite, you would not have enough to blow your nose."

Jazzlyn let out a loud bolup laugh, although Skyra did not understand anything Ripple had said.

"*That's* your crippling retribution?" Derek asked.

"We are now even," Ripple replied. "An eye for an eye and a tooth for a tooth."

The other bolups laughed at this.

Skyra still did not understand. She growled again and turned to look out over the field. Something was moving at the top of the nearest hill beyond the field. She stepped away from the others, shaded her eyes with the blade of her khul, and stared. The figure was too far away to identify. "Ripple! How many minutes since we arrived here?"

"Forty-six minutes have passed."

Lincoln stepped up beside her. "Do you see something?"

She pointed.

A few breaths later he said. "I see it—coming toward us. Ripple, can you zoom in on the figure moving down that hill?"

Ripple moved to Skyra's side and looked. A low hum came from its shell. Ripple lifted off the ground to the height of Skyra's shoulder and hovered there. "The figure you are referring to is actually two figures. They are trying to run, but one of them seems to be injured."

Skyra's heart was pounding in her chest. "Can you see who they are?"

Ripple did not reply for many breaths. "I can. This is unexpected. One of them is you, Skyra. The other—the one who is impaired—appears to be Veenah."

"Veenah? I did not bring Veenah over that hill. I tried to take her from the bolups, but there were too many, and I failed. I was alone, running from the bolup men!"

"Looks like you didn't fail this time," Lincoln said. "Remember, the last forty-five minutes have been a different timeline."

The two figures were now near the base of the hill, and Skyra could see they were trying to run. One was supporting the other with an arm around her waist, pulling her along as fast as she could."

"Oh shit!" Lincoln said, grabbing Skyra's forearm. "Things really *are* different."

She snapped her head around to glance at him then followed his gaze. She expected to see the bolup men coming over the hilltop, pursuing Veenah and Skyra's other self.

There were no men on the hill. Instead, three brown creatures were just starting down the slope, obviously stalking the two nandups. Skyra's heart pounded even harder, and her leg muscles began twitching.

She pulled her arm free from his grip. "Cave lions, Lincoln! We must help Veenah!"

THERE'S MORE TO THIS STORY!

"Cave lions, Lincoln! We must help Veenah!"

Skyra, Lincoln, and the team have used their last time jump. They've left behind their T3, as well as the chance to ever jump again. Now they're stuck 47,000 years in the past. Can they make a life for themselves there, or will they forever be at the mercy of hungry predators and murderous humans and Neanderthals?

If you enjoyed **Obsolete Theorem**, **Foregone Conflict**, and **Hostile Emergence**, don't miss the last episode of the epic *Across Horizons* series, **Binary Existence**.

Also, don't miss the series prequel, **Genesis Sequence**.

In the meantime, if you haven't read my **Diffusion series**, my **Bridgers series**, or my **Fused series**, be sure to check them out.

AUTHOR'S NOTES

I love science and science fiction, so I enjoy thinking about bizarre questions related to such things as time travel, alternate universes, and unusual creatures. Below are some of my thoughts regarding the concepts in **Hostile Emergence**. These are in no particular order, and they may not cover everything you're curious about, but here you go if you're at all interested.

I find these timelines to be confusing. Can you be a little more clear about what timeline the characters are in?

Here's a good way to start: When you jump *back* in time, you create a new timeline (a new universe). Logically, this has to be true. Even if you jump back only one hour, it starts that hour all over again. Tiny, random events make it so that different things happen during that hour. Therefore, it is a different universe than the one you jumped back from.

When you jump *forward* in time, it doesn't really create a new timeline. When you arrive in the future, you are in the same timeline you left, but it is only one possible thread out of an infinite number of futures that could occur.

In Book 1 (**Obsolete Theorem**) Lincoln's team jumped back 47,659 years to Skyra's time. Before jumping, they were in Lincoln's lab in Arizona. When they jumped 47,659 years into the past, they also jumped to a specific location in Spain—the location where researchers had found Skyra's and Ripple's remains. So, Book 1 takes place in Spain during Skyra's time. When they jumped to Skyra's time, they created a new timeline (a new universe). From that moment on they were in a new timeline.

At the end of Book 1 they jumped forward 47,659 years. Therefore, in Book 2 (**Foregone Conflict**) they are in the same timeline they were in during most of Book 1, but it is only one thread of an infinite number of possible futures. In this thread, Neanderthals did not go extinct, and when the team arrived, the world looked very different. Lincoln's lab was not there, and bolups (humans) were at war with nandups (Neanderthals).

For Book 3 (**Hostile Emergence**) they jumped farther into the future, another 47,659 years (which put them 95,318 years after Skyra's time). So, they were still in the same timeline as most of Book 1 and Book 2, but again it is only one of infinite possible futures. In this future the war between nandups and bolups was long over, and other wars have come and gone. The team members found themselves in a wilderness with a surprising assortment of plants and animals. They also saw a gleaming city in the distance. Anyway, that's how they got to this place. It is 95,318 years after Skyra's time and 47,659 years after Lincoln's original time. They are in the same location of Lincoln's lab in Arizona (although in this timeline this area is not called Arizona, and there is no United States, and there is no lab).

Now, at the end of Book 3, they jumped back in time 95,318 years to return to Skyra's time (actually, to a point one hour before the original time Lincoln's team arrived there). This jump, of course, created yet another new timeline, which is why different things happened during that hour, and why Skyra was surprised to see that her other self was not alone coming over the hill in the distance.

Remember, there are only three timelines so far in these books: (1) Lincoln's original timeline, (2) the timeline created when Lincoln's team jumped 47,659 years into the past to Skyra's time, and (3) The timeline created when the team jumps back in time 95,318 years to Skyra's time again (at the end of this book).

Why is Veenah now with Skyra's other self as they come over the hill in the distance?

Because, as stated above, different things can happen when you start a new timeline. Skyra, Lincoln, and the team arrive an hour before the time of Lincoln's first arrival in Skyra's time. Which means that hour starts again. It's not possible for the exact same events to happen during that hour. In Skyra's original timeline (at the beginning of Book 1), she attacked some of the bolups who had captured Veenah, but she was not successful in taking Veenah from them. She had to flee, and the bolup men chased her. Apparently, during the do-over of the last hour, Skyra's other self was actually successful in taking Veenah from the bolups. Now Skyra's other self is coming over the hill with Veenah (who is weak from being abused by the bolups). Not only that, but Veenah and Skyra's other self are being stalked by several cave lions. Can't anything ever be easy?

So, is there really going to be two Skyras? Will there be two Lincolns, two Virgils, two Jazzlyns, and two Dereks also?

First, since the team arrived an hour before Lincoln's team originally arrived there, there will *not* be two Lincolns, Virgils, Jazzlyns, and Dereks. Why? Because a new timeline was started the moment the team arrived there. Random events will result in a completely different future in this timeline, a future in which Lincoln will never be born, a future in which there will not be a United States, or an Arizona, or much of anything else we are familiar with. Obviously, Lincoln will never be born 47,659 into this new future, and therefore he and his team cannot jump back to Skyra's time to arrive here. For that reason, there will not be two Lincolns, Virgils, Jazzlyns, and Dereks.

However, Skyra and Ripple already exist in this place when the team jumps back in time at the end of Book 3. So, there *will* be two Skyras and two Ripples. What do you think will happen when Skyra comes face-to-face with her other self? What will happen when Ripple comes vision-lens-to-vision-lens with its other self? Hmm... good question. Book 4 in the series is titled **BINARY EXISTENCE**. That's where we find out.

Wait! Not only did they jump back (or forward) in time, they also jumped from Arizona to Spain (and vice versa). How is that possible?

It's important to realize you cannot jump through time without also jumping through space. Time travel = space travel. Jumping back in time is actually the least complex part of time travel. The most complex part is placement, or jumping through space. Remember, Earth is moving really fast. As it rotates on its axis, the surface at the equator is spinning at 460 meters per second (about 1,000 miles per hour). So, even if you jumped back in time one second, you would have to jump 460 meters back toward the east in order to appear in the same room you jumped from. But that's only one small part of Earth's movement. The planet is also in orbit around the sun, moving at 30 kilometers per second (67,000 miles per hour). Not only that, but our solar system (including Earth) is revolving around the center of the Milky Way galaxy at 220 kilometers per second (490,000 miles per hour). As if that weren't enough, the galaxies in our part of the universe are moving at 1,000 kilometers per second (2.2 million miles per hour) toward a huge, dense region of space called the Great Attractor.

So, are you starting to see how difficult it is to calculate placement if you are jumping back in time only one second? Now imagine trying to calculate placement for jumping back in time 47,659 years! The calculation is staggering. As Lincoln has said, we may someday discover deep space is littered with the frozen bodies of time travelers who failed to properly calculate placement.

Even though Lincoln's T3 is equipped with an enormously powerful computer, it still takes up to 30 hours for it to run a new placement calculation.

So, time travel is only possible if your time machine is capable of instantaneously sending you through space to a very specific location that could be billions, or even trillions, of miles away. In other words, time travel = space travel. This is very, very different from jumping between alternate universes, as the characters did in the Bridgers series. Bridging between universes does not require movement through space—you simply bridge to the exact same location but on an alternate version of Earth. Fortunately, Lincoln understands all of this, and he designed his T3 with the capability of processing immensely-complex placement calculations.

What about this alternate universes concept? This seems really far-fetched.

It's not as far fetched as you might think. This is a big topic, and I cover it in detail in the Author's Notes at the back of the books of the Bridgers series, so you may want to check those out (see what I did there?).

What is the meaning of the title **Hostile Emergence**?

This is the name Virgil came up with for a hypothesis he developed to explain the strange combination of plants and animals living in this place. He was trying to come up with an explanation for why there seemed to be such a preponderance of creatures that live at least part of their lives below ground. Also, they found some creatures, such as the prairie dogs, that apparently had adapted to eating other animals, at least supplementing their diet with animal tissue. Virgil speculated that some tragic event had wiped out all (or most) of the above-ground life at some point in the past. Instead of an event with long-term deadly effects, such as a nuclear war, he thought maybe it was something that killed above-ground life all at once, and then the effects were gone. This would very briefly result in a world where everything above ground was dead and everything below ground was still alive. With most of the plants (again, briefly) dead, those below-ground creatures would emerge to find that everything above ground was dead.

These dead things could have been a source of food, but only for a brief time until they rotted or were consumed. Then all these creatures that emerged would have to (at least temporarily) resort to eating each other or die out. Even the creatures that were previously herbivores, like the prairie dogs, would have to resort to eating animals or die out. Virgil referred to this temporary flurry of aggressive behavior of emerging creatures as a *Hostile Emergence*.

What kind of weapon could kill all above-ground life and then not have any long-term residual effects?

That is a good question, for which I do not have a specific answer. Is such a weapon even possible? I would have to say yes, simply because the "people of thought" in *Hostile Emergence* are far more technologically advanced than we are in our timeline (they did not reveal details of the weapon, and for good reason). To fit within Virgil's *Hostile Emergence* hypothesis, the weapon would have to be almost instantaneous, with effects that last only from a few seconds to no more than a few days and then disappear. One possibility would be a gas of some sort, released in huge volume, something that destroys biological tissue and then dissipates or becomes inert after a short time (without seeping into the ground or into caves and burrows). Hmm... not likely. I'm leaning more toward some kind of particle-beam weapon, perhaps fired from space from multiple sources at once so as to strike every portion of the Earth's surface. The weapon directs a beam of particles that disrupts the atomic or molecular structure of biological tissue. The beam does not penetrate rock or soil. The beam can be emitted for a short time, perhaps a few seconds, and then turned off, leaving no residual environmental effects (other than a lot of dead plants and animals). Particle accelerators are real and have been used for decades. A particle-beam weapon is a weaponized version of this. If you have other ideas for what kind of weapon could produce such effects, I'd love to know your thoughts.

Could prairie dogs really become carnivorous?

Prairie dogs, like most other rodents, are primarily herbivorous. But they do occasionally supplement their diet with animals, such as insects, and some prairie dog species are known to be cannibalistic. So, prairie dogs already have a hard-wired tendency to consume animals. This makes it much more likely for them to survive the tragic event described above. In **Hostile Emergence**, the prairie dogs likely still eat some plants, the way their ancestors did, but they also have developed the tendency to attack and kill any animals that enter their colony. In fact, these prairie dogs have evolved a way to attract swarms of insects to their colony by producing droppings (poop) with a scent that attracts the swarms. When the insect swarms alight in the dung heaps to feed, the prairie dogs charge in and eat as many as they can catch. Could this really happen? Who knows, but I think it's a cool idea!

What about that deadly colony of yellowjackets (ground hornets)?

Another cool idea, if I do say so myself. By the way, the term *hornets* is usually used for specific types of social wasps that make large nests above ground (typically in trees). The term *yellowjackets* refers to social wasps that are smaller in size and create nests in burrows below ground. Yellowjackets live in colonies of up to 5,000 wasps. They typically feed on sweet stuff such as flower nectar, ripe or rotting fruits, and tree sap (not to mention the occasional soda can contents). However, when they are caring for their larvae (the queen can lay 25,000 eggs in one season), they become carnivorous, feeding on other insects and large carrion. So, it's not too far-fetched to imagine yellowjackets responding to the environmental disaster described earlier by developing the habit of killing and consuming any unfortunate animal coming near their nest. Like the prairie dogs, they are already hard-wired to be carnivores. Also, I can tell you from personal experience that the vibrations from a lawnmower can set them off. They come swarming out to attack. So, it's not far-fetched for Lincoln to correctly assume that the killer yellowjackets could detect their footsteps. It's a good thing Di-woto had that roll of reflective material with her!

Do velvet worms really shoot sticky goo?

You bet they do! Although velvet worms in our timeline are small compared to the arm-sized velvet worm Skyra and Di-woto found, they have an amazing way to capture their prey. They squirt out jets of goo, which hardens upon contact and immobilizes the prey animals. The velvet worm can then take its time and consume the animal without risk of getting hurt or having the animal escape. I recommend you do an internet search for velvet worms. You'll be impressed by these awesome predators. I need to point out that the velvet worms in *Hostile Emergence* have become larger than normal because of an extreme abundance of insects they feed on.

Could badgers become the size of wolves?

Again, the answer is yes. There is an ancient badger-like creature called *Repenomamus giganticus* that was about the size of a wolf. The badgers of our timeline today belong to a group called mustelids. The largest mustelid is the wolverine, which is 1.2 meters long and weighs over 20 kg (45 pounds). So, it's not far-fetched to imagine badgers adapting to a drastically different food source by becoming larger.

Di-woto becomes an important character in **Hostile Emergence**. *She is just a girl—did she really have such a huge influence on the future?*

Do the following names sound familiar? Anne Frank, Malala Yousafzai, Ruby Bridges. If you're unfamiliar with any of them, you should look them up. These are young girls who changed the world. And there are plenty more: Claudette Colvin, Bana Alabed, Audrey Faye Hendricks, Jazz Jennings, and Capri Everitt to name just a few. Di-woto started a revolution of peace. In a world in which humans and Neanderthals had been at war for thousands of years, Di-woto happened to live at a time when change was probably imminent, but someone had to be the one to initiate that change. Di-woto was in a unique position to do so.

In **Foregone Conflict**, *Di-woto's mother Lo-aful betrayed Lincoln, yet in* **Hostile Emergence** *it is revealed that Lo-aful took up Di-woto's cause after Di-woto disappeared. What's up with that?*

Lo-aful was Di-woto's biological mother. Di-woto was taken from her at a young age, and Lo-aful wasn't even allowed to see her for years. You must remember that they both lived in a society of oppression and deceit. Lo-aful did not have much choice in the matter of betraying Lincoln. Apparently, though, after the initial violence and overthrow of the khami-buls (the orange-clad scientist-learner-teachers), Lo-aful decided she had the freedom to attempt to carry on her daughter's mission. Therefore, in the thousands of years after their time, both Di-woto and Lo-aful are remembered as crucial to the change initiated by Di-woto.

Why is Di-woto willing to stay behind and live forever as a "person of thought?"

Di-woto is just a girl (ten to twelve years old), but it's important to remember she has lived a tortured life. She is an alinga-ul (a hybrid with a nandup mother and bolup father), the only alinga-ul in the Kyran-yufost kingdom. She has felt alone and oppressed all her life, resulting in significant psychological challenges. She even inflicted extensive scarring on her own body as a way of dealing with her anguish. So, when she realizes she is among the future descendants of her people, and that they have only praise for her and the impact of her plan to initiate peace, she suddenly feels like she belongs. As a "person of thought," she can make her scars disappear, and she can easily brush away all her psychological disorders. Not only that, but she can now create any kind of clothing or building she can envision. We all know Di-woto loves creating clothing and buildings, right? Also, consider that Di-woto is only about 11 years old, which is an age at which drastic decisions are often made without much thought or indecision.

What will happen to Di-woto in the future?

We do not know. We learned from Kods and Thide that every person in their population has existed as a "person of thought" for over two thousand years. So, perhaps Di-woto will live that long—or much longer—in their virtual world, creating beautiful things.

Why were Kods, Thide, and the rest of their people naked?

    The people of their population, and presumably all the other populations of this world, had done away with clothing long before becoming "people of thought." Why? For the same reasons they did away with all personal belongings. Remember, Lincoln and the others did not find a single loose object anywhere in the city. These people did not like the clutter of loose objects. Over a span of many thousands of years they became interested in experiences and conversation, rather than material objects. They enjoyed walking the streets of their city and hiking into the surrounding wilderness. They also enjoyed the intellectual stimulation of talking to each other. These activities could be done without clothing or other possessions, so eventually they eliminated them. Their buildings were filled with chairs and tables that were part of the floor, arranged to make it easier for the citizens to gather and talk. Presumably, as Virgil suggested, even their computers and communication devices were built into the walls and tables. Everywhere these people went, if they wanted to contact someone else, they could stop where they were, touch a wall or table, and access anyone or any information.

But what about tools, and food, and other such things?

    These people were obviously obsessed with the aesthetics of simplicity—no clutter. Even the beds, tables, and chairs were fixed in place and could not be knocked over or shoved into disarray. Everything that involved tools and other loose objects took place in the below-ground portion of the city, and it's my guess that most of those tasks were carried out by robots, fondly referred to by Kods and Thide as *robotic caretakers*. These caretakers would build and repair the city and technology devices, and presumably they would manufacture food, prepare meals, and deliver the meals to people aboveground, to be eaten wherever the people cared to eat.

What else can you tell me about these robotic caretakers?
In my opinion, the most impressive thing about them is that they are all made of one single type of smaller robot. At first, Lincoln and his team assumed the smallest ones were the rat-sized robots, which could fit together to form much larger robots for doing heavy jobs (like building the city and capturing Skyra, Lincoln, and their friends). Later, however, they discovered that even the rat-sized robots were made up of thumb-sized robots, which were made up of fly-sized robots, which crawled into Jazzlyn's body through her arrow wounds. As Virgil pointed out, the beauty of this is that you can put all your efforts into designing and building *one* single kind of robot (the smallest of the robot hierarchy). These tiny robots can fit together in infinite ways to make all the other robots, no matter the size or configuration.

Skyra seemed to become very fond and protective of Di-woto. Why?
Interesting observation. Could it be that Skyra has a strong mothering instinct? After all, Skyra knows that Di-woto is an alinga-ul (a hybrid with a nandup mother and bolup father), and she knows if she has a child with Lincoln it will be an alinga-ul. Or, could it be that Skyra empathizes with Di-woto? After all, Skyra had a difficult childhood too. She (and Veenah) were different from the other Neanderthals, and this resulted in harsh treatment from her tribemates. Or could it be a combination of both of these things?

How were Skyra and Veenah different from their tribemates?

The twin sisters are unusually intelligent, for one thing. This is one reason why Skyra often says she and Veenah could "see what their tribemates could not see." Another reason she says this is that she and Veenah have the strange ability to detect what a person is about to do by reading subtle changes in their facial features and body language. This ability is so profound that it has saved Skyra's life many times when fighting humans and other Neanderthals. Coincidentally, Lincoln also has this ability. Lincoln is obviously also highly intelligent. These characteristics are what prompted Ripple to make a plan to get Lincoln and Skyra together back in Skyra's time. Ripple believes the alinga-ul offspring of Lincoln and Skyra could initiate the spreading of certain genetic characteristics throughout a growing population of nandup/bolup hybrids. Ripple also believes the best time to initiate this process is Skyra's original time, when Neanderthals and humans both existed and were already intermixing. Skyra's world 47,659 years in the past is the optimal time and setting for Ripple's plan to succeed.

Is Ripple crazy? How could it be possible for the offspring of one man and one woman to affect the future of all humanity?

Ripple may or may not be crazy—that's a matter of opinion. However, Ripple's plan is not as far-fetched as it sounds. Have you heard of the biological concept of a "mitochondrial Eve?" A mitochondrial Eve is the most recent female historically from which all living animals of a species can trace their ancestry. There is a lot of confusion in the media about the nature of a mitochondrial Eve. It does *not* refer to the first female of a species. For example, the mitochondrial Eve of sperm whales is thought to be a female that lived somewhere between 10,000 and 80,000 years ago. This female was *not*

AUTHOR'S NOTES

the first sperm whale (sperm whales existed for millions of years before that). There were a lot of other female sperm whales swimming around at that same time. Instead of being the first sperm whale, she just happens to be the most recent female that passed down the mitochondrial DNA that all modern sperm whales possess. All the other lineages eventually died out, and now all the living sperm whales today are in the lineage of this one female. Every animal species has a mitochondrial Eve somewhere in its past. The mitochondrial Eve of all living humans is a female who lived about 200,000 years ago.

Anyway, this mitochondrial Eve concept can help us understand how one individual has the potential to impact the entire future population of her species. Ripple believes Skyra could become the mitochondrial Eve of a future population of people who have both human and Neanderthal DNA. Ripple thinks the chances of this are greatly helped by the fact that Lincoln and Skyra's offspring will have superior traits. If they have superior traits, they will have a better chance of surviving than many other nandups and bolups of the time. They will likely find their own mates in neighboring tribes, then they'll have their own offspring. Those offspring will disperse and find their own mates in neighboring tribes, and so on. The success if each generation born from Skyra's and Lincoln's DNA will have a better chance of success than everyone else. According to Ripple, this could result in a world thousands of years later that is populated by superior alinga-uls. It is Ripple's plan to make a better world based on the legacy of Lincoln and Skyra.

It's important to point out that this is not the same thing as a genetic bottleneck (inbreeding), which would result in a preponderance of deleterious recessive genes in the population. It's not like Ripple is putting Lincoln and Skyra on an island and expecting them to create a new population just from their own offspring. That was the difficult problem faced by the characters of my Bridgers series. This situation is completely different and is the normal way that advantageous genes spread throughout populations.

In Hostile Emergence, the differences between Skyra and Lincoln are becoming more obvious. Is it possible they are simply incompatible?

Skyra is in the species *Homo neanderthalensis*, Lincoln is *Homo sapiens*—two different species. Also, they were born more than 47,000 years apart. It's becoming obvious that Skyra's mind is more concrete and less abstract than Lincoln's. She does not understand why Lincoln and his team like to talk about everything. She just wants to get things done, to see, to touch, to feel, to smell, to figure things out by experiencing them. Lincoln and his other human friends want to talk things through, hypothesize, reason out the answers, and understand what they are getting into before they do something. Of course, we cannot know if Neanderthals 47,000 years ago were more concrete than today's humans, but I'm guessing they were. I also wouldn't be surprised if the *humans* from 47,000 years ago were more concrete than today's humans.

Is this enough of a difference to make Skyra and Lincoln incompatible? I guess we'll have to wait and see, won't we?

What about Maddy? Lincoln still has Maddy's cognitive module in his pocket, doesn't he?

Indeed he does! The more we learn about Lincoln, the more we realize how important Maddy has been in his life. We also know that Lincoln can talk to Maddy when he wants to by pulling Ripple's cognitive module and inserting Maddy's in its place. I'd say there's a decent chance Lincoln is going to want to visit with Maddy at least one more time.

How many more books will be in this series?
 Book 4, titled **Binary Existence**, will be the last in the series. This book will detail the team's experiences back in Skyra's original time, and their attempts to make a permanent life there. As you can probably guess, that's not going to be easy. There will also be plenty of surprises.
 In addition, there will be a prequel, titled **Genesis Sequence**. This is the story of Skyra almost two years before she meets Lincoln, when she finds Ripple for the first time (or when Ripple finds *her*). You already know Skyra and Ripple were friends for almost two years before Lincoln and his team jumped back to Skyra's time, but there's a lot about Skyra and Ripple's story that you don't yet know.

If you ever have any additional questions about this series, don't hesitate to email me at stan@stancsmith.com

ACKNOWLEDGMENTS

I am not capable of creating a book such as this on my own. I have the following people, among others, to thank for their assistance.

First I wish to thank Monique Agueros for her help with editing. She has a keen eye for typos, poorly structured sentences, misplaced commas, and errors of logic. If you find a sentence or detail in the book that doesn't seem right, it is likely because I failed to implement one of her suggestions.

My wife Trish is always the first to read my work, and therefore she has the burden of seeing my stories in their roughest form. Thankfully, she kindly points out where things are a mess. Her suggestions are what get the editing process started. She also helps with various promotional efforts. And finally, she not only tolerates my obsession with writing, she actually encourages it.

I also owe thanks to those on my Advance Reviewer team. They were able to point out numerous typos and inconsistencies, and they are all-around fabulous people!

Finally, I am thankful to all the independent freelance designers out there who provide quality work for independent authors such as myself. Jake Caleb Clark (www.jcalebdesign.com) created the awesome cover for *Hostile Emergence*.

ABOUT THE AUTHOR

Stan Smith has lived most of his life in the Midwest United States and currently resides with his wife Trish in a house deep in an Ozark forest in Missouri. He writes adventure novels that have a generous sprinkling of science fiction. His novels and stories are about regular people who find themselves caught up in highly unusual situations. They are designed to stimulate your sense of wonder, get your heart pounding, and keep you reading late into the night, with minimal risk of exposure to spelling and punctuation errors. His books are for anyone who loves adventure, discovery, and mind-bending surprises.

Stan's Author Website
http://www.stancsmith.com

Feel free to email Stan at: stan@stancsmith.com
He loves hearing from readers and will answer every email.

ALSO BY STAN C. SMITH

The DIFFUSION series

Diffusion

Infusion

Profusion

Savage

Blue Arrow

Diffusion Box Set

The BRIDGERS series

Bridgers 1: The Lure of Infinity

Bridgers 2: The Cost of Survival

Bridgers 3: The Voice of Reason

Bridgers 4: The Mind of Many

Bridgers 5: The Trial of Extinction

Bridgers 6: The Bond of Absolution

INFINITY: A Bridger's Origin

Bridgers 1-3 Box Set

Bridgers 4-6 Box Set

The ACROSS HORIZONS series

1: Obsolete Theorem

2. Foregone Conflict

3. Hostile Emergence

4. Binary Existence

Prequel: Genesis Sequence

The FUSED series

Prequel: Training Day

1. Rampage Ridge

2. Primordial Pit

Stand-alone Stories

Parthenium's Year

Printed in Great Britain
by Amazon